NO RIGHT THING

Laura Langston

CP | CRWTH PRESS

Library and Archives Canada Cataloguing in Publication
Title: No right thing / Laura Langston.
Names: Langston, Laura, 1958- author.
Canadiana (print) 20200160648
Canadiana (ebook) 20200160680
ISBN 9781775351580 (softcover)
ISBN 9781989724019 (PDF)
ISBN 9781989724026 (HTML)
Classification: LCC PS8573.A5832 N6 2020 | DDC jC813/.54—dc2

Copy edited by Rowena Rae
Proofread by Audrey McClellan
Cover and interior design by Julia Breese

Published by
CRWTH PRESS
#204 – 2320 Woodland Dr.
Vancouver, BC V5N 3P2
info@crwth.ca
www.crwth.ca

23 22 21 20 · 4 3 2 1

Printed and bound in Canada

DEDICATION

For Carol-Anne Almquist, artist and friend

"No good deed goes unpunished." —Clare Boothe Luce

PROLOGUE

Three months earlier

Max isn't on his usual corner across from Fine Foods when I get off shift. I look for his familiar shape curled up in one of the nearby doorways, but it's dark and I don't see him. It's a lousy night to be sleeping outside. A misty rain starts to fall; it cuts into my cheeks like tiny icicles as I head for the bike rack.

Max usually stops into Fine Foods every few days to exchange his bottles and sometimes splurge on a cup of coffee, but he hasn't been around lately. I wipe the seat of my bike, tuck the bag of bread and cheese under my jacket and start to pedal. I circle the block a couple of times, pedalling slowly down Second Avenue, checking the doorways of the galleries and cafes, but I still don't see him. I could ride home, but Max will be hungry. He always is.

Max shouldn't go hungry when I can help him out. When I'm working in the bakery I save him day-old muffins and pastries. I have a bag for him today, plus a wedge of triple cream brie I picked up at the deli. Max loves expensive cheese. I don't know where he got a taste for the finer things in life. He has his secrets, Max.

I get that. I have my secrets too.

I ride back down Memorial and hang a right on Crescent Road East. A few minutes later I coast to a stop at the entrance to Heritage Forest. The entrance gate looks oyster white under the street light. The path beyond the gate disappears into darkness. My breath hitches. Dad would lose it if he knew I was here.

I've gone into the forest hundreds of times, but I've never cycled the path at night. And I've never gone to Tent City—the open area in the middle where the homeless have been squatting for the last eight months.

People are afraid of the homeless the way they're afraid of the dark. They build things up in their minds and imagine a threat where there isn't one. Max has taught me the homeless are people like you and me. But I'm not stupid. A few can't be trusted; some are addicts and some have mental health issues.

Still, Max hasn't been around for over a week. And Dad and Parker are tired of all the day-olds I've been bringing home. So before I can overthink it, I ride into the forest.

I shiver, from nerves and cold. With the light from my bike, I can make out the shapes of trees and the winding path that hugs the drop-off on my right. I'm not sure how I'll find Max when I get to Tent City. I only know I have to try. An owl hoots in the distance, a soothing counterpoint to the squish of my tires on the rough path. After a few minutes I start to relax.

I reach a curve and hear the metallic ping of a bike chain up ahead. My heart skips a beat. I take the turn wide. A shape looms out of the darkness. It's coming right for me. I jerk my bike out of the way.

"What the hell?"

The voice has an unmistakable British accent.

"Max?" My back tire grazes his as I wobble past. I manage, just barely, to avoid falling as I stop. "Where'd you get the bike?"

"That's not the question, Catie." He lowers his bike to the ground and his beige trench coat billows as he lifts a long leg awkwardly over the handlebars to extricate himself. He's a thin man with ropes of grey hair. "The question is what are you doing here?"

"Looking for you." I unzip my windbreaker. "I haven't seen you around lately."

As he approaches me, the pungent scent of cigarette smoke, raspberry vodka and body odour hits me like a slap. I step back. "Been a bit under the weather," he says. "But I'm okay now."

"I brought you some day-olds." I hold out the bag. "And a wedge of brie."

"You're a good lass." His hand trembles as he takes it. "Thank you."

"You're welcome."

He shoves a scone into his mouth. His eyes widen as he chews. "Ginger," he says, crumbs spraying out of his mouth. "Delicious."

"I know, right?" Max and I talk about food a lot. Max because he dreams of raspberries out of season and quince preserves, and me because I adore all things food and want to be a chef. The first time I volunteered at the community breakfast sponsored by Fine Foods, Max was there. He raved about the extra sharp cheddar I'd convinced the cook to use, and we struck up a conversation. After a while we became friends.

"Did you get your applications off?"

The scone is gone; he pulls out a blueberry Danish.

"Yeah." Max has been encouraging me to apply for cooking school even though Dad is totally opposed. Max is all about following your heart no matter what anybody says.

"Good." He stops mid-bite and peers into the darkness. "Where's yer fella? Richard? Randall?"

"Robert." I retrieve my bike. "He's not here." And he's not my fella either. He never was.

He stares at me, a knowing look on his face.

Max is astute. Normally I like it. But Max thinks I need a man to complete me. And Max is wrong. "I gotta go, Max. It's getting late." I'm not talking about guys with him. He's old enough to be my father. "I'll see you around." I wave and push off into the night.

1

He steals the peach so fast I think maybe I've imagined it. Fine Foods is busy—no surprise for a Saturday just before noon—and when I glimpse Max I'm wrapping up an order for a dozen lemon crunch muffins and a loaf of crusty sourdough. All I see is the flash of a pale hand and a blushing peach disappearing under his dirty coat. A minute later my customer leaves and I have a clear view of the produce department.

Max is still there.

I watch him as I straighten the sweet rolls in the bread case. He saunters around the peach display, his striped shoulder bag swinging in a carefree arc. He stops, glances over his left shoulder and then his right. Seconds later he snatches a second peach, pocketing it as quickly and as matter-of-factly as if it were a set of keys.

I clench the sweet roll tray. Stealing is wrong. But so is going hungry. Besides, the stock guys throw out more rotten produce than the homeless could ever steal.

Tegan marches up to the bakery counter, obstructing my view. "Tell me you didn't," she hisses. My best friend works cash at Fine Foods and we're scheduled for the same lunch break today. I've been looking forward to it since I signed in this morning, but the way Tegan's glaring at me I know this won't be fun. She points to a cheesecake brownie. Her usual. "Tell me you didn't break up with Carter!"

"Shh." Even in whisper mode Tegan is loud. I lean over to get her brownie and glimpse Max again. He's wandering past the tower of radishes and heading for the dairy. Oh crap. Peaches are one thing. Even out of season they aren't that expensive. But aged Stilton is.

Don't press your luck, Max. I will myself to send him a telepathic message. *If you get caught again, Peter will call the cops.* The store manager is predictable that way.

"Well!" Tegan demands when I slide her brownie into a takeout bag. "Did you?"

"Yeah, I did."

She stares at me, her dark eyes unblinking. Tegan reminds me of an owl: round face, round hoops in her ears, round head made rounder by her short hair. Well, short except for the chunk growing out the left side. "Are you nuts? Prom's exactly three weeks from today!"

That has nothing to do with anything.

"And why didn't you tell me?"

"Meet me across the street in fifteen and I'll fill you in." I hand her the brownie. "I have other news too." Something way more important than Carter.

"Good news or bad news?" Tegan asks.

Luckily she gets a text and I am spared from answering.

As I put a *Happy Birthday Nate* cake on the counter for a customer, I see Max talking to Noah Fox. My heart skips a beat. Mr. Shoulders. He's captain of the Spider Lake Rowing Team and weekend produce manager. Noah's on the quiet side and hard to read. I don't know what he'll do if he saw Max take the peach.

NO RIGHT THING

The customer taps a claw-like red nail on the counter and frowns. "It's not quite what I ordered, is it?"

I pull my attention back to her. "It's not?"

She pouts. "No."

It's a beautiful cake. Twinkly yellow stars, orange and red planets, all carefully outlined in white marzipan so they pop against the dark blue background. "I'm sorry you're not happy with it." I put hours into this cake—my fingers still sport faint blue tinges—and I *know* I followed her instructions; I read them over a billion times. "Let me get the book and see what we wrote down."

My cell phone vibrates in my pocket as I turn away. Carter again. I suppress a sigh. That's twelve texts since we broke up last night.

I pull out the order book. Now Max is at the snack bar buying a coffee. I incline my head to the door. *Leave,* I try to convey. *You don't want Peter to catch you.* I hope he'll take the hint.

Max wanders over. The soles of his worn runners slap the floor like flippers. Spotting a discarded gum wrapper in front of the doughnut case, he leans over, picks it up and shoves it in his pocket. The woman shoots him a dirty look.

"The cake needs more stars," she says as I page through the orders. "You've only given me three."

Because Nate is turning three and she specifically asked for three stars. *The customer is always right.* My manager's mantra.

"Give me at least five more," she orders.

I study the cake wondering how I'll fit on more stars.

Max peers over the counter. "The colour's all wrong on that cake," he says. "Outer space is black. Not blue like the ocean."

Thanks, Max.

The two of them have surprisingly similar profiles: high foreheads, long hair, ski-jump noses, but there the similarities end. The customer has a glossy sheen that comes from being well-fed, well-groomed and well-dressed. Max has a dismal, dumpster-diving look: rotten teeth, ripped sweatpants, ratty old trench coat. That faded old bag slung over his shoulder.

Ignoring him the woman turns back to me. “And make it fast.” She carries a butter-coloured leather purse with a designer logo. “I’ll be back in five minutes. I’m in a hurry.”

Of course she is. Every mother who orders their kid a birthday cake is in a hurry. And they’re usually rude too. Is this the difference between mothers who order and moms who bake? I wouldn’t know. Mothers are aliens as far as I’m concerned.

Max smirks at her. “Hurrying is bad for your blood pressure.”

The customer rolls her eyes and stalks off.

“You didn’t have to say that.” I hand him a few day-old buns I’ve set aside. He puts them into his bag.

“Why not? It’s the truth.”

Max speaks his truth no matter what. I lower my voice. “You should go. The new manager’s here today.”

“Ah.” Max nods. Peter has been coming down hard on the street people. He boots them out of the store, and he cancelled the monthly community breakfasts, which got him a lot of bad press in the local paper. “Right, then.” But he makes no move to leave.

I drum my fingers on the counter. I want Max to leave before he gets picked up for shoplifting. I want to fix the cake and get outside to Tegan. I need her advice.

"No ginger scones today, Max. Sorry."

"Oh." Disappointment shadows his red-rimmed eyes. "I have money." He fumbles in his pocket. He looks paler than usual, a little thinner too.

"Save it and buy yourself breakfast tomorrow." I pluck a cookie from the glass jar on the counter. "If Peter says anything tell him to come and talk to me."

"Thanks." He slides the cookie in with the buns. But he still doesn't move. "Are you all right, Cate? You seem off today."

Off doesn't come close to describing it. I've been offered the biggest opportunity of my life. Only it comes with an outrageous price tag. Plus, Carter will not stop texting me.

"The cake," I say with a wave of my hand.

"Don't be worrying. That woman's a thickie is what she is." Maybe, but she's a paying thickie.

"Thanks, Max. Don't eat your cookie all in one bite."

"I won't." He turns to go. "Toodle pip, Catie girl."

"Toodle pip, Max."

"I don't care how you salvaged that cake," Tegan says when I make it outside ten minutes later. She has snagged us a bench on the green space between Fir and Veterans Way. Scoring a seat is a coup on a busy Saturday. "Why did you break up with Carter?"

I don't want to go there yet. The sun warms my shoulders as I pop the lid on my Italian soda and take a sip. It's the first nice Saturday we've had this spring. Across the street in the Petro-Canada lot, students are holding a fundraising car wash. The sound of bluegrass music drifts over from the Saturday market. I watch a group of tourists wander up the hill toward the galleries, restaurants and boutiques that line downtown Qualicum Beach.

"Well?" Tegan prompts. She picks half-heartedly at her standard lunch: Caesar salad minus the dressing, croutons and Parmesan cheese. In other words, washed romaine with lemon juice and capers. "What was it this time?" Before I can form an answer, her cell phone bleeps. She looks down. "Owen."

Big surprise. Tegan can barely go an hour without talking to her boyfriend.

She giggles into her phone. "Yes, I got your text but I'm talking to Cate about Carter and I haven't had time to answer." She pauses, gives me a significant look. "They broke up last night."

Oh *man.* Nothing is sacred with Tegan. She's the live version of Twitter. I pick up my sandwich and glance down the hill, searching out the peekaboo view of the Strait of Georgia and Lasqueti Island. A slight breeze carries the scent of salt, seaweed and French fries. A cawing seagull rides the current, swooping and dipping on the air before flying off toward Village Theatre. My cell phone vibrates again, a faint flutter in my pocket. I don't even look.

"Stop it, Owen. Don't be gross. I'll text you later. Bye. For sure. Yes! Bye!"

Tegan pokes my back. "So, what's going on?"

I lick a smear of Dijon from my finger and turn around. A dairy truck rumbles down the road. I spot two clerks from the deli crossing the street, takeout bags in hand. Noah Fox ambles behind them, carrying a pizza box and still wearing his striped produce apron. He's the only guy on staff who has the confidence to wear his apron on break. And not care what anyone says.

"Come on, spill!" Tegan has a chunk of green stuck between her two front teeth.

"I told you a month ago I didn't think it would work out."

"And I told you a month ago to stop being stupid. Carter is perfect for you."

Says the girl who apparently found perfect in grade six and hasn't dated anyone since. "There's no such thing as the perfect guy, Tegan."

Her hair chunk bobbles as she leans close. "Not perfect enough for you obviously."

The two clerks pass us and head for a patch of grass by the Legion. Noah flops on the grass a few yards away, beside a cedar tree. Keeping my voice low I say, "What's that supposed to mean?"

"Come on, Cate, you know exactly what I mean. You go through guys like cars go through gas and—"

"Not really. I dated Carter for nearly three months."

"And Robert before him for a month!"

Noah glances over. I give him a little wave. He inclines his head and looks away.

I don't need this. I have more important things to discuss. Except Tegan thinks the entire world should be coupled up. "Robert smoked too much weed, remember? He was constantly stoned. And he lied."

"Carter doesn't. He's totally honest. And he's dependable too."

She's right. Carter is dependable, agreeable, likeable. If Carter were a vegetable, he'd be a potato. Not even a fancy blue heirloom. He'd be a plain old russet. I sneak a peek at Noah. What kind of vegetable would he be?

He lifts a wedge of pizza and his bicep strains against his white T-shirt. *Man.* Noah's no vegetable. In the food store of life, Noah Fox is dessert. A rich tiramisu or a chocolate ganache torte. He catches me looking and raises a brow. Heat hits my cheeks. I pull my gaze away. Definitely the kind of dessert I avoid.

"What was it this time?" Tegan asks.

She knows me too well. It's the same with every guy I date. I start out with good intentions but after a while things start to bug me. Little things like endless throat-clearing or wearing the same shirt two days in a row. Or, in Carter's case, telling me I shouldn't have a second beer at Owen's party. Honestly, if I needed a babysitter I'd hire one. When I start to get resentful, I know it's time to end things. "It was a bunch of stuff. I did him a favour. It was the right thing to do."

She rolls her eyes. "You and your right thing to do."

"Forget Carter," I say. "You won't believe what happ—"

"What about prom?" she interrupts. "It's three weeks from now."

"I don't need to go to prom with anybody. I've told you that."

"But we're going together, remember? Me and Owen, you and Carter?"

I worry about Tegan sometimes. She lives in a fantasy world. One day Owen's going to dump her and she will be crushed (I have seen how he drools over the barista's boobs when we go for coffee). I, on the other hand, will never have to face that because I never let anything get too serious. People leave. It's a fact. Better to be the one walking than the one left behind.

"We've been planning it since grade six."

Correction, Tegan has. Grad has never been a huge deal to me. It's a pile of money for icky buffet food and mediocre music followed by an after-grad where everybody gets wasted. On the other hand, it *is* my last big school celebration so I'm not going to miss it. But I prefer to keep it low-key. Which Tegan hates. She freaked when I rented my dress instead of buying one. As a concession, I agreed to do the spa thing with her beforehand. And rent a limo for the prom parade. "I'll be there, Tegan. Tickets go on sale Monday. I'll get one. Don't worry."

With a look of disgust, she slaps the lid onto her salad and shoves the container into her bag. "Come on, Cate, nobody goes to prom alone."

"I won't be alone. I'll be with you guys. I'll still pay for my share of the limo. And I'm sure I can find somebody to pay for Carter's seat. Lots of people go in groups."

"That's lame."

"No, it's not." I pick at my ham on rye. "You're always telling me to quit trying to please people. So now I'm pleasing myself. I'd appreciate a little support."

She pulls out her brownie. "I support you. It's just—" She stops. "You're weird," she finally mutters.

"Call me weird, call me crazy, call me whatever you want. It doesn't matter because—" I pause for effect "—I've been accepted by Chef's Apron!!"

"What?" Brownie crumbs spray from her mouth. "That's amazing!"

"I know, right?" Chef's Apron is one of the best private culinary schools in North America. Their application process is rigorous, and their acceptance rate is only thirty percent.

Tegan grabs my arm. "You're going to be the best chef

ever. And you'll be moving to L.A.! I can come down for long weekends." The pressure on my arm makes me wince. "We can go celebrity spotting!"

"I know. But first I have to convince my dad to let me go. And find the money. The tuition for the first year is twenty-one thousand dollars."

Her mouth gapes. "Seriously?"

"Yeah. I need to send them ten thousand by June fifteenth and eleven thousand by September first. I've only got five thousand dollars saved." I need to find five grand in about six weeks. And that's just for tuition. I don't even want to think about living expenses.

She drops my arm. "Don't you have an education fund?"

"I'm not sure Dad will let me use it." Dad's an English prof at Vancouver Island University. He wants me to get an academic degree. Cooking, he says, is a life skill not a life plan.

"You could get a student loan."

"Chef's Apron isn't an accredited school under the government program. I checked."

"What about a private loan?"

"They need co-signers. Dad would never sign."

"That's so bogus. Ask Parker to talk to him. He'll stand up for you."

"Parker says it's Dad's decision." My dad's partner is sympathetic, but on parenting issues, he defers to Dad. Maybe because he didn't come into our lives until I was five.

Tegan's phone chirps, signalling a text. She glances down. "It's Owen again. He says Carter still wants to go to prom with you even if you're not together."

My stomach tightens. "Forget prom! What am I supposed to do about Chef's Apron?"

"Talk to your dad again. You want to be a chef, not a pole dancer."

"I know but—"

"Owen needs to confirm numbers for the limo. I'll tell him to write you down for two people." Before I can form the word no, Tegan is back on her phone. "Hey, babe."

I crumple my sandwich wrapper, grab my soda and stand up. When I whirl around, I almost plough into Noah Fox. Or more specifically into his chest. A very nice chest, even if it's mostly hidden under that dumb produce apron.

"Whoa!"

I stumble backward. My soda sprays all over him. Oh crap. "Sorry." *Awkward.*

"Hey, no worries. I knew you were going to dump soda on me. That's why I wore the apron."

A flush hits my cheeks. "So either you think I'm a klutz or you can see the future."

His lower lip twitches. Then he grins. And I stop breathing because Noah Fox smiling is a beautiful thing. "You're definitely not a klutz." He studies me with smoky green eyes framed by thick, black lashes. Natural guyliner.

I'm self-conscious about my ugly work pants and blue bakery shirt. And I probably still have the imprint on my forehead from the hairnet they make us wear. "So, you're psychic then."

"Totally." He winks. "Hang with me long enough and I'll tell you your fortune." And then he pulls off his apron.

I try not to stare but I can't help it. Noah Fox is stacked. It must be all that rowing. "You got some on your sleeve." I point. *Focus on the sleeve, Cate. The sleeve.*

"It'll dry fast. Things dry twenty percent faster outside than they do in a dryer, did you know that?"

I roll my eyes, relieved to be thinking about something other than how hot he is. It's weird. Normally I'm immune to hot guys who mimic dessert. "I don't do numbers, remember?" Noah and I sat beside each other in math last year, and he always finished at the top of the class.

He falls into step beside me as I walk to the nearby trash, his long legs easily keeping up with my shorter ones. "Why the hurry?"

"Tegan's hassling me about prom." I throw away my garbage. "Better to leave than fight with her."

Noah flattens his pizza box and tosses it into the recycling bin. "What's to fight about?"

"I'm going alone. She's flipping out."

"Well, it is social suicide to go to prom alone."

I study him out of the corner of my eye. I assume he's joking, but with Noah it's hard to tell. During math we had this ongoing discussion about where to find the best pizza in town. I never could decide if he was flirting or arguing. It was a flirtgument for an entire semester.

"But," he says, "sometimes it's the logical thing to do. I'm going alone."

I'm surprised. I know he broke up with Riley last month, but lots of other girls would be happy to be his date.

"Huh." I don't ask him why. I'm curious but I don't want to pry.

We head for Fine Foods, sidestepping a man in plaid shorts walking a black pug, and a jogger pushing a baby stroller.

"There's a rowing regatta the next day," Noah says after a minute, "so I can't make it a late night, and I didn't think that was fair to a date." His hair dips over his forehead; he flips it back. He has great hair. Thick and curly, the colour of chocolate cake. "I'm probably bailing on after-grad completely."

"Too bad."

"Not really," he says. "It's a big drunk up and I'm not into that." We stop at the corner and wait for the traffic to pass. "Hey, since I'm going alone and you're going alone, we should go alone together. What do you think?"

He smiles down at me. My heart skips a beat. I think I should lighten up about Noah Fox, that's what I think. Seriously, what is *wrong* with me? I don't react to guys this way, ever. Maybe I'm low in B vitamins or something. "You tell me," I tease as we cross the street. "You're the psychic."

He laughs. "You think it's a great idea."

"I do?" A dozen feet away, I see a familiar figure with a striped bag. It's Max. He's on his bike, bags of bottles and litter hanging from his handlebars. He's getting ready to ride across the street.

"You know it would be the best date of your life," he adds.

I'm about to tell him his ego is on steroids when I see Max push away from the curb. He's heading straight for oncoming traffic. "Max!" I shout. "No!"

Noah follows my gaze. "Oh crap!"

We both start to run.

2

It all seems to happen in slow motion. The screech of brakes. The swerving truck. The panicked shouts of bystanders. The thud of flesh meeting metal as we yank Max back.

His bike bounces and flips into the air. Bottles, cans, stale buns and litter take flight. Max crumples to the ground like a puppet whose strings are suddenly dropped. I bend over him, my body shaking uncontrollably as if I've been hit.

If we hadn't yanked him sideways…I fight back a wave of nausea. *Don't go there*. "Max! Are you okay?"

His eyes are shut and his skin is the colour of cement. His right leg is twisted in a weird way. I think I see bone. *Gross.* "Someone call an ambulance!" I yell. I can't do it. I'm too shaky.

"No ambulance," Max mutters.

"He's conscious," Noah says. "That's a good sign." He undoes a button on Max's shirt and checks his airways. When Max tries to get up, Noah gently but firmly holds him in place. "You need to stay still."

"I need my bike," Max moans. "I need to get outta here."

"You need to see a doctor first," I tell him.

Didn't you see that truck? What were you thinking?

A crowd gathers. A man in a grey suit starts directing traffic. A few people take pictures with their phones—of the intersection, the truck that's sideways across the road, Max's rusty old bike twisted and mangled on the boulevard. One of the deli workers puts Max's canvas bag down beside him. Someone else lines the empty bottles up on the curb. A few people collect the litter.

"Cover him." A woman passes us a brown sweater. "I know it's warm but he's probably in shock."

Noah drapes the sweater across Max's chest. His calmness amazes me.

A barrel-shaped man in a T-shirt and jeans hurries over. "He rode right in front of me like he wanted to get hit!" It's the truck driver. His flushed face is beaded with sweat. "He came out of the blue." He mops his forehead with the corner of his T-shirt. He stares at Max. "How is he?"

"I'm fine," Max whispers. "I need to go."

But Max's voice is thready. And weaker than it was a minute ago. My heart starts to thrum.

"You need to wait, Max, okay? The ambulance will be here soon." I hope. The health centre is on the Alberni Highway at least ten minutes away.

"I've radioed my company," the driver says. "They're sending a representative. They'll want witness statements."

"Don't worry," I tell him. Poor guy looks like he's been hit by a truck too. "I'll make a statement."

"Me too," Noah says. "We saw everything."

Tegan rushes over. "I saw the rescue part," she says. "You guys were amazing!"

"You pulled him away just in time," says a guy wearing a Mariners ball cap. "I got the whole thing on my cell."

"If it wasn't for you guys, Max would have been killed," Tegan adds, a tinge of awe in her voice.

I hear the faint whine of a siren. Thank goodness! Two police officers on bicycles ride up and dismount. "Do me a favour?" I ask Tegan. "Tell Peter we'll be late getting back to work."

Tegan's eyes widen. "*Late?* Are you kidding? You're gonna need the rest of the afternoon off. I'll tell him." She hurries away.

The female officer joins the man directing traffic. The male officer kneels down beside Max. "Took a spill did you?" He has a deep, reassuring voice.

Max mumbles something in response.

"What day is it today?"

"May eighth. Or maybe the eleventh. Who knows?"

The officer chuckles. "Bingo. It's the eleventh. Where do you live?"

I wait for Max to tell the guy it's none of his business or to say the whole world is his home, but he surprises me by naming a street about six blocks away. He's lying. When Tent City was disbanded last month, he and some of the other street people started staying at Rathtrevor Beach. It surprises me sometimes, the ease with which they're able to travel back and forth between Parksville and Qualicum.

"What's your name?" the officer asks.

"Max," he mumbles. "Just Max." He struggles to sit up but the officer holds him down.

"Take it easy there, Max. Not so fast."

Gently the officer rips the already torn fabric on Max's sweatpants, exposing the wound. My stomach flips. That *is* bone. I look away. The ambulance shoots around the corner, lights flashing. Another ambulance follows quickly behind. The two vehicles emit a final blast of their sirens before coasting to a stop a few feet away.

Two paramedics wearing bright yellow vests hop out and head for Max. Two more, a sleek blond and a man wearing aviator shades, take Noah and me over to the boulevard. They look into our eyes, ask us questions and take our vitals. "No physical damage," says the blond, "but shock can come later." She starts to talk about secondary victims and secondary shock, but I'm more focused on Max. His agitation is growing now that a paramedic is unloading a stretcher from the ambulance.

"Get that thing away from me!" he yells.

"Calm down, sir," one of the paramedics says. "We're taking you in so the doctor can check you out."

Max fists the air. "I'm not going anywhere."

"What do we know about the victim?" the blond paramedic asks the police officer.

"He says he lives over on Thetis. No last name yet. He won't tell me if he has next of kin." The officer picks up Max's canvas bag. "There might be something in here."

"Hey, hey, hey!" Max hollers when he sees them rifling through it. "That's private property. You have no right—"

"We're not taking anything, Max. Just looking for next of kin."

"Never mind!" Max shouts. "Give me that. I'm going home." He catches sight of me. "Tell them, Catie. Help me!"

Oh Max. I move toward him but Noah touches my arm. "Don't." He gestures. "Let them do their jobs."

I follow his gaze, see one of the paramedics holding a needle. My stomach flips again. *Max, what is happening to you?*

Another paramedic pulls a scrap of paper from a faded brown wallet.

"It looks like his name is Max Le Bould," he says.

"Jesus, Joseph and Mary!" Max's bellow is quickly followed by an angry howl of pain as the needle hits its mark. With a snap of metal, the stretcher is lowered to the ground.

"That can't be right." The cop snatches the paper out of the paramedic's hand and stares at it. "I can't believe it." He looks at Max and scratches his head. "Apparently that's Max Le Bould."

A moment of silence and then someone shouts, "Did you hear that? The guy on the ground is Max Le Bould."

Behind me a dozen voices talk at once.

"Max Le Bould."

"It can't be."

"...tragic what happened."

The man in the Mariners cap elbows his way past us. "I gotta get a shot of this!" He snaps a picture as the paramedics transfer Max onto the stretcher.

"Who's Max Le Bould?" I whisper to Noah as the guy turns and takes our picture next.

He shrugs. "No clue."

The guy in the ball cap gapes at us. "You guys don't know?"

We shake our heads.

"Max Le Bould! Only the most famous musician since John Lennon," he says. "He's been missing and presumed dead for fifteen years."

I want to go with Max in the ambulance but the paramedics won't let me. Instead, Noah and I speak to an official from the trucking company, and then we make statements to the police.

While we're waiting to make our statements, Noah gets on his phone and googles Max Le Bould. He reads for a few minutes, then hands me the phone. On the screen is an article from the *Guardian.* Max had been lead guitarist for the Magpies, a British rock group up there with the Stones. My dad plays their music sometimes, and he's mentioned the bus crash that claimed the lives of the band members. It was headline news for days as rescuers searched the Montana mountainside for bodies. According to the *Guardian*, Max's body was never found.

By the time we're done, Max is gone and the crowd has thinned. The only people left are a couple of officers still examining the accident site, and a reporter from the local TV station, KONO.

"How does it feel to save the life of someone so famous?" she asks us. Stacey Kosinski is tall and thin, with cropped blond hair and large giraffe teeth. She doesn't wait for our answer. "Not to mention aid in the discovery of his whereabouts?"

I'm not sure I buy it. The whole thing is so movie-of-the-week. It doesn't happen in real life. "He's just Max," I tell her. Max, who likes fancy cheese and picks up litter and recycles bottles and makes pithy statements about life and the world. But reporters don't care about homeless guys who sometimes drink too much raspberry vodka. People like that don't make headlines.

"It wouldn't have mattered anyway," Noah adds. "We did what anyone would have done."

Her blue scarf slips, revealing a low-cut peach top. Impatiently she flicks it back into place. "You don't understand. Back in the day, Max Le Bould was as famous as Justin Bieber. Only Le Bould had way more class. To have him alive and well and hiding in a small town on the west coast is momentous."

Is he hiding? Really?

She gives us a too-wide, too-fake smile. "Tell me again what happened." She is fawning and I don't like it.

Noah starts at the beginning. Unwilling to relive the accident, I walk across the boulevard to where the police are now examining Max's bike. I hear one officer say, "Imagine if it's true and he really is Max Le Bould."

A second officer snorts. "Yeah, and Elvis is alive and well and living in Toronto."

The second officer doesn't believe Max is *the* Max Le Bould either.

One of the officers, the man with the reassuring voice, looks up at me. "Can we give you a ride home?"

"Thanks, but I'm good." I gesture to Max's bike. "Would it be okay if I took that with me?" The frame is bent at a ninety-degree angle. A chunk of plastic bag is caught in the handlebars, ripped in half by the force of the truck sideswiping the bike. Tears clog the back of my throat. *If Noah and I hadn't been there*...I force that thought away. "I know it's in bad shape but Max will probably want it." I don't know how I'll get it home, since I rode to work. Maybe Peter will let me store it in the staff room overnight.

The officer shakes his head. "I'm sorry but we need to take it down to the station. The bike is evidence."

I thank him and wander back to Noah and Stacey, who is too busy firing questions at Noah to acknowledge me. "What can you tell me about Max? I understand he frequents this store often?"

She's sniffing for a story like a pig hunting for truffles. Only pigs have more class. Before Noah can answer, I say, "Any comment on that would have to come from our store manager, Peter Schwartz."

"He said he was too busy to talk."

"Then you'll have to talk to Max. We can't speak for him."

She jabs her pen into her notepad and slaps it shut. "There's no way I can get to him now. The paramedics said they'll probably need to operate on his leg."

My heart skips a beat. Operate?

"And we're on the air in three hours."

Max will need somebody in his corner. He wouldn't tell the cops his next of kin. He probably won't tell the doctors either. But he might tell me. At the very least I can hold his hand while they prep him for surgery. I look at Noah. "I need to get to the health centre and I rode my bike to work. It will take too long to ride there."

"I could drive you," Noah says.

Relief waterfalls through me. "That would be great, thanks."

Stacey frowns. "But I have more questions. And my tech will be here any minute to get footage. I want you both on camera."

"We have nothing else to say." Noah puts his free hand on the small of my back and steers me across the parking lot to his car like he's done it a thousand times before.

~

The Oceanside Health Centre, once only an urgent care clinic, was recently expanded to include a fifty-bed hospital. That's the good news. The bad news is the parking lot expansion is months away. Luckily Noah manages to squeeze his Civic into the last spot.

We hurry inside. The entrance is crowded with paramedics, representatives from the trucking company and a guy wearing jeans and a linen jacket firing questions at a cop. He's taking notes. My neck prickles. Another reporter.

"Come on." I weave through the crowd to the double doors that lead to the new emergency and hospital wing.

A security guard holds up a square hand. "Whoa, young lady, just a minute there."

Beyond the doors I hear Max. His voice is slurred but recognizable. "I'm leaving," he protests. "Stupid bastards. You can't keep me here." My heart lurches. He sounds miserable.

"I can't let you go back there." The guard has a belly that's seen way too many honey crullers. "Family members only."

I hesitate for only a second. "My uncle's in there. Max Le Bould. I'm his next of kin."

The guard frowns. "I don't—"

"He was hit by a truck in Qualicum a few minutes ago," I interrupt. "He needs an operation and I'm the only family here. I need to see him before they cut him open." I grab Noah's hand. "And my boyfriend needs to come with me because he keeps me calm, which is important because I'm diabetic and if I get stressed my sugars go through the roof."

Behind the doors, Max grunt-howls. He sounds like a wounded dog.

"That's not—" the guard starts to say.

"And if my sugars go through the roof I could collapse

right here and my father is a lawyer." I smile my sweetest smile. "A lawyer with a very bad temper."

The guard looks from me to Noah and back again. "I don't have time for this," he mutters, waving us through.

Admiration flickers across Noah's face. "Nice one, Sheridan. I didn't know you had it in you."

I drop his hand as we push through the doors. I don't know whether to be flattered or annoyed. The thought dissolves when I see one of the paramedics talking to a doctor and a nurse. My heart sinks. That guy was at the scene. My "I'm his niece" story won't fly here.

"Cate!" Max is on a bed a few cubicles away. He's wearing a baby blue hospital gown and a scowl. "Get me the hell out of here, Catie girl!"

I hurry over before the medical staff can stop us.

"They say I need a pin in my leg." Max's voice is thick and laced with pain. His eyes are at half-mast and his grey hair is spread out on the pillow like skinny little garter snakes. "They might send me to Nanaimo if they can't find a surgeon. I don't want any operation."

I reach for his hand. He's freezing. "Let them fix you." I rub his gnarled fingers to try and warm him up.

"Bugger that. I don't need fixing. Nothing wrong with me."

Noah wanders off. "You need a pin in your leg." I parrot Max's words back to him. "It sounds like your leg is broken."

Seconds later, Noah comes back carrying a brown blanket. It's heated I realize as I help him unfold it. "Nice one, Fox," I murmur. "I didn't know you had it in you."

He grins. "I was in here the second week they opened with a guy from the rowing club. I know where they keep them."

"That feels good," Max mutters as we tuck the blanket around him. He shuts his eyes. A few seconds later they fly open. "Get me outta here, Catie. I want to go home."

"You don't have a home," I whisper. "Remember?"

"Do so," he whispers back. "I've got everything I need out by Rathtrevor."

At least he's not lying about living on Thetis Avenue. "You need an operation, Max."

"They can give me a splint. Some drugs." His voice starts to climb. The paramedic and the nurse look over at us. "I can heal at home." His eyes flicker shut again.

"They can't keep him here against his will," Noah says softly.

I can't believe he just said that. "Are you nuts?"

"They can't," he repeats. "He's over nineteen and in his right mind."

That's debatable. Ignoring him, I turn back to Max. "Is there someone we can call for you, Max? Family maybe? Or a friend?"

His eyes pop open. "Just Tillie," he murmurs. "Tell her what happened."

Tillie is one of the few homeless people Max associates with, but as a resource she's even less reliable than Max, and that's saying something. "There must be somebody else I can contact." *Especially if you are who they say you are.*

Max swears under his breath. His eyes droop shut.

"You checked Google," I whisper to Noah. "If he's really Max Le Bould he must have friends and family. People who loved him." I look down at Max's hollowed cheeks, his dirty, matted hair. "Unless it's all a mistake."

"I don't think it is," Noah whispers back. "Remember

the picture I showed you? Add forty pounds and clean him up…" His voice trails off.

Max takes a laboured breath. His mouth gapes, flashing rotten teeth. He doesn't look like a man who walked away from a life of privilege. "I can't leave him here by himself."

"He's not by himself," Noah says. "He has the hospital staff."

I glare at him. One minute he gets Max a warm blanket, the next he's telling me to ditch my friend. "You know what I mean. Until we find his next of kin he has nobody." Except me.

Max is awake again. "I need to get my bike and go home." He struggles to sit up. "I left my cheese out. I need to put it away."

"Lie down, Max." Gently I ease him back against the pillow. "Your bike is broken. It needs to be fixed."

"I can fix it." He tries to sit up again but he's so weak he falls back. "Let me see it."

"It's already at the shop," Noah says. He doesn't clarify what shop he means. "Don't worry about that." I shoot him a grateful look.

A plump nurse carrying a clipboard walks up to the bed. I drop Max's hand and step out of the way. "Good news, Mr. Le Bould. The surgeon will be here shortly. All we need is your signature here." She raises the top half of his bed. "Let's get you sitting up."

"Bugger that," he protests. "Lemme go home."

The nurse adjusts the pillow behind his head and turns to us. "He's lucky," she says. "The break could have been much worse. But he needs surgery to retain his mobility." She bites her lip. "If it was up to me, I wouldn't let him leave without the operation."

As a homeless man, Max is already marginalized. Without surgery his life will be even more difficult. I pick up his hand. “Max, please have the surgery. For me.”

He stares at me, his eyes dull with pain and fear.

“It’ll be okay,” I whisper. “You’ll be healed up and riding your bike out to Rathtrevor in no time.”

“What about my stuff?”

“I’ll take care of it,” I tell him. “And I’ll find Tillie and tell her what’s happened.”

The nurse holds out a pen.

Max eyes it like it’s a snake ready to strike. Finally, with a sigh of defeat, he manages a wobbly signature. Even upside down I can read it. *Max Le Bould*.

“Cate is like kin,” Max tells the nurse. “She’s the only family I got.” He hands her the clipboard and closes his eyes.

“You’re Cate Sheridan?” the nurse asks. I nod, wondering how she knows my last name. My confusion must show because the nurse says, “Your details are on the accident report. I’ll list you as the primary contact for Max.”

“Good thing.” Noah nudges me. “’Cause we need to go.”

I turn and meet the stern gaze of Mr. Honey Cruller, the security guard. “We have a problem,” he says.

Heat hits my cheeks. “I know.” I’m not sure which lie to admit to first so I start small. “My dad’s not really a lawyer and I’m not diabetic. I don’t think.”

“Whatever.” The guard rolls his eyes. “Prepare yourself. There’s a heap of media waiting in the lobby. And they want to talk to you.”

3

My breath catches as I peer through the glass doors leading into the lobby. There are a dozen people out there. With TV cameras. I step aside so Noah can take a look.

He lets out a low whistle.

"I can't go out there." A bead of sweat rolls down my back. "I have nothing to say."

Noah gazes at me, his eyes calm and steady. "So say nothing."

"How does that work?"

"You say 'no comment.' You did it with that reporter from KONO earlier."

"Yeah, because she bugged me. If someone asks a question, it's polite to answer."

"You don't have to."

His calmness irritates me. "Are you always so logical?"

He grins. "Only ninety percent of the time." I roll my eyes. "Let me do the talking," he says. And for the second time that day, Noah puts his hand on the small of my back. But this time he leads me into hell instead of out of it.

Lights flash. Cameras whir. Reporters rush forward, surrounding us like a pack of hungry dogs. Several thrust big black microphones under our noses.

"How is Max Le Bould?"

"What's he been doing for the last fifteen years?"

"Sky is prepared to offer you an exclusive." Someone touches my arm. I jerk away. "What are your terms?"

Noah pushes his way forward; I follow his lead.

"Did he say anything about the accident that claimed the lives of his band members?" shouts another reporter.

"No comment," Noah says.

The reporters do a crab-walk backward, dangling their microphones in our faces, shooting questions at us.

"There are reports he's had a stroke."

"We understand he's had multiple transfusions and is on life support?"

Where do they *get* this stuff?

"We can't comment on his medical condition," Noah says. "That's up to the doctors."

"You saved his life," says a familiar voice. "How tragic if he dies now." It's Stacey, the reporter from KONO. She has a camera operator with her.

Bile burns the back of my throat. "He's not going to die." *He can't. I promised him he'd be fine.*

Noah increases the pressure on my back in warning. We reach the outside doors. The fresh air is a relief as we hurry across the parking lot. A few reporters follow, peppering us with more questions.

"Is Max mentally ill? Suffering from amnesia?"

"Does he realize people have been looking for him all this time?"

How should we know? *And how do you know it's Max Le Bould in that bed?*

"No comment," Noah repeats for the millionth time as we bolt across the parking lot to the safety of his car.

Noah pulls onto the road and boots it toward the inland highway. "Put on your seat belt." He peers into his rear-view mirror. "Those guys from KONO are following us."

As he passes Buckerfield's, I look at my phone. I've got three voice messages and a pile of texts.

Dad: *Parker saw an ambulance on Memorial. He heard there was an accident and you saved some man's life. Call me.*

Tegan: *Cate! Peter said KONO interviewed you. Is that TRUE??? Send deets!!!!*

Noah shoots past the exit for the highway, makes a sudden left on Bellevue and guns it for the side of the Petmania lot.

Dad, again: *A reporter from KONO called for you four times. She's annoying so I've taken the phone off the hook. She says you'll be on the news. Call my cell.*

Whoa. "We're gonna be on the news."

Noah doesn't answer. He's staring into the rear-view mirror, drumming his fingers on the steering wheel. There's a flash of red as the KONO van barrels past us. "There they go." He pulls out of the lot and heads back toward the highway. "We've lost them, but not for long."

"That KONO reporter called my house," I tell him after he's merged onto Highway 19. "If she has my phone number, she probably has my address." My breath hitches. "What if this *is* big news? What if they keep bugging us?"

"No comment is a complete sentence," says Noah. When I don't reply, he adds, "And like I said before, you don't have to talk to anybody if you don't want to."

I wonder what it's like to be so sure of yourself. I stare out the window as he drives. "I live on Belyea, off Garrett Road," I tell Noah after he takes the exit for Qualicum Beach. My house can be tricky to find from the inland highway. "Head down Rupert to Arbutus."

"Got it," he says.

I fire off a text to Dad and then one to Tegan. When I'm done, Noah says, "You promised Max you'd go and get his stuff. You mean out at Rathtrevor Beach?"

"Yeah. I'll go out tomorrow."

"Do you know where he's squatting?" Noah asks. "There's a lot of land out there."

He's right. With two kilometres of sandy shoreline and a huge swath of forested area, there's plenty of room for people to spread out. "They're at the far end, by San Pariel. Tillie will know where Max's camp is." If I can find her. Tillie bounces between Rathtrevor and Foster Park when she's not hiding out at the library.

He drums his fingers on the steering wheel. "You shouldn't go out there alone. You could get yourself in trouble."

"Only if you're government," I joke. Being a provincial park, Rathtrevor is administered by Park Services. But sometimes when park authorities ask the homeless to move, the homeless claim another government department gave them permission to be there. It makes for constant conflict. The first month there were fights almost every day. One guy even got stabbed.

"I'll be fine," I tell Noah. The afternoon sun slants through the car window, soothing and warm on my arm. "Max says most of the troublemakers have moved on. They're squatting by the Berwick well fields now."

"Chances are, Max will move on," says Noah. "He won't want to squat at Rathtrevor now that people know who he is. Especially not when the summer crowds show up. He'll have no privacy."

"I'm not sure he really is Max Le Bould."

"I'm betting on it," he says.

A prickle of unease runs down my spine. I don't know why the idea of Max being *the* Max Le Bould bothers me, but it does.

When Noah turns down my street, I scan the block for news vans or unfamiliar cars but the only activity is Mr. Lipinski pruning his cherry tree. "Mine is the grey house with the white porch," I tell him. "On the right."

He coasts to a stop behind Dad's Prius. "I'll grab your bag from the back." He pops the hatch.

I get out of the car and stare down the hill at the familiar backdrop of the coastal mountains. In the distance a sailboat glides across the strait. It's a common sight. I've seen it hundreds, maybe even thousands, of times. But this afternoon it looks fresh and new and more beautiful. Saving Max's life has made me appreciate my own.

Noah hands me my bag.

"Thanks." At the sound of my voice, Duke starts to bark. Oh great, now Dad's going to come out. That's the last thing I need. "And thanks for taking me to the hospital."

"No worries."

"That was really close. Max could have been killed." In my mind's eye I see the accident again. Max at the curb, pushing off into the path of the truck. I shove the images back. "He's lucky."

"Or not," Noah says.

"What do you mean?"

"Maybe he didn't want to be saved."

A pressure in my chest makes it hard to breathe. "I don't get it."

He hesitates. There's a bleak look in his eyes. "What if Max rode into that truck on purpose?"

"No way." Duke barks again, twice. Even the dog agrees with me. *No*, he is saying. *No. No.*

The front door opens. Duke races across the grass and throws himself against my legs. My knees buckle; I grab at his fur. "It was an accident. Max wasn't paying attention."

"Maybe," Noah says softly. "Or maybe Max knew exactly what he was doing."

The idea sucks the oxygen out of me. I stare up at him. Noah looks sincere. He believes what he's saying. "He just wasn't thinking," I say.

He turns to go. "I hope you're right."

I clutch Duke and watch Noah walk to the car, the cold truth flirting around the edges of my consciousness.

Noah's wrong. He has to be.

"Five minutes until the news!" Dad yells into the kitchen.

Perfect timing. I retrieve the strawberry rhubarb crisp from the oven and set it on the trivet to cool. The sweet smell of brown sugar and cinnamon fills the room. I take a deep breath. For a moment Max is forgotten and all is right in my world.

Earlier, after giving Dad the short version of events, I'd headed for the kitchen. Chopping and measuring and mixing soothes me, and I desperately needed soothing.

The accident had unnerved me. Seeing all those reporters had unnerved me. So had Noah's suggestion that Max had deliberately ridden into the path of that truck.

"How did the crisp turn out?" Dad asks when I wander into the TV room. He's sprawled in the recliner, reading. Duke thumps his tail as I lean down to give him a pat.

"Good, I think." I stretch out on the couch and stuff a cushion under my head. Duke settles with a contented groan at my feet. "Where's Parker?" Parker's a landscape designer. He puts in long hours during the growing season, but he's usually home for supper on the weekends. And he loves my desserts.

"One of his clients is taking him out for dinner."

"I hope they take him for steak or burgers and not sushi." Parker's a dedicated meat-and-potatoes guy. Which is good because if Dad were a food, he'd be steak. Filet mignon, probably. High class, the king of steaks, a cut that deserves respect. That's Dad.

The familiar KONO news jingle floats out of the TV. An announcer wearing a bright fuchsia jacket and huge fake pearls appears on the screen. "Coming up tonight on KONO, a musical legend resurfaces in Qualicum Beach!"

Her image fades to footage of the accident. I glimpse the ambulance, the truck that sideswiped Max, two of the cops. "In what eyewitnesses describe as an electrifying rescue, two local teens are being touted as heroes for saving the life of Max Le Bould, the musician who's been missing and presumed dead for almost two decades. We'll have details momentarily."

The music swells; the red and blue KONO logo appears.

"If it *is* Max Le Bould," Dad says, "that'll *really* put Qualicum on the map."

"Last time I looked we were on the map."

He grimaces. "We're a town of 9,000. We're known for the Father's Day Show 'n' Shine and the Brant Wildlife Festival. This could be a big deal for us."

"Good evening. I'm Pamela Holtz and this is KONO News at Five." Pamela is sitting at the desk beside Stacey, the reporter who talked to us. My hand tightens around the pillow. "Stacey Kosinski is with us tonight, and she brings us details on the Max Le Bould story. Stacey, what do we know about today's events?"

The camera tightens on a close-up of Stacey. "Pamela, according to eyewitnesses, just before one this afternoon, a man on a bike was crossing Memorial at Harlech Road near the new Fine Foods shopping complex when he unexpectedly veered into oncoming traffic. Two teenagers, employees of Fine Foods, pulled him back to safety. One of the witnesses recorded some of the events on a cell phone."

Noah and I appear on the screen, backs to the camera. I watch us jerk Max away from a head-on impact. There goes his bike, flipping and crashing to the pavement. I see us bend over him. My movements are jerky; Noah's are smooth and calm. Suddenly I'm back there, heart pounding, trembling with fear. I suck in a breath. Duke lifts his head and gives me a curious look.

"Eyewitnesses say the cyclist is British rock star Max Le Bould," Stacey adds. "Le Bould was lead guitarist for the Magpies. Band members were killed in a Montana bus crash almost sixteen years ago. However, Le Bould's body was never found." The footage is more professional now. My stomach clenches as I see shots of Max's bike and of Max being loaded into the ambulance.

A picture of the hospital entrance flashes on the screen.

"Police won't confirm the man's identity," Stacey says. "The victim is in fair condition and is currently at the Oceanside Health Centre undergoing surgery for a broken leg."

He cannot die. I promised him.

"This is very much a developing story," Pamela interjects.

"That's right," Stacey says. "We've lined up interviews with people who know Le Bould, including Grammy-winning music producer David Foster, the editor of *Rolling Stone* magazine and representatives for Paul McCartney and Eric Clapton."

My heart skips a beat. "Whoa!"

"I told you it would be big news," Dad says.

"At this point, however, people are waiting until the cyclist's identity is confirmed," Stacey adds. "KONO will bring you up-to-date information as we receive it."

"What do we know about the two rescuers?" Pamela asks.

My breath stalls.

"Their names are Cate Sheridan and Noah Fox."

Noah and I appear on the screen. Last year's annual pictures. Where did they get those?

Now they're showing us outside the hospital, my short legs scrambling to keep up with Noah's longer ones.

"Multiple eyewitnesses have spoken about the brave rescue, saying if it wasn't for these two young people, the man in question would have been killed."

Noah and I look like criminals as we run across the parking lot hounded by reporters. I see the guy in the linen jacket shove his card at me.

"Sheridan and Fox declined to comment and downplayed their role in the rescue, saying anyone in their position would have done the same thing. However, a friend of one of the homegrown heroes had this to say."

A familiar face appears on screen.

I gasp. "Oh my God!"

Tegan's round eyes blink furiously as she stares into the camera. "Cate Sheridan has been my best friend since grade one." She looks even more like an owl than usual. "I'm not surprised she saved that guy's life. Of course she's a hero." Blink, blink, blink. "She's always doing everything for everybody and making sure people are all right and she still manages to be a straight A student."

I groan. Not true.

"That Tegan." Dad shakes his head. But his lips twitch.

Tegan is on a roll. "And she loves to bake. She sometimes brings cupcakes to school just because it's raining."

I only did that once and only because the debate club teacher got engaged.

"And she's been accepted to the most prestigious cooking school in North America, Chef's Apron..."

Dad frowns. "What?"

Crap! Dad hates surprises.

"...and one of these days you're gonna see Cate Sheridan on *Iron Chef America*. I just know it."

"Really, Cate? You applied without telling me?" Dad asks.

I nod. On the screen, Tegan is gone. The two women are talking again.

"*And* you got *accepted?*" Dad's voice is climbing. His jaw is set in a familiar I'm-trying-not-to-lose-it way.

"Yeah."

"When were you going to tell me?"

"Soon," I say. "It's just—"

In the pocket of my sweats my cell phone vibrates. "There's a lot going on lately." *And I knew you'd be upset and I didn't want that.*

I look down at the screen. It's a text from Tegan. *Was I great or was I great???? Call me ASAP. We're both heroes. We have to celebrate.*

"We have to talk," Dad says.

"You're not throwing your life away in a restaurant kitchen," Dad says. "You're too smart for that."

It's my life. Shouldn't it be my decision? I push a chunk of marinated broccoli around my plate. We've been going over this since we sat down to eat. "It's what I want, Dad. It's what makes me happy."

"I want you to be happy, and I'm glad you have a passion for cooking. It's an important life skill and a great hobby. But you don't want to do it for a living, Cate. You think you do, but you don't. The hours are long, the working conditions are terrible. Drug use is rampant in restaurant kitchens."

"Drugs are everywhere, Dad. I'm not into them. You know that."

"The restaurant pay scale is appalling. You need a career that will support you. You need to be sensible."

"I *am* being sensible." At the tremor in my voice, Duke lifts his head and wiggles forward on his mat.

"Down!" Dad reprimands.

Clearly disgruntled, the dog flops back, rests his head on his paws, stares at me.

I chew my broccoli, hardly tasting it. "There's no point in spending money on university when all I want is to be a chef."

"Your English skills are amazing. You could teach. Or write for a living."

"Boooring."

"What about social work? You're always looking out for other people."

"That's a life skill." I quote his words back to him. "Not something I want to do for a living."

"I'm sure something will occur to you when you get to university." He's trying to placate me. "You don't need to figure it out right away. You've got options."

I feel a twinge of guilt. I do have options. I have a healthy education fund. A father who loves me, even if he totally overcompensates. There are kids who would give anything to be in my place. "Nana thinks I should go."

"Of course she does. But your grandmother is hardly a role model." Dad calls Nana a free spirit. After her first marriage failed, she supported Dad by running a bed and breakfast and selling handmade jewellery. Later she started travelling and volunteering in Third World countries, only cutting back when Dad needed help raising me. Right now she's in Japan with her new husband, teaching English. We text and email regularly.

"Nana is happy. And she always gets by."

"I don't want you to 'get by.'" Dad emphasizes the last two words with air quotes. "I want you to thrive, to have a million and one opportunities. Get a post-secondary degree. You can always pursue cooking later."

I know how that would play out. If I get the degree Dad wants, the pressure won't stop there. Afterward he'll insist I get a decent job. He'll say I need to use my education to my best advantage. He'll never see professional cooking as a viable career for me.

"I'm trying to do the right thing as a parent, Cate. Think of this as my last parental gift to you."

Some gift. Tears prickle behind my lids. At times like this I wish I had a sibling to share the joy—or a mother to take my side. But I'm it, and if I don't stand up for myself, I'll end up the proud and miserable owner of an English degree. I'll be trapped.

"That money in my education fund is mine, right?" Dad refuses to meet my eyes. He's told me for years that money is mine. "Let me use it for cooking school. Let me follow my dream."

I know this is the right choice for me. In the kitchen I am my best self. Maybe it's those early memories of visiting Nana and helping her bake scones at her bed and breakfast, the scent of their fruit-studded sweetness wafting out from the oven. Seeing Nana carry them to the table and place them ceremoniously beside the glistening dishes of homemade jelly. Watching her guests scarf them down. I want that feeling back. I want to create and share food with others. It's my gift. It's what I was born to do.

"It's a mistake, Cate."

"Then it'll be my mistake. And if it doesn't work out and I decide to go back to school, I'll pay for that myself."

Dad sighs. "You'd be in debt forever. I can't let you take that chance. An academic degree will set you up for life."

Some life. I shove my plate aside and swallow my anger. If I disagree, I'm insulting his choice to become a professor. And I don't want to hurt him.

"We've gone over this," he says. "We agreed you'd get a post-secondary degree."

I didn't agree. I just didn't disagree. At least not out loud.

"And I'm disappointed that you went ahead and applied to Chef's Apron without discussing it with me."

I had to; I knew how the discussion would go. It would be more of an argument. And I don't like arguing with Dad. I also knew I would lose, and I didn't want to be disappointed. Now I've disappointed him, which is worse. "I'm going to my room."

"What about the rhubarb crisp?" Dad asks.

"I've lost my appetite."

Dad rubs his eyes. "Don't be silly, Cate."

Silly?

"This is just the accident talking," he adds. "You're traumatized."

It's not trauma, but the accident has affected me. If we hadn't jerked Max back from that truck, he might have died. Life can end with one turn of a bike pedal. I don't want to waste a second of it. For sure I don't want to waste four years of it. But Dad wouldn't understand.

"Come on." He reaches for the bowls. "Let's have dessert together."

No way. I'm so upset I'd probably choke on a piece of rhubarb. I shake my head and stand. Duke rushes to my side, presses against my leg. "I'll get mine later."

Dad presses his lips together. I've disappointed him again. Maybe I need to get used to that. Because if I end up becoming a chef, Dad will probably be disappointed for the rest of his life.

4

Blue Skies Nana to CD Sheridan: *Oh sweetie, how terrible. I'm glad the man is alive. RE: your father. He'll come around. Give him time.*

CD Sheridan to Blue Skies Nana: *I don't have time. The first tuition payment is due June 15.*

Blue Skies Nana to CD Sheridan: *Things will work out. They always do.*

Duke's barking wakes me before eight on Sunday morning. I hear the squeak of the front door and a low, masculine rumble as Dad's voice floats up the stairs. Rolling onto my side, I snuggle under the duvet and wonder if there's coffee. Duke barks again. Dad's voice carries into my room. He sounds irritated. The front door slams.

I jump out of bed and pad to the window. My insides turn to mush. Three news vans are parked on the street.

When I head downstairs, Dad's in the kitchen grinding coffee beans. The back door is open and Duke is out on the grass. Droplets of dew glisten in the early morning sun. It's a perfect day to look for Tillie at Rathtrevor Beach.

"We've got company," Dad says when the grinder stops running. "They want you to make a statement."

"I have nothing to say."

"I told them that."

Duke bounds up the stairs and wags his tail as Dad pours kibble into his dish. My stomach lets out an angry growl. I open the fridge and survey the contents. I'm hungry but I don't know what I want.

Footsteps sound on the back stairs. Duke looks up from his breakfast and races to the deck. It's Parker returning from a doughnut run.

"Those bastards practically accosted me." He's carrying a familiar red Tim Hortons box. My mouth starts to water. I'm no food snob. I love homemade, but I also love Timmy's. Especially their apple fritters. I shut the fridge and grab mugs and plates from the cupboard.

"I read them the riot act," Dad says grimly. "If they don't leave soon, I'm calling the cops."

Parker gives Dad's shoulder a squeeze. The two of them are so different. In looks and in personality. Parker is tall, husky and red-haired; Dad is short, wiry and dark-haired. Dad's an intense control-freak academic. Parker's laid-back, funny and happiest outside digging in the dirt. Opposites must attract because the two of them have been together and happy since I was in kindergarten.

"How do you feel about doing our hike after lunch?" Parker asks Dad. "An order of shrubs came in at Cultivate and I need to pick them up and buy perennials for next week's job. I'd rather get that done this morning."

Talk about good timing. The Parksville garden shop is a ten-minute drive from the beach where Max has been squatting. "If you're driving out that way, would you mind dropping me at Rathtrevor?" Before either of them can ask why, I add, "I need a beach walk to clear my head."

"Why not walk the beach in Qualicum?" Dad asks.

I gesture to the window. "Those guys might follow me."

"Not if I can help it," he says grimly.

"I don't mind driving you out to Rathtrevor," Parker says. "I'll probably be close to an hour at Cultivate. That give you enough time?"

"Perfect, thanks."

I chase the apple fritter with a double chocolate doughnut before changing into jeans and a sweater. Thankfully the reporters are gone by the time we leave. While Parker drives the lower highway along the water, I unload about Dad's insistence that I get an academic degree. And about Max and how worried I am about what lies ahead for him. Parker doesn't say much, but he's a good listener. His quiet understanding makes me feel better.

"Why don't you drop me by the San Pariel access point?" I strive to keep my tone casual. "It's closer to Cultivate." It's also closer to where Max and the others are squatting.

"You sure you're just going for a walk?" Parker asks.

Parker is the mac and cheese in my life. The rich, homemade kind. Steady, comforting and true. He's also a straight shooter and he expects the same from others. "Max wanted me to let one of the homeless people know he's in the hospital, so if I run into them..." I shrug and let my voice trail away. I can't lie to him, but I don't want to worry him either.

Parker stares at me. "You have your cell phone?"

I nod.

"Stay on the trail or the beach," he says. "Don't go into the forest. And call if there's a problem."

I nod again.

"I'll pick you up here in an hour."

"Thanks!" I jump out of the van and give him a wave.

A two-minute trail walk leads me to the beach. In the distance, shrouded in morning mist, is Lasqueti Island and the Sunshine Coast. The tide is coming in. I breathe in the salty air and feel my shoulders relax at the soothing sound. The shoreline to my left is banked by houses. Predictably there are no squatters there. But to the right I see tents, woodpiles and people. One person is wearing a familiar striped poncho. Tillie.

I start to walk, passing day visitors setting up beach mats and coolers. Two children are searching for crabs under rocks. Brown-and-white sandpipers dive near the water line, pecking at the sand for breakfast.

Two minutes later I reach Tillie's camp. It's a bare-bones affair: a propane stove on a couple of bricks, a faded green tarp and a couple of plastic shopping bags. "Well, well," she says. She's got badly cut shoulder-length grey hair and skin weathered from hard living. Hands on hips, she studies me through narrowed eyes. Her tummy, accented by the orange and blue stripes of her poncho, juts out in front of her. "What are you doing here?"

Tillie isn't one for small talk. "There was an accident yesterday. Max almost rode into a truck." A few feet away a dreadlocked guy wearing army fatigues puts his book down and watches our exchange. I glance past him to the other camps, wondering which one belongs to Max. The one with the dirty white tarp hanging over a blue tent maybe. It looks deserted.

"Ah." There's a knowing look on her pie-shaped face. "Well, we all reach the last frontier eventually."

The last frontier? Has she been drinking? Or smoking weed? Whatever. It's not my place to judge. "He wanted me to get his book and cheese and stuff. And I thought I'd see if he has a spare pair of pants since the paramedics cut his off."

Her eyes widen. "He's alive?"

Last frontier. She thought he was dead. *What if Max rode right into that truck?* My breath hitches. No. Just no. "He broke his leg and they had to operate. He'll be fine. But he's worried about his stuff."

She starts to walk. "Why didn't you say so?" She leads me down the beach and up a steep incline covered in Oregon grape and ferns. She's probably a hundred pounds heavier than me, but she moves so quickly that by the time we stop at the edge of the trees, I'm out of breath.

"Max wasn't staying on the beach?" I ask, thinking of Parker's order to stay out of the forest.

"No. He likes solitude." She starts walking again. "Nobody bugs him here."

I step over a log and follow her. The woods smell like cedar and moss and wet earth. They smell peaceful. And safe.

After a few minutes, Tillie stops in a clearing. A round brown pup tent is set up at the base of a thick old tree. Low-hanging branches frame it like arthritic fingers cupping a walnut. A rusty metal chair with rotted webbing sits in front of a cold firepit. A piece of twine is stretched between two trees. "Here he be." She holds the tent flap ajar and gestures me inside.

The tent smells like mildew, and even though we haven't had rain lately, Max's sleeping bag is damp. It takes me less than a minute to determine that he doesn't have a spare pair of pants. Max doesn't have spare anything. An ache goes through me. I rock back on my heels and survey what he does have. One sleeping bag, a burgundy sweatshirt he obviously uses as a pillow, a mouldy piece of cheese, a chunk of stale bread and two books: *Thoughts Without a Thinker* and *Teaching a Stone to Talk.*

Tillie insists I take down the tent. "If you don't, as soon as word gets out that he's in the hospital, somebody'll come along and grab it."

It takes us less than five minutes to break Max's camp. I pack up his tent and sleeping bag, the books and his sweatshirt. I tell Tillie to take the chair. I'll buy Max a new one when he gets out of the hospital. I figure I'll toss the food but when I see Tillie eyeing it, I offer it to her. "Sorry, it's a little old."

"I've eaten worse," she says.

Max's belongings weigh almost nothing but they're bulky. It occurs to me as we leave the shadow of the forest and head down the beach that I'll need to come clean with Parker and Dad. It's not exactly normal to return from a beach walk with camping gear.

"Say hi to him for me," Tillie says when we reach her camp. She unfolds the chair and puts it by her stove.

The last frontier. Clutching Max's damp sleeping bag, I ask, "Did Max ever talk to you about the last frontier?"

Tillie's hand, busy unwrapping Max's bread, stops moving. She's in profile; I can't see the expression on her face. She stuffs a chunk of bread into her mouth. "Me and Max talked about lots of things," she mumbles.

I open my mouth to ask her another question, but she gives me a wave and turns away. Her message is clear. I've been dismissed. And that is both a relief and a disappointment.

Parker says nothing when he picks me up fifteen minutes later, though he raises an eyebrow when he sees Max's tent and sleeping bag.

"Don't ask," I say, so he doesn't.

Instead he drives me to Fine Foods where I retrieve my bike. At home I stash it in the shed along with Max's things. I spend the rest of the day checking out scholarship options and compiling a list of companies that offer loans for chef training. It's a long shot because I know Dad won't co-sign, but looking for solutions beats sitting around worrying. Or thinking about Max and wondering why Tillie didn't seem surprised about the accident.

Monday morning, when I leave the house, the street is still a reporter-free zone. But when I get to school I spot a Sky News van along with a red one from KONO parked on Village Way. I hang a quick right and ride across the field before locking up my bike by the gym entrance.

Seconds after I reach my locker, Tegan appears, cell phone in hand. She's wearing a sleeveless floral dress over tight black leggings with brown combat boots. "You're late. Where have you been?"

"I had to call the hospital to check on Max. The surgery went well and he'll be ready for company tomorrow." I spin my combination and open the door.

"This Max thing is big," Tegan says. "The story's everywhere. Even the teachers are talking about it."

Tegan exaggerates.

"No way." I slam my locker.

She nods. "Yep." She starts to walk. I fall into step

beside her. "And Jared wants me to interview you for the *Messenger*."

The *Messenger* is our school paper. Tegan contributes a monthly column, though her stuff runs more to the TMZ side of things than actual journalism.

"I pretty much have the story mapped out. I just need a few quotes. We can do it after school."

"I'm seeing Kaneko then." Mrs. Kaneko is the career counsellor. I'm going to pick her brain about tuition for Chef's Apron and ask if she'll talk to Dad. She's supportive of careers in the trades. Maybe Dad will listen to her.

"How about we talk at lunch? There's a food truck coming today. Let's meet by the trail."

There's no way I can stop Tegan from writing about Max's accident. She's as obsessive about writing as I am about cooking. If Tegan were a food, she'd be hot salsa. She's up front, in your face and impossible to ignore. "Okay, I'll meet you at lunch." If I cooperate maybe I can influence how she spins things.

Before she turns to go she says, "Don't forget to buy your prom ticket. And talk to Carter. You seriously need to put the guy out of his misery and give him another chance."

In English, Mrs. Moreau claps her hands. "Well done, Cate." She beams at me. "I'm looking forward to hearing all about it after class."

My face flames. Titters break out. A couple of guys snort-laugh. I slouch down in my seat, hugely relieved when she picks up last week's lesson on the work of Anton Chekhov. Today she's talking about *The Cherry Orchard*. "Each character is involved in a struggle to remember," Mrs. Moreau tells us, "but more importantly they're also struggling to forget certain aspects of their past."

I don't have to forget my past. I never think of it, at least not much. Except Mother's Day is coming. The muffin I had for breakfast cramps my stomach. I slap a lid on my thoughts and focus on what the teacher is saying.

When class ends I bolt before Moreau can ask me any questions. I stop in the office to buy tickets for prom and then head for the door. When I turn the corner, I practically plough into Noah Fox. He's standing in the middle of the hall talking to a group of girls.

He reaches out to stop me from stumbling. "There you go again, trying to run me over!" He drops his arm casually across my shoulder. Two of the girls smile. Riley, the third girl, doesn't.

"So that's how it is." Riley's eyes narrow. Tall and slim with long white-blond hair, Riley is the unofficial leader of the Chip Trail Squad, the kids who spend more time hanging on the trail smoking than in class.

Back in elementary school, Riley was my friend. She was fun. Then in grade six her father was charged with embezzlement and sent to jail. Soon after, Riley's humour turned mean and she began picking fights. After a while I got tired of the drama.

"I didn't know you guys were together," Riley says.

"We're not," we say in unison. But we say it too fast, too loud, too *something* because Riley rolls her eyes in obvious disbelief. "Sure you're not." She pauses. "Well, we can't all have good taste." She shoots me a haughty look before turning to go.

I look at Noah. "She thinks we're dating."

He grins. "Maybe she's psychic too."

"Give it up. You're not psychic and we're not dating."

"Why not?" He dips his head almost bashfully, a

chestnut curl flopping over his forehead. "I'd be up for it."

My stomach goes all squidgy. Noah Fox is a smorgasbord of gorgeous. "I'm off dating right now."

He frowns.

"It's like being off dairy," I clarify. "Or gluten."

"We can hang out then." He steers me down the hall. "You're a nice person."

My heart constricts. Nice is such a four-letter word. I slide out from under his arm. "If you want to hang out, do me a favour? Tegan wants to interview me about the rescue for the *Messenger*. We're meeting by the trail. Do it with me?"

"Sure. Hungry Rooster is here and I am starving."

We join the crowd waiting at the food truck. I order the slapdown, a grilled cheese perogy sandwich with bacon and onions. Noah opts for a double order of the Mexicana perogies, a deluxe smokie, two chocolate chip cookies and a wedge of banana bread. I stare at his massive shoulders. I guess all that food has to go somewhere.

Tegan is waiting for us at the edge of the field. She's typing on her cell as we sit down on the grass. "Riley says you and Noah are together but I'm telling her she's wrong." She glances up at us and quickly looks back down. "Right?" She keeps typing.

I look at Noah. Noah looks at me. He has a mouth full of smokie so I speak for him. "Wrong."

Tegan stops texting. She looks up. "What do you mean, wrong? Right wrong, or wrong wrong?"

Before I can answer, Noah says, "It's complicated."

Tegan's eyes go owl-in-the-headlights wide. "Oh man. You guys sure didn't waste any time. I gotta tell Owen!" She starts texting again.

"Tegan, he's kidding!" I say.

Noah's shoulders shake in silent laughter. *Quit messing around,* I mouth.

Tegan looks up after she finishes texting Owen. "So how long?" she asks.

My chest tightens. "We're not rea—"

"Not really wanting to talk about it," Noah interrupts. I glare at him. He's finished his smokie and is starting on his perogies. "It's kinda private. Besides, we'd rather focus on Max's rescue. Cate says you want to talk to us for the *Messenger*."

"You're right." Tegan smiles at Noah. "I do." She pulls a notepad and pen from her bag. "Tell me everything you remember."

Noah has amazing recall. I barely contribute anything. By the time he's done, Tegan is stoked. "It'll be a great story," she says as we stand up. "Thanks." She gives me a meaningful look. "Call me later. We clearly have some catching up to do."

She heads for the school; Noah and I follow slowly behind. Tegan is my best friend, and I love her like a sister, but she doesn't get the whole "I don't need a guy" thing. Her body rejects it like an allergy to wheat. If I try to explain Noah was teasing, she'll think I'm kidding and the next thing I know she'll upload our pictures to Instagram with some cutesy lovesick hashtag. I need that like I need a bad rash.

"Have a good afternoon," Noah says when we reach the doors. And then he grabs my hand, turns it palm side up and scribbles something with a black pen. "Here's my cell number. Text me yours, okay? It makes sense to have them if we're hanging out."

As I watch him walk away, all long legs, big shoulders and messy hair, I wish we were dating. But I'm being dumb. Dating gets complicated. And I like simple.

Case in point: Carter. I see him the minute I walk into Environmental Studies. He has saved me a seat. Russet potato dependable, that's Carter. I slide into the seat beside him. "Hi."

He just looks at me. Carter has short sandy brown hair, a narrow face and a pale, potato-white complexion. Or normally he does. Right now his cheeks are mottled a plummy red. "You could've told me there was someone else."

"There isn't. I swear."

He folds his arms across his chest. He is the picture of grievous disappointment.

"Honestly, there's no one."

Carter is clearly skeptical. "The guys warned me when we started going out, but I figured you'd be different with me."

My spine stiffens. "What do you mean, they warned you?"

"That you were, you know, a commitment-phobe. Unless I needed food or was living on the street or something—then I'd have your undivided attention."

That was the other thing about Carter. He hated Max. Whenever I said hi to him, Carter would raise hell with me about talking to a homeless guy.

"They told me you couldn't stay with anybody."

Heat creeps up my neck. "That's unfair." I remember Tegan's words. *You go through guys like cars go through gas.*

Carter leans forward. He's so close I can feel his hot breath against my cheek. "Come on, Cate, we're perfect together. I can see us years from now, telling our kids how we met in high school and—"

Little potato-lings? I don't think so.

"—how you were a little bit wild but I settled you down and—"

"I had *two beers* at Owen's party! That's not wild! And you settled me down? Really?" I won't say more. I don't want to fight. "Friends, Carter. Take it or leave it." I offer him my hand.

He eyes it like a scorpion has materialized at the end of my arm. "Friends," he finally mumbles. But he doesn't take my hand or look at me for the rest of class. As soon as it ends I jump out of my seat and bolt out the door before he can argue his case for our future offspring.

Thoughts of Carter quickly fade later that afternoon in Mrs. Kaneko's office. She's sympathetic to my need for tuition money and promises to search out scholarships specifically for food studies, but she recommends trying to work things out with Dad. "I could talk to him but it's better for you and your father to come to an agreement. Your dad only wants you to have options. I'm sure you can convince him cooking school will secure your future."

I wish I shared Mrs. Kaneko's optimism. By the time I leave her office, the halls are empty. I dump my books in my locker, grab my English homework and head outside to the bike rack.

The afternoon is cool; it feels like rain. A breeze ruffles my hair as I put on my helmet and do up my coat. I'm unlocking my bike when I hear a voice shout, "There she is!"

I look up. Half a dozen reporters rush toward me, microphones and notepads in hand. I can't believe they're on school grounds. Isn't there some kind of law? Then I spot the camera operators behind them. Their equipment is hoisted to their shoulders; they're ready to film. My heart kicks into overdrive.

What should I do? Abandon my bike? Go back inside? What?

I decide to take a tip from Noah. Say nothing and keep moving. I wheel my bike out of its stand, climb on and start to pedal, almost crashing when a large black microphone is dangled in front of my face.

"Ms. Sheridan, slow down!"

"Two minutes, Ms. Sheridan, please?"

Another microphone is thrust into my face. I veer left, onto the gravel. "What's your reaction to the news?"

What news? But I don't ask. I pump furiously, desperate to get away, but the gravel makes for slow going. And they're running along beside me.

"It's been confirmed," says Stacey from KONO. "The man in the hospital is Max Le Bould."

Adrenalin surges through me.

"You single-handedly brought a musical legend back to life."

My bike wobbles. Not single-handedly. Noah was there.

"How does that feel?"

Go away. "No comment."

One of the men starts to ask another question. I cut him off. "I said no comment. Leave me alone!" Finally I reach pavement. I lift out of my seat and push down hard on the pedals. My bike shoots forward. And the reporters are left behind.

5

"Cate! I don't get you," Tegan screeches into my ear later that night. "Anybody else would jump at the chance to be on TV. Embrace your fifteen minutes of fame. Talk to them."

I'm stretched out on my bed, a pile of English homework and notes for my Environmental Studies paper spread out around me. Duke is lying beside me, snoring softly. "I don't have anything to say."

"They want to know about Max. He walked away from his life. He's homeless by choice and that's kinda weird. People want to know why."

According to Google, Max had a fiancée when he disappeared. He had friends, colleagues, a sister. People who loved him. How could he walk away from that? Why does anybody ditch a life? Ditch family? A cold chill rocks me. *Don't go there*. I grab my fuzzy pink throw and pull it over my legs.

"Tell them about his funny sayings. The insights he has about people. His love of cheese and how he picks up litter. The media will love it."

I trail my fingers through Duke's fur. "That's private."

"You told me."

"Yeah, in confidence. And I don't want to talk to them."

"I'll talk to them then," she says.

"Don't you dare!"

She snorts. "If the opportunity presents itself, I'd be nuts to turn it down."

Tegan wants to be a reporter. The way she networks and manages to find out everything about everybody, she'll probably make it.

"People are dying to know about him," Tegan adds. "Have you googled the guy? He was majorly hot back in the day. A total megastar. And now he's living on the street. The question is why?"

I've wondered the same thing. So many lost years. "Don't say anything, Tegan. Just don't. Let me talk to Max first. That's only fair."

"Fine." Three seconds of silence and then, "Speaking of fair, it's not exactly fair that you didn't tell me you'd hooked up with Mr. Shoulders. What is up with *that*?"

Duke's eyelids are twitching. His tail thumps against my leg and he lets out a tiny whine. He's dreaming. "We haven't hooked up. Noah was goofing around. We're just friends."

"I know why you're saying that. You don't want to admit you're going out because you don't want me bugging you when you break up with him."

"That's totally not true!" I stuff another pillow behind my head and try to convince Tegan that life does not depend on having a guy.

With Max's identity confirmed, the reporters become more aggressive. Tuesday morning they show up at Noah's rowing practice; the coach tells them to leave. There are four news vans outside our house first thing in the morning too. Dad calls a couple of neighbours who let me cut through their backyards until the media frenzy dies down. When he and Parker leave for work, I slip out the back, retrieve my bike from a neighbour's shed and get away unnoticed.

Sparrows chatter as I ride past the towering maples on Hoylake Road. My phone rings when I reach Arbutus but I don't stop. In the distance I spot two sailboats floating lazily across the water. It's going to be a beautiful day. My phone signals a voice message as I ride down Harlech but I keep going. I'm on a roll, enjoying the sunshine and my downhill speed.

Rather than coming down Village Way, I take the back route along the trail so I can use the entrance near the gym again. I'm on edge as I ride up, but there are only a couple of jocks shooting hoops and a few kids trailing in through the back entrance.

I lock up my bike and listen to my voice message: "*Cate, my name is Mrs. Chen. I'm the social worker at Oceanside Health Centre. I'm calling about Mr. Le Bould. He wants to sign himself out and we don't want him to do that. You're down as his contact, and I'm wondering if you could come in and speak with him. Ideally I'd like to meet with you first. I'll be here until three thirty today. Thanks.*"

Max can't go back to Rathtrevor Beach. He can't heal if he's living in a tent.

When I get to English, Mrs. Moreau says, "Mr. Statski would like to see you in his office after class, Cate." Why would the principal want to see me? But her face gives nothing away.

Walking to the office after English I spot a cluster of reporters across the street. Just steps past the school grounds. When I sit across from Mr. Statski a few minutes later, it's obvious they're the reason he called me into his office.

"The reporters want statements from you and Noah Fox." He frowns and strokes his bushy white moustache. "I can't ask you to make one but I'll be making one myself at eleven thirty today about what great students you and Noah are and how proud we are of your roles in the rescue." He pauses. "Are you okay with that?"

"Of course."

"Good." He straightens his thick black glasses. "I've had to kick them off the school grounds twice this morning. And now they've parked themselves on Village Way and I'm getting calls from disgruntled drivers. With any luck my statement will make them go away."

Or not. *If you don't talk to them, I will.* Tegan's words roll through my mind and I think about the danger of letting her do the talking. "I could speak to them too, but I need to clear it with Mr. Le Bould first." I tell him about the call from Mrs. Chen and Max's threat to check himself out of the hospital.

"Could you see him at lunch?"

"I don't think I could make it there and back in time." I hesitate. "But I have a spare this block so if I leave now..." Technically spares are supposed to be used for school work.

"Under the circumstances, I think that's fine." He clears his throat and leans back in his chair. "The reporters aren't the only reason I called you in this morning." There's a weird look on his face. My heart does a tap dance.

"As you may know, every year one lucky graduate is the recipient of the Ruth Mackie Holland scholarship."

Everybody knows about the RMH scholarship. It's given to the student who goes above and beyond in helping others, in demonstrating community spirit. "Yes."

"The committee met before school this morning and the decision was unanimous. I'm happy to say this year's recipient is you. Congratulations, Cate."

And just like that, I cannot breathe. "That's amazing!" My excitement billows and gathers force like cotton candy being spun onto a stick. But then comes the gut-dropping realization of what this means. "I, um. I'm honoured but I don't think I'm the right person." I'm unsure of what else to say, of how to get out of this.

Mr. Statski misunderstands my hesitation. "You're a fine student with good grades, you've volunteered in our community many times and you have a reputation for being extremely caring, all qualities we like to see in RMH recipients. Your rescue of the homeless man underscores that."

The homeless man. His name is Max, I want to say. Max, who likes fancy cheese and out-of-season raspberries and always picks up litter.

"That action puts our school in the spotlight for all the right reasons," he adds.

They're asking me to do it because I rescued Max? How can one good deed have so many ramifications? "Maybe, but—"

Mr. Statski won't let me finish. "The Ruth Mackie Holland scholarship is worth eighteen hundred dollars."

Eighteen hundred dollars! It would take me months to

earn that. My fear dissolves in a wave of giddiness. I do a quick mental calculation. With the five grand I've saved, plus another eighteen hundred, I'd only need thirty-two hundred more for the June fifteenth Chef's Apron payment. That just might be doable!

"Of course, as you know, the winner gives a speech before the valedictorian at the convocation ceremony."

I crash back to earth. I'd have to speak in front of the entire student body, and their parents too. I grip the side of my chair. "I, um, I don't know if I have time to write one." The speech is important. It's supposed to be empowering. As good as the valedictorian speech, only shorter. I force the words out. "I'm working a lot of shifts right now so I can save for post-secondary."

"The speech won't take you long to write and Mrs. Moreau will help." He's smiling broadly, like I've won the lottery. "Please don't say anything until the formal announcement is made at lunch today." He stands. "But after that, feel free to comment as much as you like, especially to those reporters outside." He chuckles. "With such a newsworthy Ruth Mackie Holland recipient maybe now the school board will approve our budget increase request."

Thirty minutes later I'm sitting in Mrs. Chen's office. "Thanks for coming in so quickly, Cate." She's a petite middle-aged woman with tired eyes and a brisk manner.

"No problem." My stomach growls. There's a cafeteria somewhere in the building and the smell of French fries and hot soup is making me hungry.

"Max wants to leave, but he can't do that until he's up and walking." Frowning, she flips through a pile of file folders on her desk. "They may remove the catheter and get him using a walker tomorrow if they can get his other issues under control," she says.

What other issues? I'm about to ask when her face clears. "Here we go." She pulls out a file and picks up a pen. "Max insists he has somewhere to go when he's discharged but he won't tell me where that is. He won't tell me about his next of kin either. He says you're like family, so I'm hoping you can provide me with some information."

"He's been squatting out at Rathtrevor Beach. That's all I know." I hesitate. "Other than what I've heard on the news."

"I was afraid of that." She tosses the pen onto her cluttered desk and gives me a level look. "This is a complicated case. And very much in flux. Mr. Le Bould may have resources we aren't aware of as well, but let me explain where we're at right now."

"Okay."

"With his admission to hospital, Max is in our system. Short of discharging himself, there are only two ways he can leave. He can be discharged to a house or apartment for support and out-patient rehabilitation." She pauses. "But if he doesn't have an address to go to, the government will send him to whatever rehab facility has an opening, possibly hundreds of kilometres from here. If that happens his case gets turned over to a public guardian or trustee."

"Why would a public trustee be involved?"

"That's the process for homeless people in his situation. The trustee assigns them to a facility, checks on them and supervises their care. The trustee also makes decisions on their behalf if they're found mentally unfit."

"Max would hate that."

She grimaces. "Most people do. However, if Max ignores doctors' orders and returns to Rathtrevor Beach before he's healed, the government will likely declare him unfit."

What a mess. "But if the news reports are true, Max has family back in England," I say. "A sister, they said."

She nods. "Yes, and I'm trying to reach her but so far I've had no luck. I'll keep trying. In the meantime we need to keep him here until he's well enough to leave." She hesitates. "I'm hoping you can convince him. I'm also hoping you can find out if there's somewhere he can stay after he's discharged. Time is crucial because he could be ready to leave next week."

"That soon?"

"If he co-operates with the physiotherapist and has a place to go, yes."

As I ponder that, she adds, "I don't want to worry you, Cate, but Max walked away from his life once before. He could walk out of this hospital and disappear again."

My heart sinks. She's right.

"Given his precarious physical state, I don't have high hopes for the outcome if he does that. So I'm hoping you can get through to him."

No pressure. "I'll do my best."

Max is in a room by himself. His door is open, and when I stop in the doorway, he turns his head and smiles.

"Cate." His voice is still hoarse but he has more colour in his cheeks than he did on Saturday. His blue eyes, normally bloodshot and watery, are bright and clear. "I knew you'd come."

I grab a chair and pull it up beside his IV line. His right leg is on top of the covers; its lower half is encased in an air cast. There's a heart monitor machine on the other side of his bed. "How are you, Max?"

"I'd be a hell of a lot better if I could get outta here." Somebody has pulled his hair into a neat ponytail and it makes his cheekbones stand out. "They won't let me up to take a piss. They've got me hooked up to a tube. They're always in here poking me with something." He gestures to the food tray beside him. "And they've got me on a godawful low-salt diet because they say my blood pressure's high." He frowns. "O'course it's high. The stress of being in here is killing me."

I fight back a smile. "The social worker says you'll probably be up walking tomorrow, which means they'll take out the catheter and you can go to the bathroom on your own too."

He snorts. "Taking a piss in private is my right. So is my right to go home and be left alone."

"Being alone might be hard. There's a ton of reporters in town. They say you're the last surviving member of the Magpies. That you've been missing for years."

"What a load of bullshit."

I stare at him, hard.

"I haven't been missing," he mumbles after a minute. "I've been where I wanted to be."

"I saw the footage of the accident on TV. Clips from your sister. Your fiancée." He turns his head away, but not before I see pain flicker in his blue eyes. "We could call them, Max. I'm sure they'd come and help you. Then you wouldn't need a social worker."

"No."

I study his profile, his ponytail on the pillow like a grey exclamation mark. "What happened, Max?" It's none of my business but I'm desperate to understand why someone would walk away from their life. "Why did you disappear?"

He doesn't answer.

I find myself inexplicably close to tears. "There were people who loved you," I say thickly.

"No doubt." He sounds so British—cool and matter-of-fact.

Did you not love them? I want to ask. *Did you not think of the pain you might cause? Did you not wonder how their lives were unfolding without you?* But going down that road could flatten me. I take a deep breath and change tactics. "I know you want to go home, Max, but you're not well enough to leave, plus you have nowhere to go."

"I can go back to Rathtrevor."

"You can't get down to the beach with a broken leg." He starts to say something but I talk over him. "Or into the forest. It's not practical. And the social worker just told me that they won't discharge you without an actual address to go to."

He picks nervously at the white sheet. "I don't need a discharge. I can walk myself out."

It's time to level with him. "If you do that, they'll get a public trustee involved. You could be sent to a government rehab facility. Or declared mentally incompetent."

Colour floods his cheeks; he swears under his breath.

I feel a level of responsibility. I insisted Max have the operation. If I hadn't done that, he wouldn't be in this situation. "I'd invite you to stay with us but our bathroom is upstairs and so are the bedrooms."

"Thanks, luv, but I don't want to stay with anybody."

"You need to go somewhere."

He doesn't respond.

"Where does Tillie go when the shelter's full?"

"The library if she can hide from the security guy."

That won't work either. There has to be somebody. "What about that guy down at French Creek Marina? The one you did some work for?"

"Gabe?"

"Yeah. Could you stay with him?"

"Nah. He sleeps on his boat most of the time. No room for me there."

Stumped, I fall silent.

"But he has a fishing shack on the water close to Nanoose that he rents out. I helped him haul wood there last fall."

I look at his leg. How will he manage with a broken leg in a shack? "How accessible is it?"

"It's not, which is a goddamn good thing. I don't want people around."

"I'm wondering about stairs and stuff like that."

"There are no stairs. It's one big open room. Even the bathroom's barely private. Just a curtain separating it from the rest of the place."

That sounds doable. "How much does it rent for?"

"'Bout a hundred bucks a month." He gestures to the cupboard beside his bed. "I've got seventy quid in my bag.

Could you take it to Gabe and ask him to rent me the place for the month? I'll owe him the rest. He knows I'll be good for it."

I should let Mrs. Chen handle it. But she did ask me to find out if Max had options. If I find this Gabe guy and he agrees to rent his shack to Max, Mrs. Chen can take it from there. "He's out at the marina?"

"Yeah. He sells crabs off *Miss Shelley*, his boat."

The marina is a forty-minute ride from here and another thirty minutes back to school. I can't miss class. I'll go after school.

"Best time to get him is between ten and two," Max says, killing that plan.

Today is out. Maybe Noah could give me a lift at lunch tomorrow. We could go to Lefty's after. "Sure, Max." I put the chair back and retrieve the seventy dollars from his bag. "By the way, the reporters want me to make a statement. And they want to talk to you too. They have questions."

He won't meet my gaze. "Well, I have no answers." His chin is set in a stubborn tilt. "Say whatever the hell you want, just don't tell those idjots about the fishing shack. I don't need them showing up there." He shuts his eyes. "Toodle pip, Catie."

"Toodle pip, Max." As I head back down to the main floor I realize I forgot to ask Max about the accident. Not the accident that happened fifteen years ago. The one that put him in the hospital this time. The accident Noah believes wasn't an accident at all.

6

Blue Skies Nana to CD Sheridan: *Congratulations, sweetie! That scholarship is a huge honour. Maybe now your father will agree to release your education fund.*

CD Sheridan to Blue Skies Nana: *I'm taking on extra shifts at Fine Foods and looking at other scholarship options. Dad won't change his mind and I don't want to fight.*

Blue Skies Nana to CD Sheridan: *Your father is stubborn, but the first step to owning your dream is being prepared to fight for it.*

French Creek Marina, between Parksville and Qualicum, is home to a variety of marine vessels: sleek motorboats, stately sailboats and barnacle-crusted fishing boats. The cool wind whips my hair across my cheeks as Noah and I head to dock A during our lunch break on Wednesday.

"Tell me why we're doing this again?" Noah asks.

The dock sways gently beneath our feet. He has such long legs I have to take three steps to his two.

"I needed a ride. Since we're hanging out and you're one of my only friends with a car, you're the obvious choice." *Plus, I didn't want to go alone.* "And if Max doesn't have a place to stay, he'll discharge himself and then the public trustee would get involved, and that would be terrible."

"Right." He's eating a granola bar; a couple of crumbs speckle his white T-shirt. "But leaving would be Max's choice."

I step over two cables lying across the dock. "It would be a dumb choice. Sometimes people don't know what's good for them."

"Maybe, but people should have the right to choose. Even if they make mistakes."

"The social worker asked me to help so I am." He opens his mouth but I don't want to give him a chance to say anything more so I speak before he can. "You've got crumbs on your shirt. And one on your top lip too."

He grins. "I don't function well when I'm hungry." He brushes his shirt and licks his lip. Heat unfurls in my belly. *Don't be silly. You don't need to fall for Noah Fox.*

Miss Shelley is a black fishing boat sporting a Canadian flag. A large *Buy Your Seafood Here* sign is propped up beside an orange life raft. The door to the cabin is closed. My heart sinks. I assumed Gabe would be here.

Before I can figure out what we should do, a gruff voice shouts, "You here to buy crab?"

We turn. A man with a bushy salt-and-pepper beard is a few feet away at the edge of the dock. "Got 'em right here." He crouches down and hauls a wire basket out of the water. It's filled with purple-shelled crabs scrambling to get out.

Involuntarily I step back. "Actually, we're looking for Gabe."

He offers up a toothy grin. "I'm Gabe. Best crab on the island." His face beams with pride. "Twelve bucks a piece. Two for twenty."

"Thanks, but we don't need crab. We need to talk to you about Max."

His grin fades. He lowers the trap back into the water. "What kinda trouble is he in this time?"

"You haven't heard?" Noah asks.

He shakes his head. "I haven't seen Max in months. I hired him to help with repairs on *Miss Shelley* but the third time he showed up drunk I had to let him go."

Disappointment knots my stomach. Oh crap.

"What happened?" Gabe asks.

I give him the bare bones of the accident and Max's surgery, leaving out the part about the Magpies. I can tell Gabe wouldn't be impressed with Max's sudden celebrity status. "He needs a place to recuperate. He'd like to rent your fishing shack for a few months."

Gabe pulls off his cap, runs a hand over his thinning hair and puts his hat back on. "Busy season's coming. Got guys arriving late June through the end of August."

It's only early May. Gabe could rent to Max but he doesn't want to. He's trying to let us down gently. I pretend not to understand and pull the money from my purse. "Max wanted me to give you this." I hold up the bills. "Seventy dollars. I know you charge one hundred for the month but—"

"Two hundred," he interrupts with a scowl. "And I could probably get three if I wanted."

I look at Noah, but he only shrugs. I turn back to Gabe. "Max needs help."

"Max has needed help since I met him," Gabe says. "Let that crusty old bugger figure things out for himself."

"If he doesn't have a place, he'll end up back on the street and he may not make it."

"We all gotta die sometime," Gabe says gruffly, staring out over the water. "And Max is a big boy." He taps his foot impatiently against the dock. "I don't know why you're getting involved."

"Because everybody deserves a warm place to sleep at night," I say. *Without a public trustee telling them what to do.* "And a place to heal. Even crusty old buggers."

His brown eyes soften; he tugs at his beard. He's weakening, I can tell.

I pull out my wallet. All I have is a twenty and a ten. I add it to Max's seventy. "Here's one hundred dollars." I wave the bills in his direction. "I'll bring you another hundred by the end of the week if you'll let Max have the fishing shack through June." I'll take the money out of my savings if I have to or maybe Dad and Parker will each kick in fifty bucks. "I'll let the social worker know—"

He frowns. "What social worker?"

"I need to let the hospital social worker know Max has somewhere to go. It's no big deal, just a technical thing."

"I don't want social workers crawling around the place. It's a mess. I need to clean it up. Buy sheets for the bed, a new frying pan too."

"We could clean it up for you."

"Nah, I need to do it myself." His frown deepens. "I don't have time for this crap right now."

I clutch the bills in my sweaty palm. This *has* to work. If Max discharges himself, he could die. "Max needs a friend. It would just be for a couple of months. That's all."

Gabe stares at me, his brown eyes unreadable.

"We'll help get the shack ready." I look at Noah. He nods, reluctantly. "Buy the sheets or the frying pan. Whatever you need."

"I'm a goddamn softie, that's what I am." Gabe sighs. "All right. You clean it and buy a frying pan. A good cast iron one. Max can stay until mid-June. No longer."

Relief makes me lightheaded. "Thank you so much." I hand him the money. "I'll get you another hundred by the end of the week."

"I'll need more than that," he says.

"What do you mean?"

"He's not staying in the shack unless I'm paid in full up front." Nerves clutch my stomach. "If he wants the fishing shack until mid-June, I want another two hundred by Friday."

~

"I have the money in the bank," I tell Noah twenty minutes later after we're settled at Lefty's. The restaurant is popular for its thin-crust pizzas, amazing desserts and outdoor patio. "But I'm trying to save for chef school and two hundred bucks isn't small change." I'm overwhelmed with the task I've set myself.

The waitress swoops down with our food—a hefty beef burger with double cheese and extra fries for Noah and a quesadilla with a side salad for me.

"I'll have a slice of lemon meringue pie for dessert," Noah says as she turns to go. "Please."

Smiling, she hurries away. Noah picks up his burger. It's the size of a cantaloupe. How's this going to work? He opens his mouth and takes a huge bite. No spills, no messy collapse, no squirts of mustard. I am amazed. Clearly he has had practice. I bite my quesadilla. Cheese oozes out the end and a chunk of pepper falls on my plate. No fair.

After a minute he says, "Let the social worker pay. She probably has a budget for that."

"Maybe. But she'd have to go through a pile of hoops and do a bunch of paperwork and that takes time."

He dips a fry in ketchup. "And Gabe won't want to wait and you're worried that Max will lose out."

"Exactly."

"It's not your problem."

He sounds cold and heartless. But cold, heartless guys don't retrieve warm blankets for cold hospital patients. "Max is a friend. And you don't bail on friends when they need you. We have built-in support systems. Friends, family, teachers even. Max has nobody until they find his next of kin."

At the table behind us a little boy bangs his fork; his mother shushes him. My heart pings at the laughter and the obvious love in her voice. I shut out their conversation. "I could take up a collection at school. Ask my dad to contribute and—" I stop. I don't usually tell people about Parker until I have a sense of how they'll react. It's amazing how many people still judge. Or pretend to accept but make homophobic comments and jokes. Especially guys. "Some of his friends too."

"What about your mom?"

I put my quesadilla down. "Not in the picture." Before he can quiz me, I decide to level with him. He'll either accept it or he won't. I pick up my fork and poke at my salad. "My dad's gay." When people learn about my dad, they assume I was adopted or bred to order with a surrogate. It usually prevents further questioning.

He licks a trail of ketchup from his finger. "Cool."

There's no sarcastic undertone to his voice, nor was he

too quick to speak. I wait for him to clear his throat or crack a disgusting joke but he only says, "Taking up a collection is a good idea."

"Thanks." I've been clutching my fork so tightly my hand is cramping. I loosen my grip.

"But that takes time. I still think you should talk to the social worker again."

The waitress appears with his pie. Quarter pie is more like it. With about eight inches of meringue. She plops it on the table, slaps our bill down and moves on.

"I will, but Max won't want her involved. He's wary of everybody. I tried to introduce him to Parker once, but there was no way Max would talk to him."

A shadow drops across his face. "Who's Parker?"

I take a breath. "My dad's partner." This is usually enough to weed out the pretenders.

His face clears. "Oh." He pushes his fries toward me. "Help yourself. I'd rather have the pie."

Relief rushes through me. He doesn't care about my dad. For a minute I watch him eat with enthusiasm. I'm reassured when a glob of meringue sticks to the corner of his mouth. Wouldn't want this guy to be too perfect.

I ask Noah about rowing and his plans for after graduation. He wants a career in sports medicine, he tells me.

"You'd make a great doctor. You were so calm when Max was hit."

He lowers his eyes, dips his chin and smiles. A tiny dimple I haven't noticed before flashes at the corner of his mouth. How cute is *that?* "Thanks." He shoves the last piece of pie into his mouth.

I could seriously fall for a guy like Noah Fox. I change the subject.

"The bell's going in twenty. If we leave now, we'll just make it."

"Right." Noah stands and picks up the bill.

"Wait a minute. You drove me to the marina. Let me pay."

"Nah. You can get it next time."

Next time. I flush. Like I'll make a habit of going out with Noah? I don't think so. "Thanks, but you don't have to." I dig in my purse for my debit card.

"I know I don't have to." His green eyes twinkle. "I want to."

Heat spreads down my neck. "Seriously, it's my treat."

Noah steps closer. His white T-shirt brushes my arm; a shiver of awareness ripples down my spine. "No, it's my treat today."

His breath is hot on my cheek. It smells of lemon meringue pie. "Let me at least leave the tip then."

He stares at me like he's looking for the answer to a puzzle. Finally he says, "You're the first girl I've met who'd rather give than get. I kinda like it."

Thank goodness I'm looking through my purse and Noah can't see my face. Thank goodness he's moved away and I don't have to answer. Thank goodness because I am speechless and I don't like feeling that way.

Noah takes the shortest route back to school, which means driving down Village Way. I think nothing of it until I see reporters parked along the side of the road. There are at least two dozen of them now.

"There they are!" someone shouts as we cruise past.

"We should have parked a block away and walked down the trail." Gravel crunches under the wheels as Noah turns into the parking lot. "Sorry." He parks and kills the engine.

In the side mirror I spot one of the reporters running toward us. It's the same guy we saw in emergency a few days ago.

"It's okay," I tell him. "Max doesn't care if I talk to them. And maybe if I make a statement, they'll go away."

"I'll come with you."

"Thanks."

The reporter knocks on my window. He's the only one nervy enough to approach the car. "Miss Sheridan. Mr. Fox. Will you make a statement?"

I lower my window. "Yes, if you promise to go away after."

"Of course." He whips out a pad and pen from his jacket pocket. "How is Mr. Le Bould? I understand you went to see him at the hospital."

How does he know that? "We'll meet you at the front entrance. Give us two minutes."

"I just need a few—"

Man, the guy is nervy. "*Two minutes.*" He starts to say something else but I roll up the window and cut him off.

Noah whistles. "Nice backbone, Sheridan." He's slouched against the driver's door, his right arm stretched along the back of his seat.

"I'm not a total pushover." In the mirror I watch the reporter sprint back to the others. "And I have an idea that might help Max."

My mouth is stupid dry and my legs feel like spaghetti as Noah and I walk across the parking lot to the school entrance. A few feet from the crowd I stop. I'm second-guessing myself and wishing I hadn't agreed to this. Before

I can take another step they rush forward, a blur of cameras and microphones and faces.

"Has Le Bould said anything to you about his lost years?"

"What will Max do when he's released from hospital?"

My heart hammers in my chest. Noah gives my arm an encouraging squeeze.

If I look at the whole group I'll lose my nerve, so I take a deep breath, moisten my lips and pick one face to focus on: Stacey, from KONO News.

"Max came through the surgery fine. He'll probably be up walking tomorrow." I don't think Max would mind me saying that.

A male voice from my left asks, "What about the accident that claimed the lives of his band members?"

"Did he tell you where he's been?" another reporter yells. "Why he's been hiding?"

"Max doesn't want to talk about the past, and it's important he be given space and time to heal, so I haven't pressed him." I don't know where the words are coming from. I sound so calm.

"Where will he go when he's released from the hospital?"

"That's private. But he'll need to pay rent and buy food. He may need medicine too. And he has no money, so I'm taking up a collection to help him through his recovery."

"He's a rock star," one reporter shouts. "He'll have money coming to him now."

The comment throws me. "We don't know that for sure. And he needs money now, for his recovery."

"How can people help?" asks Stacey from KONO.

"If they want to donate, they can send cash or a cheque to Mid-Island Credit Union, care of Cate Sheridan. I'll be setting up an account tomorrow."

"We understand you're this year's recipient of the Ruth Mackie Holland scholarship," says the reporter who approached Noah's car. "And as such, you have an important speech to prepare."

Don't remind me.

"How will you find the time to administer the fund for Mr. Le Bould and fulfil that obligation too?" he asks.

"The speech is short. It shouldn't take up much time." I hope.

"And we'll ask the credit union to administer the fund for Mr. Le Bould," Noah adds.

We will? As I try to process the meaning of the word "we," a woman from the back of the group says, "The mayor has announced that you and Mr. Fox will be invited to a civic awards ceremony scheduled for this Saturday. You'll be receiving a bravery award for saving Mr. Le Bould's life."

My blood stops. I know that voice. British. Well-modulated. And a bit husky.

I am suddenly, inexplicably, freezing. I stare blankly at the crowd and think, *Really?*

"What is your reaction to that?" the British woman asks.

I can't speak. My heart is galloping in triple time. Noah comes to my rescue again. "We hadn't heard, but obviously it's an honour." He continues, but his words are white noise. I pull my gaze from Stacey and scan the crowd.

There she is. In the back row. Sleek white-blond hair, blue blazer, pearls at her neck. She's standing apart from the others, and she's looking right at me.

The woman I haven't seen since I was two.

My mother.

7

She approaches me a few minutes later when things wind down. Her perfume, something exotic and vaguely musky, hits me like a slap.

"Hello, Daisy."

Her presence is so surreal my legs start to shake. "I use my middle name now. I go by Cate. Cate Sheridan." I deliberately emphasize the last name, underscoring the fact that the surname she gave me—Patrice-Sheridan—no longer applies.

Her lips curve into an enigmatic smile. "Right."

The afternoon bell rings, saving me from this conversation. I don't know where to look, how to feel, what to say. After all the cards and promises to visit, here she is. I turn to Noah. "This is my mother, Cynthia Patrice. She's with the UK News Group."

Noah extends his hand.

"It's nice to meet you," she says.

I gulp in the shape of her face (high cheekbones, pointy chin), the entire length of her (long and lean, greyhound slim), hands that are close enough to touch (elegant fingers, peach-coloured nails). She's wearing rings. One looks like a diamond. Is my mother married?

My mother. The phrase sticks in my brain like chewing gum on the bottom of a shoe. It does not belong there. It is foreign matter.

This whole situation is foreign. And yet. As she stands beside the flowering cherry tree talking to Noah about the upcoming award ceremony, as she nods and stands with her left hip angled out, there's an odd familiarity. Maybe because I've seen her on the news? Maybe because those movements are printed on my DNA? Who knows?

"...to get together?"

Noah nudges me. I snap to attention. They are both looking at me.

I'm trembling like a half-set bowl of Jell-O. I hate that I'm so rattled. I've imagined this moment so many times. In my fantasies it has been filled with joy. Instead I am full of questions. *Why now? Why not on my first day of kindergarten or when I got my period or the first time I went on a date? Or when I asked you to come to my grade seven graduation?*

"Tonight?" There's a hopeful sheen to her blue eyes. "I was hoping to take you to dinner."

She's acting like we're friends who haven't seen each other for a while. It's weird and I don't like it.

"You could choose the place." She laughs. "You'd have to choose. I don't know what's good around here."

My shoulder blades tighten. Of course she doesn't know. She doesn't know anything about me. Sharing a meal will only drive home the fact that we're strangers. "I'm busy tonight. I have a shift."

She frowns and pulls on her ear. "A shift?"

My breath hitches. That's what I do when I'm confused; I pull on my ear. "At Fine Foods, where I work."

"Ah." She smiles. "Well. It doesn't have to be tonight. Another night then."

How long is she staying? I want to ask but I'm not sure I should. I'm grateful for Noah's presence beside me. I'm grateful too that there's activity around us. A Fed Ex driver bolts through the school entrance; a couple of students straggle in late. "Sure. Maybe. I'll have to see. Things are kinda busy right now." *With a life you know nothing about.*

"I'll be in town for a while. To see you get the award, certainly, and possibly afterward too."

One question answered, a million more to go. "Okay." I wonder if Dad knows she's here. "I should go. I have a class."

"Yeah," Noah says. "Me too."

"Of course." She presses a business card into my hand. "I'm staying at the Crown Mansion. Call my cell when you have time. We have a lot of catching up to do."

Seriously? She thinks we can catch up on fifteen years of *everything* over dinner? An awkward silence stretches between us. My mother is standing in front of me in, like, the first time ever, and I don't know what to say. What is *wrong* with me? "Sure." My tone is light and I give her a smile. But for some reason my eyes prickle with tears as I turn and head for the door.

The halls are nearly empty when Noah and I go inside and head for our lockers. "Will the credit union really administer the fund for Max?" I ask. Talking helps me avoid the one thought that will not leave.

My mother is in town.

"Probably. At least until Max is out of the hospital. My dad knows the branch manager. I'll see what I can find out."

When we reach my locker I expect Noah to say "see ya" and keep going, but he stops and watches me spin my lock. My ears start to burn. "Shouldn't you be going to class?"

"In a minute." He continues to stare at me. "Are you okay?"

"I'm fine. Totally." I grab what I need for French and root around for a pen.

"Then why," he asks quietly, "are your hands shaking?"

My mother is in town.

I shut my locker and turn to face him. Noah has his arm up on the neighbouring locker and he's standing in such a way that I can't see into the hall. I can't see anything but him—his too-big shoulders, his crazy curly hair. If Carter blocked me in like this I'd be totally pissed. With Noah, not so much. Maybe it's the concern in his eyes. Maybe I need a minute after the adrenalin rush of seeing her. Maybe it's because standing in his shadow makes me feel oddly sheltered.

"My mother left when I was two."

His eyes widen.

"And I haven't seen her since." *Except on the cable news channel, which I don't watch anymore because when I did I'd wake up in the middle of the night with my heart racing from a horrible dream I couldn't remember.*

"She called you Daisy."

Heat floods my cheeks. "It's my first name but my family—everybody—calls me by my middle name. They have since—" *Since she walked out*. "Since I was two."

"I'm surprised."

I shrug. "Why? Lots of people use their middle names."

"That's not what I meant."

I know but what can I say about a mother who leaves a baby when I don't understand it myself? "My parents couldn't make it work," I finally tell him. "Families fracture. People leave. You can't count on forever." I'm lucky I learned that lesson early.

"But not to see your mother in, like, fifteen years? That's harsh."

"Not really." I shrug. "I'm used to it." *Kind of.*

"I guess." His eyes skirt away. He opens his mouth, shuts it again.

"What?"

His gaze slides back to me. "I didn't think you had a mother in the picture because...you know."

"Because my dad's gay?"

"Yeah. I mean, I just figured—"

"That my dad found me under a bush somewhere?" I tease.

He jerks back. "Geez. No! Nothing like that." His face fills with colour. "I figured, you know." His blush deepens.

I am charmed. Noah is earnest and sweet and the best distraction I could have. "That I was a made-to-order baby? Or had a surrogate mother?"

"Yeah. Or that you were adopted."

"No." I hesitate. How much should I tell? According to Dad, he'd been conflicted in those days, and while my mother apparently knew he'd been attracted to men, she was convinced he was also attracted to women. And he was, at least long enough to fall in love and conceive me. But not for long after.

"They were married for a while." My voice falters. "It's not something I talk about."

My mother is in town.

"We all have secrets," he says.

He looks so serious. My heart starts to thrum. Oh no. I've had enough drama for one day.

He bends close. His breath is warm and still lemon-pie sweet. "When I was five I was sure I saw the Easter bunny in my bedroom. And after that I needed the light on to go to sleep for an entire year."

I start to laugh. "You?" My mood lightens. Mr. Logic was afraid of the Easter bunny? "Seriously?"

He laughs too. "Yeah." He drops his arm and we start to walk. "Since we're hanging out, I figured you should know."

"Thanks." Talking to him has made me feel better.

He stops in front of his locker.

"I wonder if I should go to dinner with her?"

"That's a no-brainer."

His head is so far inside his locker I'm surprised he heard me. "It is?"

He backs out, slams his locker shut. "Of course." He winks. "Nobody in their right mind turns down a free meal, Sheridan."

I have a spare last block on Wednesday. I call Mrs. Chen and bring her up to speed on Gabe and the fishing shack, I meet with Mrs. Kaneko again about scholarship options and then I head home. I need to google Cynthia. With my shift at Fine Foods not starting until four thirty I have time for a little internet stalking.

Before school I'd filled our slow cooker with garlic, apricots, pork chops and peach nectar. The mouth-watering smell hits me the second I get home and open the door. Between that, Duke's slobbery love-filled greeting and the soothing quiet of being alone, my shoulders loosen and I start to relax.

In spite of my urge to pull Cynthia up online, I'm reluctant to boot up my laptop. Instead I change into my work clothes and grab some hummus and crackers. I'm about to write a note to Dad and Parker when Tegan texts: *HEY. How is it that your mother is Cynthia Patrice and you NEVER TOLD ME?*

My shoulders tighten up again. I never told anyone. Tegan is the only person I've told about my mother, period. And all I said was that my parents divorced when I was a baby and that my mom lives overseas.

Seconds later Tegan texts again: *You there?*

I don't answer. Instead I sit down and start writing.

Hey guys, the Mayor's giving us an award for rescuing Max! I consider writing, "Now will you let me use MY education fund the way I want?" But I don't. Even though I'm still looking at every option possible for Chef's Apron, I haven't had the nerve to bring it up with Dad again. I sit for a minute, unsure of what to write next. Finally I settle on: *Cynthia's in town. She showed up at the school today with the other reporters.*

Then I boot up my laptop and type her name into the search bar. As I hit enter, I wonder what it'll be like to see my parents together. Parents, plural. For most kids, parents come as a pair. Even if they're divorced, it's usually still Mom and Dad. For me it's always been Dad, period.

The screen fills with dozens of hits. My eyes are drawn

to the box on the right. It's bare bones: her name, her place of residence, a few professional credits. But there are seven images: three of her on-camera reports, two in a studio and two personal shots. One looks quite recent.

I click on it.

My breath stalls. She looks like a movie star. All sparkles and smiles. Her long red gown is asymmetrical and her right shoulder is bare. Her blond hair is up; silver earrings dangle to her chin. A bearded man in a tux stands beside her, his arm draped possessively around her shoulder. I study their hands for rings. Are they married? Living together?

Obsessively I click through the links, hungry for personal details. Her professional life is easy to find (previously reported for the BBC, now working for the UK News Group; a Courage Under Fire award; an international commendation for a documentary called *Sarajevo Then and Now*) but I want more. One story references her car, an Austin Mini Cooper Deluxe. Another refers to the passing of her mother two years ago.

I have another grandmother. Or I did.

Stunned I lean back in my chair. Do I have aunts or uncles? Cousins? I stare around the kitchen, at the green kettle on the stove, the goofy pictures on the fridge, the stack of well-thumbed cookbooks. Everything is the same.

But it feels so different.

I lose track of time and I'm ten minutes late for work. Since I'm usually early, my supervisor brushes off my apology with a wave of her hand. "It happens to the best of us," Karen says.

The first few hours fly by. It's always busy between four and six with people stopping in after work for garlic bread or a takeaway pizza shell or a bag of cookies to pad out dinner. After the crowd thins I busy myself tidying shelves and decorating a sheet cake for a retirement party. When I take my break around seven, I check my phone. There's nothing from Dad but Tegan has texted: *Cynthia Patrice, are you freaking kidding me? We need to talk. I can't believe you NEVER told me.*

I consider responding with "you never asked," but that's confrontational-bordering-on-bitchy and I don't want to fight with Tegan. But ignoring her isn't fair either. So before I go back on the floor I respond with: *No time. Super busy. Will call later.*

For the next hour there's a steady stream of customers. At one point two women ask to see the sample book of wedding cakes. I can tell they're mother and daughter. They have the same reddish hair, the same wide smile. I can almost see invisible strings of belonging that weave like a web and bind them together. An ache rolls through me. They seem to talk and laugh in code too. I feel like someone has punched me, leaving a hole where my stomach should be.

My mother is in town.

How am I supposed to make sense of that?

By eight thirty it's quiet enough for me to cash out, clean the bagel bins and start tidying up. I'm in the back stacking trays when I hear a familiar voice out front. "Hello! Can I get some service out here?"

I recognize that voice. Riley. I wipe my hands on a rag and straighten my hairnet. She's about as appealing as a slab of liver. I take a deep breath and walk out to the front counter.

My heart sinks. It's Riley and her friends. They stare at me, all blond indignation and drippy lip gloss.

"We'd like five lemon-filled, three apple fritters and two chocolate-glazed doughnuts," Riley says.

"We're out of chocolate-glazed," I tell her.

"Oh my *God.*" Riley rolls her eyes. "Then give us three maple-glazed, four lemon-filled and six apple fritters."

"What's up with that stupid hairnet?" I hear one girl mutter as I collect a set of tongs and some bags. "Is she a hundred and five or what?"

"A total loser," Riley says. Her voice dips and the only words I catch next are "slept with" and "RMH scholarship."

My heart somersaults. I can't believe what she's implying! I shove their doughnuts into the bags and slam them on the counter. "I've cashed out for the night," I tell them, feeling a small burst of delight at their obvious displeasure. "You'll have to pay at the front."

But Riley has to have the last word.

"Why am I not surprised?" She grabs the bags and with a flash of her black-tipped nails she flounces away.

The sun is setting in a swirl of orange and raspberry as I wheel my bike around the back of the house to the shed. The curtains are open in the family room; I see the TV reflected on the wall. I can't sneak in. Whoever's watching will see me. And I don't know what to say. The whole thing with Cynthia is weird.

My cell rings as I'm climbing up the stairs to the back deck. Tegan's number flashes on the screen. I press talk.

"I know you've been busy, Cate, but I might hate you if you don't tell me what's going on with you and Cynthia Patrice!" She drags the last word out as *Paaaatrreeeeece.*

I hesitate. The sun is almost at the horizon; the sparrows are madly chirping the last of their evening song.

"*Come on!*"

I pull up a chair and sit down. "I don't want you sharing this with anybody."

"I won't." Her promise is quick and expected.

"I mean it, Tegan. This can't go in the paper, on Facebook or Instagram or anywhere else. It's too important." I'm counting on Tegan's loyalty to override her need to be Twitter Queen of the Universe.

"Okay."

I watch an ant crawl across the glass-topped patio table. "You can't even tell Owen."

"Not even Owen?" Her voice is small.

"Not even Owen." She'll probably tell him, but Owen is as discreet as Tegan is open. And by asking her not to, I'm underscoring how serious I am. "Things are too..." I hesitate. Too what? "Too delicate at this point."

"Oooh." I can tell she loves that. "Spill."

"Promise me first."

She sighs. "Okay. I promise."

I skim quickly over the facts of my birth, my early life, my mother leaving when I was two.

"I can't believe you haven't seen or heard from her since," Tegan says.

"She sent cards sometimes," I say. "But they were always way too juvenile. Like she thought I was three or something." And she always signed them the same way too: *Have a happy day, Cynthia.*

"Well, at least she tried," Tegan offers. "That's something, right?"

"I guess." I don't tell Tegan that every year my mother

had said she would visit soon—and she never did. She never got my name right either. Not once. What mother doesn't know her daughter's name? I'd shoved every card in the back of my underwear drawer and tried to forget them. Every once in a while, though, my fingers brush against the envelopes and they rustle like bits of dry yeast waiting for water and sugar to bring them to life. I should probably throw them out. But I can't. Dry yeast holds promise.

I tell Tegan about my mother's arrival at school today and her offer to take me to dinner. "I haven't talked to Dad yet, but I'm sure he didn't know she was coming. He would have told me." I hear Duke whining at the kitchen door.

"I can't believe you kept her a secret for so long."

Some things are too confusing to share.

"Cynthia Patrice is right up there with Christiane Amanpour. She's been to Afghanistan. To *two* royal weddings." Her voice is climbing. "And she's interviewed two—or maybe three—members of the royal family. You must be so excited!"

"I guess. Maybe."

"I would have been daydreaming about our mother-daughter reunion for years."

When I was little I used to. But now? Not so much. In my mind, Cynthia's return was a one-in-a-million possibility, up there with winning a lottery or being head chef in a Parisian restaurant. It was the stuff of dreams. And dreams are for little girls.

After a minute Tegan says, "It must be kinda weird too, right?"

This is why I like Tegan. She's a mouthpiece, but she's also sensitive. "Yeah, and I don't need people talking about it and making it more complicated. Plus, I don't know what—" *my mother* "—what Cynthia even wants me to say about it." She didn't seem fazed when I introduced her as my mother to Noah, but I don't tell Tegan that.

"I won't say anything," Tegan promises again. "I can't wait to meet her. Cynthia Patrice! She's who I want to be when I grow up." She sighs.

"You'll meet her. For sure. In a while, though, okay."

"Of course it'll be a while. She has other priorities, right?"

"I guess." The sun slides below the horizon; the sky looks like a mashed plum. "I'm not sure what those priorities are. Or even why she's here."

"I know why she's here," Tegan says.

"You do?" Inside the house, Duke woofs and scratches harder at the kitchen door. I push back the chair and stand.

"Of course I do," Tegan says firmly. "She's here to cover Max. Your famous mother is reporting on the biggest story this town has ever seen. How cool is that?"

My mouth is dry. "Way cool." But as cool as it is, I don't want my mother here for Max. I want her here for me.

8

Blue Skies Nana to CD Sheridan: *RE: Cynthia. Well, that's a surprise. Keep your wits about you, sweetie, and remember there are two sides to every story. xo*

Administration @ Chef's Apron to CD Sheridan: *Regarding your enquiry, we do not have provisions for a monthly payment plan. Annual tuition is due in two installments: June 15 and September 1. There are no exceptions.*

"What a day you've had!" Dad says twenty minutes later when I sit on the couch in the family room with a plate of food. Dad and Parker ate hours ago but I am starving. "Learning you're getting a bravery award." An awkward silence falls.

Your mother arriving. He doesn't have to say it. It's the proverbial elephant we've been dancing around since I got home.

"Yeah." I cut my chop into bite-sized pieces and start to eat. Duke settles at my feet, an expectant look in his brown eyes.

"And this after learning yesterday that you're the recipient of the Ruth Mackie Holland scholarship," Dad adds as he mutes the commercial. "That's amazing too!"

"I guess." I chew a piece of pork. The scholarship is

pretty much all Dad has talked about for the last two days.

"You don't seem very excited but I'm thrilled for you. It's a tremendous honour." His voice is laced with pride. When I don't respond he adds, "I thought you'd be ecstatic." He's studying me over the rim of his mug.

"Not really. The winner has to do a speech and I don't want to. I tried saying no but Mr. Statski shot me down. I let myself be railroaded." Maybe not railroaded, but I let myself be bought. For eighteen hundred dollars.

"Oh, Cate." He sounds as if he's being strangled. "I'm sorry you feel that way."

I know I've disappointed him and that makes me uncomfortable. Other than my career choice (and dating Robert, who never hid his pot habit from my dad) I rarely disappoint my dad. "It's an opportunity," I tell him as I focus on the positives. "It'll help with tuition for Chef's Apron." I stop and wait for his argument but he is silent. "Mrs. Kaneko thinks it might lead to other scholarships too."

"I see." His disappointment lingers like a sore bruise. After a sip of coffee he says, "Your mother is thrilled for you as well."

I stare at him. "You talked to her? Why didn't you tell me?"

"I'm telling you now. She called about an hour ago. We had a nice chat."

Nice *chat?* Like she's an old friend? "About what?"

"This and that." He puts his mug down and rubs his chin, an unfamiliar look in his eyes. "I'm glad you left me that note. God knows how I would have reacted if she'd called me out of the blue to say she was in town."

There's an edge to his tone that startles me but his face gives nothing away. For the first time I wonder what my parents' relationship was like, how it ended. Nana said there are two sides to every story, but whenever I've asked her about Cynthia all she says is "I hardly know the woman." Dad is like Switzerland. Carefully neutral. And Parker always changes the subject when Cynthia is mentioned. Maybe he's jealous of the history she and Dad shared.

I finish my chop and reward Duke with a small piece of fat. His raspy tongue licks at the traces of gravy on my fingers. "What does 'this and that' mean?" I finally ask.

"She asked about you of course," Dad says with a little laugh. "We talked about how well you are doing in school. The fact that you were selected as the Ruth Mackie Holland recipient. Your part-time job. That kind of thing. She asked about your friends. About Max."

My heart does a funny little flip. *She's here to cover Max.* Of course she is.

"She wants to see you, Cate. I gave her your cell number. I hope that's okay?"

"Sure. But..." I hesitate. "I don't know what I'm supposed to say to her. I don't even know her."

Dad nods. "I understand. And I know you've tried over the years to reach out and you felt rejected when she didn't respond."

He's right. When I was little I used to write her a letter every time I received a card. I remember Dad wasn't keen. He tried to discourage me from answering but I was insistent. The last time I contacted her was before elementary school graduation. I emailed and asked her to come to the ceremony. She never responded.

"You're her daughter. She says she wants to get to know you."

Why not when I was five or ten or back when I was two? "Yeah, now that she has a story to cover and it's convenient for her to be here."

He frowns. "You don't know that, Cate. You're jumping to conclusions."

It's too much to hope that she's only here for me. "It's not exactly a stretch."

He tilts his head, studies me for a minute and says, "You know, you can go through life believing the worst of people or you can trust that people are inherently good and are doing the best they can."

It feels like he's taking her side and I don't like it. I look away, watch the orange juice commercial playing on the muted TV. Is this what kids with two parents go through?

"I know you miss her," Dad says softly. "It's only natural for a girl to miss her mother."

Tears well behind my eyes. I blink them away and try to lighten the mood. "Not a chance. You and Parker are all the parents I can handle." When I see that the news is starting, I grab the remote and jack up the volume. I need the distraction. I don't like where this conversation is going.

"Good evening. I'm Pamela Holtz and this is KONO News. Tonight, more information on the dramatic rescue of music legend Max Le Bould."

His image flashes on the TV. He's on stage and much younger. A catchy guitar riff fills the room. Seconds later a gravelly voice begins singing about love in the fast lane. I smile. It's Max all right, though I still have trouble reconciling Max the musician with the Max who picks up garbage and recycles bottles.

After a minute Max's face is replaced with a shot of Peter, the manager at Fine Foods. He's wearing a dumb brown suit jacket and his hair is slicked back from his forehead. He looks like a wet weasel.

"Mr. Le Bould has been coming into Fine Foods for most of this year," Peter says, flashing an awkward smile into the camera. "We've always tried to support him by giving him free coffee and pastries and newspapers."

My mouth drops open. "I can't believe it!" I listen while Peter talks about what a fine person Max is. "He's lying," I tell Dad. "He doesn't give Max anything. He always kicks him out. How can he get away with that?"

"People get away with lots of stuff. Get used to it, Cate. Max is a celebrity now. Everybody's going to want a piece of him."

I pick up my plate and stand. I've seen enough. "Well, they're not getting it." I toss the remote to Dad. "Not if I have anything to do with it."

"You're not Max's saviour, Cate. I hope you know that." When I don't respond, Dad continues. "It's admirable that you're trying to help him, but I don't want you feeling solely responsible."

"I don't. I'm not. I'm just helping out till his family shows up." He doesn't believe me. I can tell. "I'm Max's friend, Dad. And friends help friends." I look at the TV. Peter is still talking about Max, pretending to be his friend. "And right now, Max needs all the *real* friends he can get."

On Thursday morning just before eight thirty, Dad drops me outside the credit union. Noah is supposed to meet me but he's coming from rowing practice so I'm not surprised when he's a few minutes late.

Seconds after Noah arrives a woman unlocks the door and lets us in.

"I was watching for you," Janie Lancaster says as she ushers us into her corner office. The savings and loans officer has spikey red hair and a wide smile. "We've received five thousand dollars in donations already. It's phenomenal!"

"That'll totally help with Max's expenses," I say. And it will. But as we sit down, all I can think about is the other phenomenon in front of me—the outrageous curls in Noah Fox's wet hair. Clearly he was in a rush and didn't have time to dry it after practice. My gaze drops to his knee. It's bare, tanned, muscled—and it's almost touching mine. I shift in my chair to put more space between us.

"Here we go." She pushes a piece of paper across the desk. "This is a living trust agreement for Mr. Max Le Bould. I'll need some information from whoever will be the trustee in charge."

"I thought we could open an account in his name," I tell her.

"And that the credit union could administer it," Noah adds.

"It's not that easy." She launches into a convoluted explanation of bank policy and the various account and trust options. By the time she's done my head is reeling. "I understand Mr. Le Bould's situation," she says. "And a trust is the natural choice." She taps the sheet of paper in front of us. "By appointing one of you trustee, you'll temporarily administer the account for Mr. Le Bould. No one else will have access."

"Can we put Mr. Le Bould's name on the account too?" Noah asks.

"Yes," Ms. Lancaster says. "And once he's out of hospital, he can come into the bank to sign the papers and take it over." She gives us a bright smile. "Now, which one of you is going to be trustee?"

Noah points to me.

"Okay. I need you to fill out this part of the form and provide me with ID. Once that's done we'll deposit the five thousand dollars and issue you a debit card."

As I dig in my purse for my wallet, I remember Gabe and the money we owe him. "Could we get a few hundred dollars in cash today?"

"Of course."

Ten minutes later we're done. I have enough money for Gabe and for clothing, food and other supplies. "We'll need to get the fishing shack cleaned up," I remind Noah as we pull out of the parking lot. "I'm seeing Max after school to tell him he can stay there. And after dinner I'm driving to Woodgrove to replace his clothes. Wanna come?"

"I can't. My dad's helping the neighbour put up a gazebo. I said I'd lend a hand."

Disappointment flutters through me. "No problem." My experience with men's clothing is limited to buying Dad and Parker stuff at Christmas, but I'm sure I'll manage. "He'll have to get to the bank to sign the papers when he's released too." Max isn't allowed to sign the papers from his hospital bed. Bank policy, Ms. Lancaster said.

"You don't sound happy about that."

"He could end up with a lot of money." Another seven hundred dollars showed up as we were leaving and Ms. Lancaster said donations could hit fifteen grand by the weekend. "What if he gets out of hospital, takes over the account and drinks all the money away?"

"What if he does?"

"That wouldn't be productive."

"People are entitled to make their own decisions."

I don't want to think about the kinds of decisions Max might make. "What about the people who donate? What do I tell them?"

The light up ahead turns red. Noah coasts to a stop. He turns to look at me. His hair has dried into a tangle of curls most women would pay big bucks to duplicate. And he smells ridiculous. Good ridiculous. Better than lemon meringue pie ridiculous. "Why worry about it?"

Why not? "Don't judge."

"I'm not judging you. I'm concerned. We're friends. At least until you get over your allergy to dating."

My insides do a squidgy dance at the idea of dating Noah Fox. "Forget it, Fox. I have a lousy track record with guys."

"So I heard."

Oh man. Thank you, Carter.

"Don't worry." He grins. "We'll have staying power."

I laugh. "For the rest of the week maybe."

"My psychic powers say way longer than that."

He's teasing. I decide to play along. "How much longer?"

The light changes but he makes no move to drive. He looks at me instead, his green eyes as deep and mysterious as a forest at dusk. "How long have you got?"

My skin tingles. My mouth turns dry. Maybe he's not teasing. Maybe I've misread him. Behind us a car honks. And before I can come up with a response, Noah steps on the gas and the moment is lost.

I have English first block. When I walk into class, Mrs. Moreau calls me to her desk and hands me some papers. "I've printed off a few student speeches to get you thinking," she says. "And I've included a couple of YouTube links of speeches you can watch for inspiration. I know the ceremony isn't until June but it doesn't hurt to start early."

As I take the sheets and tuck them into my bag, Mrs. Moreau says, "You could always ask your parents for input."

My head jerks up. *Parents? Does she mean my mother?*

"The speech has to be your words, of course, but I'm sure they'd have some advice for you about maintaining a life-work balance." She smiles.

Any balancing my mother did didn't include me. But Moreau can't know that. "Thanks," I say. "I'll consider it."

For sure I'll pick Dad's brain but I'm not asking Cynthia for help. Under normal circumstances—normal being that she hadn't left when I was two—I would. But now? I don't think so.

"I'm not even looking at the speeches Moreau gave me until next week," I tell Tegan later in Foods class as I retrieve eggs from the fridge. We're making an asparagus soufflé and I managed to snag the cooking station with the best oven. "I need to get through the bravery award first. The mayor's office confirmed everything a few minutes ago. The ceremony's at ten fifteen Saturday morning."

"Cool." She's supposed to be washing the asparagus but mostly she's checking her phone. "You and Noah will go together, right?"

"I don't think so."

She's grinning and typing furiously. Owen, no doubt. After a minute she says, "You're going to prom together though, right?"

My heart flips. I wondered how long it would take for her to bring that up. Prom's two weeks away. Aside from renting my dress and buying my ticket, I haven't thought about it.

"Right?" she repeats.

I murmur something noncommittal in response, grab two bowls and begin separating the eggs. *We'll have staying power*. Noah was kidding. He knows I'm off dating.

"Everybody's talking about Max," Tegan says as she puts her phone down and begins drying the asparagus. "They want to know if he's hiding out here. If he's running from something."

"Maybe he just wants his privacy." I pick up another egg, crack it gently against the side of the bowl.

She leans close and lowers her voice. "Noah told Owen he thinks Max deliberately rode into the truck. That he was trying to kill himself."

My fingers tighten; the eggshell snaps. "Damn!" I feign annoyance as I fish the broken piece out of the bowl.

"Some Buddhists believe suicide is an option as long as it's done for the right reasons and your mind is at peace," Tegan adds. "My mom believes that. It's kinda like assisted dying, I guess."

I glare at her. "Max was *not* trying to kill himself."

"Maybe, maybe not," she says. "But he's definitely hiding something. Like how he got over the border from Montana for one thing. No wonder the press is here."

"They're here because he's famous," I tell her. "Sometimes accidents are just accidents."

"And sometimes people hide things. You do."

I open my mouth to tell her she's being stupid but quickly shut it. If I argue, she'll bring up my mother.

"You've always been super private," Tegan continues. "You're the first person to help somebody out but you always hold a part of yourself back."

Tegan lives in full-disclosure mode. That's not me.

"Like in grade one when your dog died and you didn't tell me for an entire month!"

Apollo. The most gorgeous Great Dane I've ever known. It was a month before I could talk about him without crying. And who wants to cry in front of people? "I was six. Give me a break."

She sets the asparagus aside, reaches for the hand mixer and inserts the beaters. "Fair enough but we're not six now." She gives me a pointed look. I know she's referring to my mother.

My lungs constrict. Tegan might be a megaphone but she's also my best friend. If you can't trust your best friend, who can you trust? "Cynthia and I have been playing phone tag," I quietly admit as I put the egg whites in front of her.

Tegan turns the mixer on. "When are you going to see her?"

"I don't know."

Cynthia called my cell late last night and left a message which I retrieved this morning. I felt a little jolt when her voice first travelled down the line. "Let's go for dinner. Pick a date and a place." She hesitated and I heard her take a breath. When she spoke again her voice was lower, almost wistful. "I'd like to spend some time with you, Daisy. Please call when you can."

It was like she was whispering in my ear, tucking me in, being a mom. I told myself not to be stupid. She's a stranger.

My mom, the stranger.

She doesn't even call me by my name.

Tegan beats the egg whites so vigorously the bowl starts to vibrate. "You're going to have dinner with her though, right?"

"Sure."

She appraises me in that measured wise-owl way of hers. "Sure?" She wrinkles her nose. "So much enthusiasm. What's with that?"

She's got the beaters too high. The bowl of eggs is creeping to the edge of the counter. I take over and turn the beaters down. "Nothing's up. It's weird, that's all. I don't even *know* her." *And I should.*

"She's your mother. Don't tell me you're afraid to get close to her?"

My throat is dry. "That's a stupid thing to say. I'm not afraid."

Tegan continues to stare at me. I can tell she doesn't believe me.

"I'm *not*!" But the words jam my throat like a cork. When Tegan opens her mouth to respond I turn the beaters back to high. "Grate the cheese," I say. "We need one cup of Gruyère." She starts to say something else but I push the mega-boost button on the mixer and drown out her words.

I'm not afraid of Cynthia. But I am afraid of disappointing her.

I wasn't enough for her when I was two. What if I'm not enough for her now?

9

I could call Cynthia back at lunch but I don't. Instead I hang out with Tegan, Rachel and a few other friends. I tell myself I don't have enough privacy to return her call, but I know I'm in avoidance mode. The whole thing is awkward and uncomfortable, and I'm not sure what to say to her so I say nothing.

After school I ride over to the hospital. I expect to see news vans or reporters near the entrance, but it's a reporter-free zone. When I get to Max's floor, though, I spot two police officers standing on either side of his door. A blip of unease skitters down my spine.

"Sorry, Miss," says one of the officers as I approach. "No one is allowed in without clearance."

I peer into the room. Max is sitting in a wheelchair, his head down, his shoulders slumped. He looks defeated. A third officer, a woman, is crouched beside him, writing on a notepad. She says something. Max looks up to answer and sees me.

"Cate! You gotta get me outta here!" His face is infused with colour. His eyes are bright. "Those goddamn reporters won't leave me alone."

The officers step aside and allow me into the room.

"What happened?" I ask.

"If you don't mind waiting," the female officer interjects, "I'm almost done here and then he belongs to you."

"I don't belong to anybody," Max says belligerently. "And Catie's not going anywhere."

"To clarify," the officer says as she flips the page on her notepad. "You were in the hall and this man spoke to you first so he didn't technically accost you, correct?"

Max's flush deepens. "I was in the hall walking *on doctor's orders* because the only way they'll release me is if I prove I can walk and talk and feed myself and wipe my own ass."

I wince. "Continue," the officer says.

"I was walking down the hall *minding my own bloody business* when this wanker popped out from around the corner and stopped me."

"Wanker?"

Max wrinkles his nose. "Wanker. Twit. Arsehole. Call him whatever you want."

"So he didn't accost you but got in your way, is that correct?"

Max snorts. "He was so close I could smell the stink of his breath. And the next thing I knew another guy with a camera was in my face, asking me how it felt to be found after being missing for all these years."

Oh no.

"And when I told him to sod off and tried to turn my walker around, he grabbed my arm and started asking me questions that are none of his damn business." Max's voice is starting to climb. The colour in his face has spread down his neck. "In my books, that's called accosting a person," he finishes in a near shout.

The officer is writing.

"They took pictures of me too," he adds, his voice low and tremulous now. "I know they did. I heard the camera."

"Did they hurt you?" the officer asks.

"O'course they hurt me!"

"Physically, I mean?"

Max hesitates for one heartbeat. Two heartbeats. "I almost fell over my walker when he yanked on me," he says gruffly. "Me arm's killing me. Probably have a bruise tomorrow."

After a few more questions and clarifications from Max, the officer puts her notebook away and stands. "I'm sorry you had to experience that, Mr. Le Bould. I understand the hospital is going to move you to a more secure room which should help."

"They should release me. That will help."

"I'll be in touch if I have any other questions." The officer gives me a sympathetic look as she leaves.

Max gestures toward the window. "Take me over there, would you, Cate?" His hand is shaking. I thought he'd be through the worst of his alcohol withdrawal by now.

His room overlooks the hospital's new courtyard. It's a compact space filled with Japanese maples, dark green benches and planters filled with red and yellow tulips. "I'm sorry you had to go through that," I say as I pull up a chair beside him.

"Yeah, well, it's over and done. It's history. History belongs to a bunch of old farts, Catie. All we've got is the here and now."

Given that attitude, it'll be hard to find out about his past so I start with the present. "Good news. Gabe says you can stay in the fishing shack for the next couple of months."

His shoulders straighten. The flush is receding from his face. “You gave him the money then? Told him I'd be good for the rest?”

“Actually, he's been paid up front for two months.”

Max's mouth drops open. “How'd that work? I didn't have the money.”

“Since word of your accident got out,” *and word of who you really are*, “people have been donating money to help pay for your recovery.”

He studies me silently, his face a careful blank. His only reaction is the slow, rhythmic tapping of his forefinger against the white hospital blanket covering his legs.

“There's enough money to pay Gabe, to buy you food and medicine until, you know, your family shows up.” His finger stops tapping. “There'll probably be enough for a place to live after you leave the fishing shack too. We're talking thousands of dollars.”

The colour leaches from Max's face like someone has pulled a plug and allowed it to drain away. He's embarrassed.

“You'll be able to rent a room when the weather gets bad,” I add.

“I don't need a room. I like sleeping outside. It gets you in touch with what really matters. It reminds you of how little any of us needs.” He might love fancy cheese and out-of-season fruit, but Max is something of a minimalist.

“But you won't have to worry about scrounging for bottles or going hungry or anything like that,” I say.

He sighs. “That money doesn't come from the heart.”

“It's a gift, Max. People like doing nice things.”

His lips thin. “They're giving me money because of who I used to be, not who I am now.”

"So what? It makes them feel good and it helps you."

"I don't want anybody's pity." He crosses his arms. Outside the window a gust of wind sends the leaves of a maple tree into a carefree dance. "I don't want to owe anybody anything."

"You won't." *Man, if somebody gave me ten grand right now I wouldn't turn it down. I need every dollar I can get for Chef's Apron.*

"Gifts come with strings, Cate. Always."

"I can't believe you feel that way."

I'm surprised to feel tears stinging behind my eyes. Does he really think all the free cookies and day-old buns I gave him came with strings? "Sometimes people do nice things just because."

"Don't be sad." He reaches for my hand; his fingers are hot. "A gift freely given is a rare and precious thing. People almost always have expectations. If you don't use their gift the way they want, they judge."

My stomach takes a tiny dive. "Yeah. Like my education fund."

"What about it?"

"It's sort of a gift too, right? But Dad says I can only use it for an accredited university. Not for Chef's Apron."

"Did you hear back?"

"I got in!"

He grins and his whole face is transformed. "That's wonderful, Cate! I told you they'd say yes. Didn't I?"

"You did."

Max was the only person who was a hundred and ten percent sure I'd get in. Everybody else—Tegan, Rachel, Mr. Russet Potato Carter—told me not to get my hopes up. Max was totally certain they'd accept me.

"You have to convince your father to let you use that money. Don't let his disappointment make you feel guilty. People do stupid things when they feel guilty."

It's the opening I need. "Is that why you dropped out of sight after the accident in Montana? Because you thought you'd disappointed someone and you felt guilty?"

He swallows. His Adam's apple bobs up and down. "I disappointed myself." His voice is so soft I need to lean forward to hear him. "People don't always want to know the truth of who you are. When you hide it and they find out, there's hell to pay."

"How did you disappoint yourself, Max? And how did you get from Montana to B.C.? That's a long way. What happened?"

"Best not to ask too many questions, my dear girl."

I wait for him to say more but he's silent. I have another question on my mind, the most important one of all. "What happened when you were on your bike the other day? Didn't you see that truck coming?"

Tell me you didn't.

A tiny frown creases his brow. "I don't remember."

Relief waterfalls through me. Noah is wrong. Before I can respond a nurse walks into the room. The name tag on his blue scrubs reads *Rudy.* "You're going places, Max my man. We're moving you to neonatal."

Max looks horrified. "The *baby* ward?"

"It's the most secure unit in the hospital. Nobody can walk those halls without clearance. We're putting you in a private room across from the nurses' station so you'll have extra people watching you."

"Brilliant." Max rolls his eyes.

"And the doctor has ordered an IV antibiotic for your

fever. We need to hook that up right away if you want to get better and go home."

Fever? IV antibiotics? That doesn't sound good.

"Send me home with some aspirin. I don't need another needle in my arm."

"Aspirin won't cut it," Rudy says. "Your fever is too high. The potential for complications is too great."

My mouth turns dry. "Complications?"

"Any infection after surgery is serious," Rudy says. "It's nothing to fool around with." He walks to the closet. "Let me get your things."

"Just my bag," Max says.

Rudy holds up the sweatpants Max was wearing when he got hit. "These too I think?"

"I forgot about those," Max says.

"They're badly ripped," I tell him. "I'm going to buy you a new pair." And a few shirts, and socks and underwear too. "Something to wear when you get out of here."

His face sags. "You need to start looking after yourself, Catie girl. Not be worrying about an old man."

Rudy releases the brake on Max's wheelchair and pushes him to the doorway. Of course I'm worried about Max. I'm worried about his infection, his lack of privacy, his future.

As we near the neonatal wing a baby cries out. That baby has a family to care for him and love him and be there for him.

For now Max has nobody but me. And I won't go anywhere as long as he needs me.

When I walk outside the hospital thirty minutes later, the air is fresh with the scent of salt and seaweed. Keeping an eye out for reporters, I head across the parking lot to the bike rack. I'm fiddling with my lock when my phone rings. I dig it out of my pocket and answer without checking call display.

"Hello."

"Hello, Daisy."

Cynthia. My stomach flutters.

"Hello?" she says again, tentative this time. I hear voices in the background and glasses clinking. She's in a restaurant or maybe a bar.

"Hi." My knees start to tremble. I lean against my bike for support.

"I'm not sure if you got the message I left earlier?"

A wave of heat hits my cheeks. "I did. Sorry I haven't called back. I've been busy. I saw Max and he was practically accosted by somebody who snuck in to get pictures."

"That's terrible."

"I know, right? The guy had a camera and got right in Max's face when he was trying to walk. They're moving him to neonatal which is supposed to be more secure, but he has a high fever and he probably won't get out of the hospital now until the weekend at the earliest." The words burst out of me.

"Poor man. How serious is the infection?"

"Serious enough that they're treating him with IV antibiotics."

"He's having such a rough go of it."

Her sympathy makes me sink to the ground in relief. Max is a neutral topic, a way to connect without touching on the more painful subject of her walking out on us. "He is and I feel terrible for him." I tell her about the money at the credit union, how it will help with his care. How I'm going to buy him some new clothes.

"I could come with you."

That reminds me of the reason for her call. She wants to see me. "That's okay. I can handle it. But thanks."

"Of course." An awkward pause and then, "I would like to see you. Are you free for dinner tonight?"

Tonight? It's too soon. I'm not ready. "I, ah, not tonight. Sorry." I need to get clothes for Max but I don't want to bring it up again in case she insists on coming with me.

"When would be a good night then?"

I stand up, lean against my bike for support and watch a green VW bug pull out of the lot. "I...um...I'm not sure," I stammer. "I'm taking a lot of extra shifts at the store right now." Where would we go? What would we talk about? How would it be sitting across from each other for an hour or longer? An idea dances through my mind. It's either inspired or insane. "Why don't you come over for dinner on Saturday? After we get the bravery award?"

"You mean have dinner at your father's house?"

It was your house once too. The few pictures I have of my mother were taken in our backyard, beside the bay tree. Back then it was a small sapling. Today it's a stately sixteen feet high. That's a foot for each year of my life. "Yes, at our house. It'll be casual. Barbecue probably."

I'm already composing a menu: ribs with Nana's special glaze, the fennel coleslaw everybody raves about, my awesome potato salad. A strawberry tart for dessert. All the things I do well. "I'll invite some friends." Tegan of course. She'll be thrilled. And Owen. A picture of smoky green eyes and a tiny dimple pops into my head. Noah maybe. For sure he'd be up for a free meal.

"That would be lovely. Although I was hoping we could spend some time alone together just you and me."

A funny kind of heat swirls through me. "I'd like you to meet my friends," I say. "One of them wants to be a journalist like you." Plus I want Cynthia to see what she walked away from. The life I've made here. *And I'll feel safer with my friends around.* The last thought is fleeting, barely there, but it's sharp enough to poke at me like a sliver of popcorn caught between my teeth.

"I'd love to meet your friends. Of course I'll come."

I'm giddy with relief. I'm not sure what I would have done if she'd refused.

"What can I bring?" she asks.

"Just yourself." Just. What a stupid word, just. "Say about six? We'll eat around seven?" That'll leave lots of time for talking afterward.

"That sounds lovely, Daisy. We'll see you then." She disconnects.

My mother is coming to dinner. The thought is so bizarre I cannot move.

Plus, I am cooking for her. And she is still calling me Daisy.

How long will it take before she learns to call me Cate?

10

Woodgrove Mall is quiet for a Thursday night. Knowing Max has simple taste and keeping the budget in mind, I head for Walmart where I pick out jeans, a pair of grey sweats, some warm pullovers and a couple of T-shirts.

I'm almost at Winners when my cell rings. My heart does a little tap dance when I read the call display: Noah. "Hey." I sit on a nearby bench.

"Hey yourself. Where are you?" His voice is deeper and more richly timbred over the phone.

"At the mall," I remind him. "Buying Max some clothes."

"Where at the mall?"

"Halfway between Walmart and Winners." I glance to my right. "By Shoe Warehouse. Why?"

"Because I'm at the mall too. And I've been looking for you."

My heart flutters. I jump up and turn in a slow circle, looking at the nearby stores, the clusters of people ambling past. "I thought you were helping your dad with a gazebo tonight."

"Change of plans."

"Where are you?"

"At New York Fries."

I giggle. "Why am I not surprised?"

"Hey, searching is hard work." But he is laughing.

I grab my bags and head for the food court. "You got my text?" Along with inviting him for dinner, I told him about Max being blindsided by the reporter.

"Yeah. Brace yourself. The footage of Max is all over the news."

Noah didn't exaggerate. Two minutes later I'm sitting across from him in the crowded food court watching the news report. Even on the tiny screen, Max's panic and fury are obvious.

"He didn't want this." I put my phone down and stare at the glistening mound of bacon cheese poutine fries sitting on the table between us. "At least he's been moved to neonatal." Carefully I pluck out a single clean fry before giving in to temptation and grabbing two more loaded ones. "He won't be bothered there." Max is momentarily forgotten as I stuff fries into my mouth. They are a crunchy, salty, cheesy taste of heaven. I'm about to swallow when I remember my conversation with Cynthia.

Heaven turns to hell right in my mouth. "Crap."

Noah frowns. "What's wrong?"

I wash down the fries with a gulp of coffee. "I told Cynthia." Noah's frown deepens. "About Max," I clarify, raising my voice to drown out shouts of laughter from the table beside us. "She called as I left the hospital and I was so rattled that I blabbed on about his fever. About him being moved to neonatal." I'm back on my phone, pulling up the site for UK News Group. "You don't think she reported that do you?"

"Reporters report. That's what they do." He pulls his cell from his pocket.

But I wasn't talking to her as a reporter. I was talking to her as a—. As a what?

"What network did you say she was with again?"

"UK News Group." Their site is cumbersome and I get stuck on a pop-up ad. By the time I get it to disappear, Noah has the story downloaded. I jump up to sit beside him so we can watch it together.

Cynthia has the same footage as everybody else: Max pushing his walker slowly down the hall, being surprised by the reporter, his angry response. But her voice-over provides details the other reports don't.

"UK News Group has learned that Mr. Le Bould has developed an infection and will require intravenous antibiotics and several more days of hospitalization to prevent the infection from spreading."

My stomach flips. Oh please. Not this.

"He will remain at the Oceanside Health Centre in the neonatal wing which will offer him the security and privacy he needs to recuperate."

Heat races into my cheeks. She's telling the entire world everything I said. "I never meant—."

Noah gestures me quiet.

"UK News Group has also learned that Mr. Le Bould's sister died three years ago after falling from a ladder in an apple orchard. Attempts to contact his former fiancée and business manager have so far been unsuccessful. But UK News Group will bring you the latest coverage as it happens."

I turn to look at Noah. The sleeve of his white hoodie brushes my arm. "I didn't think she'd report that." I didn't think, period. "I was upset. And she was sympathetic." Totally sympathetic. Like Dad or Tegan would have been.

"I know. You'd never do anything to hurt Max. What are you going to do now?"

"I'm going to see her." I retrieve Cynthia's number from my call history and hit dial. "I need to let her know what she did was wrong."

~

The Crown Mansion is something of a landmark in Qualicum Beach. Set back from the road and overlooking the town golf course, the stately white mansion was built at the turn of the twentieth century when buildings were elegant and people were expected to dress well when they entered them. I feel underdressed in my jeans and runners as I hurry up the mansion's majestic stone staircase and walk into the lobby, but nobody even looks at me.

Noah had offered to come, but I'd turned him down. Now though, as I head upstairs to Cynthia's floor, my stomach is a bag of nerves and I wish he were here.

I stop in front of her door, straighten my shoulders and knock.

Seconds later it swings open.

"That was fast." She smiles. She looks less imposing than she did the other day in her blazer and pearls. She's wearing a grey tunic over leggings. Her hair is tied back in a messy ponytail. Her feet are bare. Her toenails are the same peach colour as her fingernails. "Come in. Please."

She leads me past the bed to a small sitting area. I stare at the back of her head. We're the same height. Exactly.

I take the leather armchair beside the window. In the distance I glimpse a couple of deer grazing on the golf course. Night is falling; the street lights are winking on.

She sits on the loveseat across from me, surrounded by papers, books, an open laptop and a glass of wine. I've interrupted her work. But that work is why I'm here. "It's lovely to see you." She picks up her glass, gives me a tiny toast. "I'm only sorry I couldn't buy you dinner."

She thinks I've changed my mind and that I'm here for a visit. "That's okay. I couldn't do dinner tonight and, uh, it's a school night so I can't stay long." The leather chair is slick under my sweaty hands. I don't want to blurt it out because I'm afraid of how it'll sound. But I'm not great at small talk so that's exactly what I do. "What I said on the phone about Max was private. I didn't expect you to go on air with it."

Her blue eyes widen. Without makeup her skin is almost translucent, the wrinkles on her forehead more pronounced. "Oh my dear, you think—" She laughs. "I used *your* information?" She shakes her head. "No, no. I have multiple sources. As do the other news outlets. They're all reporting the same thing as I'm sure you know."

They are?

Amusement dances across her face. "And you didn't talk to them did you?"

"No." I saw the footage on the other networks but I didn't listen to them. I only listened to hers.

"I thought not." She picks up her glass, takes another sip of wine.

I feel small and mean and petty. "I'm sorry. I guess I jumped to conclusions. It's just that Max is my friend and he wants his privacy. When I thought I'd breached that, well, I guess I overreacted."

"I understand." She sits back, rests an elegant hand against the couch. She has long, aristocratic fingers.

Those beautiful peach-tipped nails. I have Dad's hands, square and pudgy. I'm glad I'm sitting on them. "You made an honest mistake."

She's being so gracious considering I just insulted her.

"Max is big news, particularly for us Brits. People adore him. They're absolutely riveted by the fact that he's alive. They want to know everything about him and what he's been doing all these years."

"Max doesn't want to talk to anybody," I say.

"I respect that. But the poor man has a fiancée out there somewhere, a business manager too. His sister died." She pauses. "If you saw my report you know that, right?"

I nod.

"It's terribly sad. It would have been wonderful to connect them, you know?"

"Yeah." I told Max the same thing at the hospital.

"Max has fans who care about him. Who want to see him do well. Money is literally pouring into the credit union. You mentioned that on the phone."

"Yes."

"People want to help him, Daisy."

I'm Cate now. *Cate.* But I don't want to spoil the moment. "I know."

She slides forward on the loveseat, her face glowing with enthusiasm. "Max doesn't have to sleep at the beach anymore. He doesn't have to go hungry or be cold. For him to live like that is just so *wrong.*"

She could be me talking about Max. Her feelings are my feelings. Overwhelmed I pull my gaze from hers and look out the window again. I see our reflections in the glass. *My mother and me.* We share the same DNA. We are more alike than different. We both want to help Max. The scab on my heart softens a little. "I totally get it," I say, looking back at her. "I want to help him too."

"You're a good person."

Her praise makes me flush. "It's not that. Max is my friend and helping him is the right thing to do."

"I couldn't agree more. Helping someone is never wrong. So we're on the same page as far as Max is concerned."

I may not have my mother's hands or her British accent but we share a core value. To do right by others. It's the invisible string of belonging that binds us together.

"Totally," I say. "As long as Max has his privacy."

"Max will have his privacy for as long as he wants it." She pauses. "But his privacy isn't my concern. That's not why I'm here."

"What do you mean? You're here to cover Max, right?"

"Not entirely. I'd already booked my ticket to come and see you when the news about Max broke."

Really? It's a huge coincidence. I find it hard to believe.

"And when the network asked, of course I agreed to file reports on Max. But you're the real reason I'm here."

The scab on my heart softens a tiny bit more. I desperately want to believe her. "Me?"

"Yes. I'm here to get to know my daughter." She smiles. "And I'd say it's about time, wouldn't you?"

Cynthia texts Friday morning to say she's looking forward to dinner and asks again if she can bring anything. I suggest a bottle of wine and she responds with a thumbs-up. A few hours later Tegan and I are eating lunch by the trail when Cynthia forwards a link from the *Huffington Post* about a plan to help the homeless in Philadelphia. It's my turn to send her a thumbs-up.

"Why would she send you that?" Tegan asks as she eats her Caesar salad.

I swallow a bite of my mango chicken wrap. "Because we're both interested in the homeless."

Across the field a group of guys are kicking around a soccer ball. I spot messy brown curls and long legs. My heart skips a beat. Noah.

"Huh." Tegan looks skeptical. "Homelessness isn't the kind of thing Cynthia covers."

"It is now."

"Because of Max you mean?"

I nod.

"But Max isn't homeless anymore," Tegan says. "Or he won't be. Not with all the money he's getting."

A chunk of mango sticks in my throat.

"Your mother is after a bigger story," Tegan adds before I can respond. "She probably thinks you'll give her an exclusive background piece on Max."

"Cynthia knows Max values his privacy," I tell her. And Max isn't the only reason she's here. *You're the real reason I'm here.* Why would she say that if it wasn't true? "Besides, Max is old news now."

It's true. The kids at school have stopped whispering about the rescue. The reporters have drifted away, though one network produced an in-depth human-interest story about the Magpies and naturally Max featured significantly in it. Gabe mentions it when I go to the marina to pay him for the fishing shack.

"You didn't tell me Max was Max Le Bould." He's on his deck repairing a fishing line. "I saw the news report about the Magpies and the social worker confirmed it when she came out to see the place."

"I didn't want to influence you one way or another." I hope Gabe doesn't back out. The fact that Mrs. Chen is involved means he probably won't. "I got the cast iron frying pan you wanted. And a couple of extra things for the kitchen. Max will be there Sunday or Monday."

He puts the line down. "I sure as hell don't want the media crawling around my property."

"Max doesn't want that either." I hold out the envelope with the money.

After what seems like forever Gabe accepts it. He digs out a key, tells me I'll need a ramp for the stairs and gives me directions to the property in Nanoose Bay.

Noah and I drive out there after school.

The shack is well hidden. We drive up and down the road three times before we spot a tiny piece of orange tape tied low on a tree to mark the start of the driveway.

"Mrs. Chen told me it was hard to find," I tell Noah as his Civic creeps down the overgrown driveway. "She's going to put an orange traffic cone out so the physiotherapist can find the place."

Noah pulls up in a clearing. The shack is tucked in between stands of Douglas fir, bigleaf maple and small, scrubby oaks. Its cedar siding has faded to a soft, weathered grey. There's a woodpile covered with a blue tarp. Through the trees I glimpse the inlet and a dock. I grab my bags and step out of the car. Since it's so hard to find from the road, I bet most people who stay here arrive by water.

Noah removes a large piece of plywood from the back of the Civic. "I'll set up the ramp if you want to go in and put stuff away."

The stale smell of woodsmoke, mothballs and grease hits me when I walk inside. Max was right when he described it as a large open space. A curtained-off area across from the door leads to the bathroom. An unmade bed sits in the right corner beside a rickety nightstand, and a tiny kitchen runs the length of the left wall. There's a large woodstove and a small table in front of the single window that provides a clear view of the dock and water.

Leaving the door open to air the place out, I put the fruit and cheese in the fridge and the cans in the cupboard. I place the new frying pan on a burner where Max will see it; I put his books on the nightstand and hang his new clothes in the makeshift closet. I'm making the bed when Noah walks in with an armload of wood. He stacks it carefully beside the woodstove and turns to survey the space.

"Whoa. I never expected it to look this good." He lets out a long, low whistle. "Pretty nice for a fishing shack."

My nerve endings tingle. I feel weirdly unbalanced. "Tell that to Mrs. Chen." I tuck in the top sheet and unfold the quilt I've brought from home. "I'm almost done. I need to put the towels in the bathroom and then we can go."

Noah takes one end of the quilt and helps me position it on the bed. The intimacy of our actions, coupled with the fact that he won't stop staring at me, makes me fumble. To cover my awkwardness I say, "He'll need a toaster oven or maybe a microwave to heat up the meals that'll be delivered. And I'll need to buy him a new pillow or bring one from home." I gesture to the lumpy piece of foam on the floor. "That thing is gross."

"Why don't you let him decide what he wants?"

His comment startles me. I jab the corner of the quilt under the mattress. "Are you kidding me?" I retrieve the chunk of foam from the floor. “Nobody wants this under their head.” I put it on top of the quilt as far from the sheets as possible. “I just want Max to walk through the door and be happy. To see the glass as half full instead of half empty.”

“Technically the glass is always full.”

“What are you talking about?”

“Air and water. Combined they always fill the glass.” He winks. “If you want to be specific.”

There’s his logic again. “It’s too early in the day for physics, okay? And anyway, you’re overthinking things. Mrs. Chen is trying hard to find Max’s extended family so he’ll have someone to take him to the bank, do his errands, that kind of thing. Hopefully they’ll show up soon and I can back off.” I pull the towels from the bag, give them a shake.

He smiles. “It’s great that you want to help Max. I like that about you, Cate. I like it a lot.”

My heart skips a beat.

“But why don’t you let Max make his own arrangements?”

“He won’t do it.” My words come out in a rush. “And the system can only go so far. Max is high risk. If he flounders, the public trustee will probably get involved.”

“That’s his problem, not yours.” The sun streaming through the window is turning the top of his curls a burnished caramel brown. Like crème brûlée. And I love crème brûlée. “You can’t make things right for Max. Max has to make things right for himself.”

“I’m just being a friend,” I say.

“I get that,” he says. “But when my parents pushed my grandma into assisted living and started making decisions for her, she wasn’t happy. She didn’t last three months.” A shadow falls across his face. "I loved my grandma, and the end..." He falters. "Well, it wasn't pretty."

"Assisted living or government facility is what I'm trying to avoid," I say. "And a toaster oven and new pillow aren't going to kill him!"

"Technically a toaster oven or a pillow *could* kill him."

My spine stiffens. "That's *ridiculous*. How could you even—" Then I see the smile lurking at the corner of his lips. He was teasing. "Don't do that."

"Why not? You're cute when you're mad."

The flush spreads down my neck. "You're weird, Fox."

His grin widens. "We're all weird, Sheridan. The key is finding someone whose weirdness complements your own."

I grab my purse. "Don't get any ideas," I tell him. "My weirdness is the stand-alone kind."

He laughs and follows me out the door.

11

The sun warms my face as Dad and I walk to city hall on Saturday morning. The birds are chirping in the trees; a bee buzzes in the pink flowers blooming near the fountain. It's a peaceful morning.

But my stomach is cramped with nerves.

"You'll do fine, Cate. The mayor gives out these awards every month. Just let him put the medal around your neck and smile for the cameras." Dad opens the door and we walk into city hall.

Smile for the cameras. Yuck.

"You should feel proud of yourself, sweetheart. You and Noah did a good thing. Relax and enjoy the attention." He gives my hand a squeeze. "I'll wait here for Parker. You go ahead."

My footsteps echo as I walk to the antechamber where Noah and I agreed to meet. When I reach the doorway my heart skips a beat. The place is packed. People are clustered near the coffee urn and dozens more are walking around, but I don't see Noah. I'm about to text him when a familiar voice murmurs in my ear, "There you are."

I jump. "Don't scare me li—" And then I see him and I cannot speak.

Imagine the most beautiful cake ever. The Mercedes of all cakes. A cake that is glossy and sleek and stunningly perfect. Put it under a golden spotlight. On a pedestal. And be prepared to drool.

That is Noah Fox all cleaned up.

"What?" Self-consciously he brushes the front of his shirt. "Do I have crumbs again?"

He's wearing a cream shirt open at the neck, a pair of fitted black pants and some kind of spicy cologne. I am a weakling for good smells.

Swallowing my discomfort I brush an imaginary crumb from his shoulder and say, "Yeah. What did you do? Have a second breakfast or something?"

He grins, flashing that tiny dimple at the corner of his mouth. *Slay me, why don't you?* "No, just a couple of mini pastries." His green eyes sweep over me. "You look great."

Not as great as you. "Thanks." I'm wearing a dressy denim skirt with a sleeveless wrap top and my favourite angora sweater. The sweater is probably overkill. The city hasn't turned on the air conditioning yet and it's warm.

"They're waiting for us in the mayor's office."

A surge of adrenalin rushes through me. "Let's go."

Noah puts his hand on my back and escorts me through the antechamber to the mayor's office. We meet the four other award recipients and the mayor, who tells us what we can expect over the next thirty minutes. I almost relax.

Until he leads us out of his office for the actual ceremony.

There's a hush when we walk into the council chamber, which is dominated by an imposing curved dais flanked by flags. The mayor leads us past rows and rows of chairs. Chairs filled with people who are staring at us. Sweat beads on my forehead as I follow Noah to our seats on the dais. I should have left my sweater in the car. Between the lights, the bodies and the lack of air conditioning, I'm way too hot.

I scan the crowd for familiar faces. Tegan is sitting with Owen and a couple of Noah's rowing buddies. I spot Peter from Fine Foods, Mr. Statski and a few reporters standing at the back of the room.

Dad's in the front row. He's sitting beside my mother. They're laughing. A whooshing noise fills my head. I grip the chair so hard my knuckles hurt.

It's hard to believe I'm looking at my parents. Sitting side by side. Joking with each other. Dad's wearing his usual linen blazer and khakis. Cynthia is wearing a simple black dress with a chunky turquoise necklace. As she bends her head toward Dad, I glimpse the flash of a diamond in her ear. I feel a strange mix of wonder and awe. It's like that time I saw the rare clouded leopard at the San Diego Zoo. I always knew they existed, but when it was in front of me it became more real somehow.

Seeing my parents together makes everything more real. Them. Their marriage. Sadness tightens my throat. It makes my mother's leaving more real too.

I look away. My gaze lands on Parker sitting on the other side of my father. When our eyes connect, he nods and gives me a tiny smile. The sadness lifts. I smile back. Parker is my soft place to land. He always has been.

The mayor steps up to the podium. For the next few minutes he talks about the pleasure he gets from recognizing those citizens who go above and beyond to help others. He talks about a construction worker who rescued a senior trapped by fire, the bravery of two bank employees in outwitting a robber, and the quick thinking of a woman who administered CPR to a jogger who collapsed. When he mentions Max my cheeks tingle. And when he describes, in glowing terms, our effort to save him, Noah and I exchange self-conscious grins.

We did what anybody would do.

After stepping forward to receive our awards, we get our pictures taken with the mayor and then it's over. Once we're done the mayor gives another short speech, thanks everyone for coming and invites people to mingle.

Noah and I stand. "That was painless," he says.

"It was." Mostly. "Except I'm boiling hot." I pull off my cardigan, sling it over my arm and follow Noah into a crowd of people. Seconds later we're separated. I turn in a circle looking for him but he's gone.

"Cate!" Dad materializes in front of me. He hugs me and plants a kiss on my forehead. "Fabulous job. We're proud of you."

We who? Parker is beside him on the right. Cynthia is on his left. They're both smiling.

"Thanks." An awkward silence descends. I wish I had some guidelines for this situation. Then Dad steers Parker away and Cynthia and I are alone.

She smiles. "Hello again." Her gaze sweeps my face before dropping to my shoulder. I know the moment she sees my tattoo because her eyes widen and her lips part. I expect her to do the mom thing and ask how I got it when I'm a minor, but she doesn't. Instead she fiddles with her turquoise necklace and asks, "How is Max doing? He must be going home soon?"

Tegan pops into my head. *Your mother probably thinks you'll give her an exclusive on Max.* Is Cynthia fishing for information or making conversation? I'm about to answer when I see Stacey from KONO coming toward us, microphone in hand.

"Miss Sheridan, could I have a moment?" She jabs the microphone into my face. "What's your reaction to the news that Max Le Bould could end up a millionaire?"

What? Last I heard the fund at Mid-Island Credit Union was around twenty-eight thousand dollars.

"Now isn't the time." Cynthia steps closer to me. Her black dress scratches my arm. I feel the heat from her skin and catch a whiff of her perfume.

Stacey ignores her. "The latest report says there's a trust account in his name in England and Mr. Le Bould is due hundreds of thousands of dollars."

Seriously? That kind of money would solve all of Max's problems.

"Now isn't the time," Cynthia repeats more forcefully.

Stacey lowers the microphone and frowns. "Being a bigshot from across the pond doesn't give you the right to monopolize this story. We won't let that happen." A balding camera operator and the reporter from the local paper are hurrying toward us. Tegan is following, smiling widely.

Before I can figure out what to do they're in front of us. A bright light is switched on. The camera whirs. Questions begin to fly.

"Between the trust fund and the money he's bound to receive for interviews, book deals and movie rights, Max Le Bould could return to England a very rich man," says the reporter from the paper.

Book deals? Movie rights?

"This was all in a report filed by Ms. Patrice," the reporter's gaze flicks to my mother before returning to me. "What's your response?"

My mother broke the story? I look at her but she's not looking at me. She's glaring at the reporter.

"Does Mr. Le Bould know that relatives of the crash victims want to talk to him about what happened the night the other band members were killed?" he asks.

"What are his plans, Ms. Sheridan?" Stacey asks. "When can we expect him to make a statement?"

"I don't think—"

Cynthia interrupts me. "You don't have to say a word to these people, darling."

My ears prickle. *My mother just called me darling.*

She turns to Stacey. "This is a private conversation," she says firmly.

"This is a public event," Stacey counters, "and Cate Sheridan is *our* hometown hero." Looking at me she says, "Please remember your roots, Ms. Sheridan. Don't sell the story to the Brits without giving us a chance to bid on it."

I open my mouth to speak but Cynthia lays a hand on my arm. "There's no bid. No story being discussed," she says with an edge to her voice. The prickle spreads down my neck. My mother is coming to my defense. She's trying to help me. "We are having a private conversation. Mr. Le Bould's name hasn't even come up."

I blink. Except for that question about how he was doing. Does that count?

Stacey snorts. "Right."

The guy from the paper rolls his eyes.

Tegan pushes past them. "Cate, I'm so excited to meet your mother! You have to introduce me!"

One of the reporters gasps.

Tegan sticks out her hand. "I'm Tegan. Cate's best friend. I'm so pleased to meet you, Cynthia. Can I call you

Cynthia?" She giggles. "I call my other friends' moms by their first names but none of them are as famous as you." She giggles again. "You're, like, huge. I mean, not huge as in fat huge but *important* huge. And you're Cate's mother. It's so unreal!"

The bright light is switched off. "We'll never get the story now," Stacey mutters.

"Nope, not a chance," adds the cameraman.

The three of them stalk off. My mother bestows one of her dazzling smiles on Tegan and says, "I'd love it if you'd call me Cynthia."

Tegan beams. She's in total Cynthia Patrice fan girl mode. "This is so, so cool!"

We're attracting a small crowd. Everyone is staring at my mother, giving her the same look of awe and adoration as Tegan. One woman hands her daughter a pen and a piece of paper. "I'm sure she'd give you an autograph if you asked," she whispers.

"I can't believe Cate kept this a secret for so long!" Tegan says.

"I can," Cynthia says. Her smile grows wider as she takes the pen and paper. "She is a Patrice." She winks. "And we're models of discretion."

~

Later, as I prep for dinner, I can't stop thinking about Max. He could be due hundreds of thousands of dollars in royalties. It's a mind-bending amount. An amount that will change his life forever. And my mother dug up the information.

She really is trying to help Max. I'm kind of impressed.

But I'm not impressed when she's late for dinner.

"The barbecue's hot," Dad says when he comes into the kitchen that night. "When should I put the ribs on?"

Pulling my gaze from my strawberry pie, I check the time again. It's seven minutes past six. "Why don't we put them on in about twenty minutes?"

"Sure," Dad says.

I look back at the pie and frown. Last night I meticulously positioned each strawberry in a perfect circular pattern, but at some point after I poured on the glaze, some of the berries floated out of place.

"It looks good," Dad says.

My throat tightens. "It's not the impressive dessert I wanted."

"This isn't about impressing your mother, Cate."

I flush. "I know." But this is the first meal I've had with her since I was in diapers. I want it to be special.

Dad wanders back outside. I refill the appetizer tray, top up the punch and return to the deck. Rachel and her boyfriend, Josh, are talking about university with Alana, Ben, Tegan, Owen and Noah. I refill our glasses and sit down beside Noah. Conversation swells along with our laughter. Everyone seems to be enjoying the food and there's still some warmth in the evening sun. It's all good.

Except the guest of honour is still missing.

I sneak another look at my watch. Six twenty.

Noah picks up my hand and laces his fingers through mine. "Relax," he whispers. "Everything will be fine." I feel a rush of heat at his touch, but I don't pull away. There's something incredibly comforting about holding hands. It's an act laden with promise.

And everything *is* fine because a few minutes later

Cynthia breezes into the backyard as the smell of ribs is filling the air. “Darling!” She waves at me from the bottom of the deck. She’s wearing strappy gold sandals with dress pants, a crisp white shirt and a scarf the colour of lime sherbet. In her hands is a bottle of wine. “I’m sorry I’m late but something unavoidable came up and I couldn’t get away.”

Seconds later I stand to introduce my mother to my friends. From that moment the night takes on a surreal, touched-by-fairy-dust quality. Cynthia clicks with my friends; it’s like she’s known them for years. Tegan is her usual over-the-top bubbly self and even the guys are impressed when Cynthia tells a funny anecdote about Prince Harry.

I watch for undercurrents between my parents, but other than a slightly barbed comment from Dad about a cat named Ranger and my mother’s quick switch of topics, there’s nothing. She even endears herself to Parker, confesses to having a “black” thumb and asks him about his work and the community garden out by the old firehall. My mother dazzles everybody with her charm, her modesty and her obvious interest in their lives.

The food is a hit too. “Everything was delicious,” Cynthia says as she finishes her pie. Nobody noticed that the strawberries didn’t look right. “I can’t believe you did everything yourself.”

“Cate is an amazing cook,” Tegan says. “She’ll make a fantastic chef.”

Beside me I feel Dad stiffen. Parker shoots him a look.

“It’s what I’m passionate about,” I say.

“Passion will take you places,” Cynthia says.

“I heard Anderson Cooper talking about that once,”

Tegan says. "How hard it is to be a journalist with all the travelling and how you need to really love your work because you're away from home so much."

An awkward silence descends. *Nice one, Tegan*. Dad gets up to clear the dessert plates. Parker, Rachel and Alana get up to help. Once they've gone Tegan says, "Too bad your dad is giving you so much grief about being a chef. It sucks that he won't let you use that money in *your* education fund for Chef's Apron."

My mother nods. "I read about your acceptance in Tegan's story on the rescue." She gives Tegan an approving smile. "Well done, you." Tegan beams. Cynthia turns to me. "And your father isn't happy with your career choice."

Tegan snorts. "Understatement of the year. I love your dad, Cate, you know I do, but he's being ridiculous. It's your life."

"Tegan has a point," Cynthia says. "You need to follow your own path and not worry what other people think."

Is that what you did? I want to ask but now isn't the time.

"Maybe you could talk to him," Tegan suggests to her.

Seriously, Tegan?

Cynthia stutters out a half-laugh. "I doubt my words would hold any sway. Besides, I don't want to step on his toes. He is the primary parent."

True. Until now at least. A sudden pang of indigestion grips me.

"He gives Cate such a hard time it doesn't seem fair," Tegan adds.

I glare at her. *Shut up, Tegan.*

"Really?" Cynthia's voice is laced with surprise. She gives me an appraising look. "A hard time?"

Tegan makes it sound like Dad and I always fight and

that's not true. "It's complicated." Switching gears I ask a question about journalism which takes Tegan in a new direction.

A few minutes later, when Tegan heads inside, Cynthia looks at my shoulder and says, "I like your tattoo."

"It's a daisy."

"Yes, it's pretty. And fitting given your name." She smiles.

"I'm Cate now to everybody." Heavy emphasis on *everybody.* "But the tattoo was a way of acknowledging my m—" The word jams my throat. "My other name." I'd almost said "my mother name." Talk about a Freudian slip.

"Ah. Right. I see." She gazes out across the lawn, a distant look in her eyes. "I wanted to call you Daisy but your father wanted Cate so you were Daisy Cate." She hesitates. "That was such a long time ago. So much has happened since then."

It's the opportunity I've been waiting for. "You said we have lots to talk about. When I saw you that first day at school." Was it only five days ago? It feels longer. But my shock and uncertainty have faded. I'm ready to ask why she left, why she's never been back and where we go from here.

"We do. But it's getting late and now isn't the time." She's right; the sun has dipped below the horizon. "Tomorrow's Sunday," Cynthia says. "Why don't we spend the day together?"

Goosebumps rise on my arms. I grab my sweater from the back of the chair and pull it on. Max is being released tomorrow morning. Noah and I are picking him up at ten.

"Or is Max going home tomorrow?"

She knows. I'd bet money she does. I'm tempted to call

her out on it, but I'm starting to feel comfortable around her and I don't want to ruin it. "Max has asked me not to tell anybody when he's leaving or where he's going." I want to trust her—I *do* trust her—but I'm still wary. "He doesn't like me talking about him much."

"I understand completely. I would never ask you to betray his confidence."

Relief whooshes through me.

"But I would like to talk to him about the trust fund and the royalties he's owed, darling."

Darling. The endearment wraps around me like a hug. I wonder if I'll ever get used to hearing it. "It's true then? There's hundreds of thousands of dollars in trust for him?"

"Possibly more. I assume you saw my latest report?"

I flush. "No, I was cooking today. I was going to watch it tonight."

"It doesn't matter." She scoots her chair closer to mine. "I've spent the last few days doing some serious digging. I found Max's old business partner and two lawyers who handled the band's affairs. I've spoken to all of them. Max could be due over a million pounds."

I gasp. "Really?"

"Yes. The money's been in a trust because Max was never legally declared dead. His sister refused to do it. She was convinced he was still alive."

His sister was right. I wonder if Max contacted her at some point.

"After she died the lawyers filed papers to declare Max dead, but it still hasn't happened. The fiancée is involved now and relatives of the deceased band members are fighting her. It's a legal mess. The only people making money are the lawyers." She fiddles with her scarf. "The band also invested in some property in Spain that's in limbo. It needs to be dealt with too."

Property in Spain? Trust accounts? A million pounds? I can't believe how much digging she's done and what this could mean to Max. "I'll tell him."

"Could you? Please tell him I have a lot of information. Names of people he can talk to. I'd like to sit down with him and explain what I've learned."

"I don't know if he'll want to."

"I know he needs time to recover. But there's a lot of money at stake and a pile of greedy people chasing it. He needs someone to look out for him. A good lawyer." She hesitates. "I'm only trying to help. Like I said the other night, it's never wrong to help someone."

A surge of joy floods me. How many times have I said the same thing? *I am my mother's daughter.* The thought makes me giddy.

"I want to make sure Max isn't taken advantage of," she says. "I'd hate to see that happen."

"Me too."

"I'm talking as a friend now, not as a reporter." She puts air quotes around the word "reporter." "Max is your friend and I'm concerned for him."

She looks at me, her gaze direct and sincere. Tegan's mother always fusses over me, asking me if things are going well, if I'm happy. So does Alana's mother. I'm sure it's what mothers do. When they care about their kids, they care about their kids' friends. "I'll talk to him."

"Excellent!" She beams. "And what about tomorrow? Shall we spend the day together?"

Tegan wanders out from the kitchen in time to hear me say, "I'm free after lunch."

"Why don't we go for a walk then? Say around two?"

"Sure."

"A walk?" Tegan grins. "I'd love to come and talk more about journalism."

I shoot her a "back off" look but she doesn't notice.

Cynthia drops a casual arm around my shoulder. "Maybe another time, darling. Tomorrow is a mother-daughter date."

Tegan smiles and gushes and agrees. She's under the Cynthia spell. Of course she is. My mother just called her darling too. But I'm thinking about something else entirely. I'm thinking about the fact that I'm going on a mother-daughter date.

And I thought I was allergic to dating.

12

On Sunday morning, Noah and I arrive at the hospital just before ten. He heads upstairs to Max's room while I walk down the hall to Mrs. Chen's office. Her door is open and I'm surprised to find her crouched in front of a black filing cabinet wearing jeans and a pale pink T-shirt.

When I knock she jumps up and smiles. "Cate! I'm so glad you stopped by."

"You don't have my land line and I thought you should have it. I didn't expect to see you. I was going to slide it under your door." I hand her the slip of paper.

She sits down and motions for me to take the chair opposite. "I want to thank you for everything you've done for Max. Without you he'd likely be back on the street. Having said that, I must be honest. Max is homeless by choice. He has assets most homeless people don't have. It would be unfair to direct resources to him when there are other more vulnerable people in need."

"I understand."

"I won't let him flounder. I'll keep an eye on him while he's getting on his feet. And I hope he does. With his talent I'm sure he has more to give to the world. It would be a real shame if he didn't embrace the opportunities before him."

"I know."

She shifts uncomfortably in her chair. "While I appreciate what you've done, Cate, I don't like to see you in this position." She bites her lip. "Max sees you as his next of kin. He insists we contact you in the event of an emergency. You're awfully young to assume that kind of responsibility. And technically you can't because you're underage."

"I'm okay with it," I tell her. "Once Max feels better I'm sure he'll connect with friends and family in England. Until then I don't mind being there for him."

She stands. "Max is lucky to have you. Very few teenagers would do what you're doing."

Max is a friend. Why wouldn't I help him?

It's almost ten thirty by the time Max is released and we settle him in the car. "Blimey, it's hot." He's angled sideways on the back seat; his broken leg, now in a removable cast, is stretched out in front of him. And the sun is hitting him square in the face. I crank on Noah's fan and roll down my window. "It feels like August, not May," he adds.

The passing of time reminds me that my first payment for Chef's Apron is coming up. Even with all my extra shifts and the scholarship money, I won't have enough to cover it.

"It'll be cool at the shack, Max. Trust me," says Noah.

Noah called it. As soon as we turn off the road onto the driveway, the temperature in the car falls by at least ten degrees and the scent of salt water and mossy earth wafts through the car windows.

"Ah, the smell of home," Max says. "You gotta love that."

The waxy leaves of an arbutus tree rustle in the breeze as Noah and I help Max up the ramp to the door. When we get him inside and settled in a chair by the window, his reaction delights me. "It's wonderful, Catie girl."

"You should be comfortable here, Max." While Noah retrieves stuff from the car, I unwrap the new pillow and put it on his bed. "It's warm, it's dry, it's private. And you've got a view."

He glances out the window at the peaceful water of Heron's Inlet. "That I do."

"The closet is there." I point to the curtain separating the bathroom and makeshift closet from the rest of the place. "I hung up your new clothes."

He turns to me then, his watery blue eyes red-rimmed and sad. "You didn't have to do all this, Catie. Honestly you didn't."

If not me, then who? You won't let anyone else help. "I don't mind," I say. I unpack his meds and lay the blister packs on the counter. There are dozens of them. Some for morning, some for night. Some to take with food and some to take alone. I put the instruction sheet beside the packages before sitting down at the table across from him. He's staring out the window, watching a heron wade along the shoreline.

"Remember how I told you people want to help?"

He looks back at me and nods, but a shuttered look drops across his face.

"It turns out you may be able to help yourself." I tell him what Cynthia found out about the British trust fund, the property in Spain.

He doesn't say a word and his silence is disconcerting.

Finally I say, "It's great news, right?"

"It's history, Cate. I want nothing to do with that old life."

The air disappears from my lungs. *That old life.* Is that how my mother thinks of the time when I was a baby? When we were a family? I force myself to take a slow, deep breath. "You can have a new life, Max. With money you earned. You could buy yourself a house and start making music again if you want to."

His jaw is set in a stubborn tilt. "No, thanks."

My stomach churns. "This isn't a handout. This isn't people feeling sorry for you. This is *your money*," I repeat. "Millions of dollars." He simply stares at me. "I'm not explaining things very well."

"You've explained things just fine."

I haven't. Otherwise Max would be jumping for joy. I glance at his leg. Okay maybe not jumping, but happier than this. "Cynthia can explain things better. She'd like to talk to you. She can put you in touch with the right people."

"I don't want to talk to a reporter. It's bad enough that I've got a goddamn therapist coming here every other day. I don't need another stranger coming 'round."

She's not a stranger I almost say. *She's my mom.* But Max won't care if we're related. "The media's not all bad, Max. She found out about the money you have coming. Without her digging you might never have known."

"It doesn't matter. That money belongs to the rest of the guys too. They earned it the same as I did."

"They're dead, Max. And you're not."

A world of pain shadows his face. "Exactly, Cate. All the more reason I shouldn't touch that goddamn money."

"I don't understand."

"You don't have to understand."

In other words it's none of my business. Noah walks in and pulls the new cell phone from his pocket. I give him my chair so he can show Max how it works. Predictably Max says he doesn't need a cell phone. Instead of disagreeing Noah humours him and still manages to explain how the phone only gets reception when you're beside the window and how Max will want to keep it plugged in to one of the three outlets *just in case*.

Fifteen minutes later we're back in Noah's car. "I can't believe you actually got him to try that phone," I say as Noah hits the brakes. We're driving the lower highway through Parksville and traffic is always heavy this time of year. "He was even happy about it."

"I put a music app on it, that's why. But I doubt he'll use it."

"At least it's there for an emergency, as long as he remembers to keep it charged." I'm frustrated and exhausted. I know Max is wary of strangers but I figured he'd be stoked about the trust fund. "If only I could get him to understand. Maybe I'm not being clear. Maybe Cynthia could explain it better."

"Cynthia's a reporter and Max doesn't like reporters."

"She said she'd talk to him as a friend."

He shoots me a quick look. "And you believe her?"

"She's my mother."

"So what? She hasn't been around for the last fifteen years. What do you know about her really?"

His words chill me. I stare out the window at the passing scenery. Sam's Sushi. The road to French Creek Marina. Home Hardware. "Dad says you can either believe the worst of people or the best of them," I say as we approach Eaglecrest. "I choose to believe the best. Besides, Max doesn't have to tell her anything. He just has to hear her out about the money."

"He doesn't care about it."

My irritation gathers force. "How can someone not care about a million pounds? Imagine never having to worry about money again! Or tuition! With that kind of cash I could buy Chef's Apron!"

"Max doesn't want it. Why force the issue?"

"I don't want to see him suffer." We're passing the golf course. A couple of golfers are strolling across the green, their bags trailing behind them like afterthoughts.

"I get it. I wouldn't want to live in that shack or out at Rathtrevor," Noah says. "And I wouldn't want someone I love living like that either, but Max seems okay with it."

On the other side of the street a father and son are walking a golden retriever. They probably spend more money on that dog than Max spends on food in an entire year. "Max is living hand to mouth, scrounging for food and collecting bottles. It's no kind of life."

"It's Max's life. As long as he's not hurting anybody he should be allowed to live it his way and make his own decisions."

Silence descends in the car. A few minutes later, as Noah turns down Belyea, he says, "Forcing someone to do something always backfires."

Heat hits my cheeks. Why is Noah being so argumentative? "I'm not forcing Max to do anything. I'm worried."

"Really?"

He sounds skeptical. My jaw tightens. "Yes, *really.* I'm looking out for him. If I hadn't persuaded him to have the operation, he would have gone back to the beach and he'd be in agony right now."

"Probably."

His detachment is making me nuts. "Or be dead," I say rashly. I repeat what Cynthia—my mother—said the other day. "Helping someone is never wrong."

He stops in front of my house, kills the engine, turns

to face me. “Unless they don’t want your help.” There’s a solemn, weighty look in his eyes.

My heart starts to thrum. Is he going to bring up Max and the truck again? “What are you talking about?”

“Seven months before she died my grandmother fell and broke her pelvis. She was ninety-three and frail. The circulation stopped in her legs and the doctors said without an operation she’d die. She didn’t want the surgery. She was ready to go. My parents played on her emotions and insisted on it, even though it was risky.”

My shoulders tighten. He *is* talking about Max. “You think I manipulated Max into surgery?”

“That’s not what I’m saying. Let me finish.” He drums his fingers on the steering wheel. “My grandmother came through okay but she didn’t heal right. She lost her independence. She couldn’t look after herself. Then my parents forced her into assisted living.”

He’d told me that earlier. “What does this have to do with Max?”

He holds up his hand. “My grandmother was miserable there. After three months she’d had enough. She took a pile of pills.” His voice wobbles. He looks away, stares out the window. “We don’t know how she got them but it doesn’t really matter. The point is she took them.” He pauses. “She nearly died but they found her in time.” He puts air quotes around the words “in time.” “She ended up on life support. She had three miserable weeks living on a machine before my parents finally came to their senses and took her off. She died within minutes.”

Tears sting behind my lids. “I am so sorry, Noah.”

“Yeah.” His voice is thick, like clotted cream. “The whole thing could have been avoided if my parents had let her make her own decisions. She would have died sooner but on her own terms. She suffered way too much."

"That's rough."

"It was. And I learned then that we can't know what's right for someone else."

"I feel bad for your grandma, I really do." I hesitate. I don't want to seem insensitive but there's a big difference between the situation with Noah's grandmother and the situation with Max. "But she was ninety-three, Noah."

"So?" He turns to look at me.

I struggle to find the right words. "She was near the end of her life. She was...ready to go."

"Maybe Max is ready to go too. Maybe that's what this is about."

Not this again! "Max did *not* try to commit suicide and I wish you'd stop telling people that."

"Listen I—"

"No," I interrupt. "*You* listen. There's a huge difference between your grandmother and Max. I know that assisted dying is an option for someone who is ill. I understand someone like your grandma who was ninety-three and frail and faced a terrible operation might want to refuse. I *get* that. But Max is younger. Max has options. He has a long, productive life ahead of him. Or he could if he'd smarten up and accept some help."

"You seem to have decided what kind of life Max should have. That's kind of presumptuous, don't you think?"

I am overwhelmed with fury. "Presumptuous is one step away from arrogance. Is that what you think I'm being?"

"A little, yeah. There's a fine line between helping and meddling. It's Max's life. He should be allowed to live it the way he wants."

A ball of emotion jams the back of my throat. "I'm just trying to do the right thing," I say thickly.

"For you?" he asks. "Or for Max?"

What kind of dumb-ass question is that? I fling open the door. "I've gotta go."

~

Noah's criticism still stings ninety minutes later as Cynthia and I walk Rathtrevor Beach. The sun is warm on my back. A light breeze teases the ends of my hair. It's a beautiful afternoon. I don't want to ruin it thinking about Noah. I focus on my mother and the questions I have for her.

But I don't know where to start. I pull my gaze from the distant shore and glance at the sand in front of us. Our shadows stretch out: two women the same height and build, with the same shoulder-length hair, the same oval face. Shadow twins.

She's wearing a white shirt knotted at her waist and jeans rolled up past her ankles and is carrying a pair of navy Sperry Top-Siders. I'm wearing denim capris, a white T-shirt and flip-flops. We're both eating ice cream: chocolate macadamia nut for her and white chocolate raspberry ripple for me.

"Your father and I walked this beach quite a bit back in the day," Cynthia says.

"You did?" Question number one. My questions are endless. I'm scared that once I start quizzing her I won't be able to stop. What if I piss her off? What if I don't like her answers?

"Mmm hmm." There's a soft, relaxed quality to her face

today. Maybe it's the fact that we're getting used to each other or maybe it's the easy beach vibe.

I rotate my cone. "He never told me." Up ahead a little girl with pigtails laughs as a seagull swoops close to her family.

"I'm not surprised. Your father's a private man."

I'm not sure how to take that. Does she mean good private as in "he's discreet" or "he's so discreet he didn't tell me he was gay"? "All I know is that you guys met at university during a freak snowstorm and were pretty much together after that." *Until you weren't.*

After a minute she says, "It was two weeks before Christmas. It was the first time I'd been away from home and I didn't have many friends here and, well, I was so lonely." She glances at me. "Your father was funny and smart and we started talking. I bought him a coffee, and when he found out I had nowhere to go for Christmas, he invited me home for goose. Goose!" There's a trace of awe in her voice. "Goose is such a British thing to have at the holiday and he said your Nana cooked goose every year. How could I say no?" She laughs. "I couldn't, so I didn't. And the rest, as they say, is history."

"You guys were in love then?"

"We really were." Her smile is wistful. "I thought we could make it." She stops. Underneath her sunglasses her face turns pink.

"Was it hard?"

"Of course. Breakups are never easy."

That's not what I meant. I meant was the marriage hard? Being a family? Was it me? Was I the hard part?

"We both made mistakes."

There are two sides to every story. Nana's words roll

through my mind. “I don’t understand. Did Dad do something to make you leave?” *Did I?*

She opens her mouth, shuts it, opens it again. “The circumstances of our breakup shouldn’t concern you.”

There’s something she’s not saying. Is she covering for Dad? Talk about awkward. I change the subject. “Did you always want to work in news?”

“I don’t know about that, but my mother said I was fascinated by the news on the radio from a young age.” Transfixed, I listen as she tells me about growing up in Dorset, about the British education system and about the grandparents I never knew. I soak up her words like desert sand being rehydrated after a drought. Tegan hates it when her mother talks about the past, but I can’t get enough. “Your grandparents weren’t happy when I told them I wanted to be a foreign correspondent.” She steps around a mound of seaweed. “They didn’t want me in dangerous situations.”

It’s like me and Dad, except the only dangers in kitchens are grease fires and sharp knives. Hardly close to terrorism and rocket fire. “But you did it anyway?”

She licks her ice cream and nods. “I did. And it wasn’t easy. They weren’t happy and they let me know on a regular basis. But no one can live your life for you. No one knows what’s best for you but you.”

Like Dad thinking I won’t be happy as a chef. Then Noah’s voice takes over my brain: *It’s Max’s life. He should be allowed to live it the way he wants.* But there’s a big difference between me wanting to be a chef and Max refusing to accept money that could improve his life.

“I was as committed to my direction as your father was to his.”

"Being an English professor you mean?"

She shoots me a look. "Your father wanted to be a photographer. You didn't know?"

"No." I shake my head. "He had a darkroom in the basement when I was little but he turned it into a closet. He talks about retiring and photographing different countries but I never see him take pictures. Maybe because photography has gone digital?"

"Or maybe it's too painful for him to think about the road he didn't take. It's hard to stay true to your purpose in life, to live how you want to live. But it's important not to let anyone get in your way."

Did I get in her way? Is that why she left? I'm not ready to go there yet. "You make it sound easy. But Dad insists I get a B.A. He's totally against chef training."

"I hardly think becoming a chef will ruin your life, darling. Besides, you're young. You have many years ahead of you." She finishes her cone and licks a dribble of cream from her fingers. "If you find you don't like it or it doesn't work out, you can always try something else."

My purse sways against my hip as we follow the curve of the sand around the point. Up ahead I spot the squatters with their lean-tos and shelters. "Exactly. But Dad won't let me use my education fund, and tuition's twenty-one grand. Between my savings and the scholarship I'll have sixty-eight hundred, but I don't know where I'll get the rest."

I'm hoping for motherly advice or maybe an offer to help me out but all she says is, "That's a tough one." She steps around a large rock, stops walking and gazes over my head to the trees lining the bluff. "I understand he was living in the forest before it happened?"It takes me a few seconds to realize she's talking about Max. I bite down hard on the last of my cone and it shatters into a million bits. The raspberry, once sweet, now tastes bitter. “How did you know?” The news reports said Rathtrevor Beach but they weren’t specific.

“I have my sources,” she says with a tiny shrug. “People do like to talk.” She starts to walk again. “How did Max react when you told him about the trust fund and royalty money?”

“He doesn’t want it.”

Her only reaction is a tiny lift of her perfectly shaped brows. “I’m sure it was a shock. He probably needs time to get used to the idea.”

“Maybe.”

“You don’t think so?”

The tide has turned. The waves hitting the sand are loud. I wait for a break in the swell before saying, “It’s hard to know what he’s thinking.” I want to respect Max’s privacy.

“It’s okay to speak your mind. You don’t have to worry, Daisy.”

Or did she call me darling again? I can’t tell. Her words were drowned out by the tide. “I’m not worried,” I say when the tide recedes. “But there’s nothing to say. Max doesn’t want the money.” We stop and stare out over the ocean. I wait for her to offer again to talk to Max but she doesn’t. “You said a few minutes ago people should be allowed to live the way they want to live.”

“I did, although I was referring to career.”

“But maybe that’s how Max feels. Maybe he’s happy the way things are.” I hardly believe what I’m saying. But Noah’s story about his grandmother has made me think. I don’t want to force Max to do something he’s opposed to. That’s not right. That’s not fair.

"You wouldn't let a child play in traffic would you?"

"Of course not!"

"They'd be in danger."

"Exactly."

"I think Max is a danger to himself. He's not thinking clearly. He's not making educated decisions. He's living in marginalized conditions when he doesn't have to."

That was my point to Noah. "I know."

"It's unnecessary and it's terribly sad."

We agree on that too. Maybe it's a matter of perspective. Cynthia and I are sad because we see someone turning their back on a better future whereas Noah and Max are more accepting of the status quo.

"Max just wants things to stay the way they are," I finally say.

"He may want that but it may not be possible," Cynthia says. "Things have changed for Max. He can only go forward from here."

13

Blue Skies Nana to CD Sheridan: *So glad things are working out for Max. So sorry you're still struggling with Chef's Apron. I talked to your father. He's not budging.*

CD Sheridan to Blue Skies Nana: *I have to keep working on him.*

Blue Skies Nana to CD Sheridan: *Yes, or move forward without his blessing. There has to be a way. We need to think out of the box.*

It seems the lack of interest in Max was only temporary. On Monday, CNN does a look back at Max and the Magpies. Then *People* magazine does a four-page spread on Max. There are pictures of Max as a child, Max as a young musician, Max at Tent City, an orange tabby on his knees. The story quotes the wives of the dead band members saying the trust money belongs to them. A distant cousin is quoted saying the property in Spain belongs to him because he found it, he negotiated the purchase and he contributed to the down payment. It's getting ugly.

My mother, however, doesn't mention Max again. Instead she texts about the speech I need to write and attaches a link about a school in Alaska that cut a girl's speech because they thought it was too political. She sends a cute story about America's top ten dessert restaurants. She also sends me a couple of black-and-white photos of my grandparents. I print them out and tuck them into my top drawer with all her cards. Our texts fly back and forth and I feel so comfortable I ask if she'd be willing to help with my scholarship speech.

I'd be delighted to, she texts back. *How about 3:30 tomorrow? At Qualicum Sushi.*

Perfect, I reply.

In spite of the joy I feel reconnecting with my mother, Max is never far from my mind.

"The story just keeps on going," Dad says when he sees me reading the *People* magazine article after dinner on Tuesday.

I'm on the couch in the TV room. Duke is curled up by my feet. I'm supposed to be working on my speech—the papers are scattered on the coffee table in front of me—but I'm having trouble focusing. Even baking dessert didn't help my focus, and time in the kitchen usually does. "I hoped everything would die down by now."

Dad sits down and helps himself to one of my lemon squares. "There's millions of dollars at stake." He points to my papers. "How's the speech coming?"

"Okay. Mom offered to read it and give me some feedback." *Mom.* The word still feels foreign on my tongue.

Dad takes his time chewing. "I'm sure she'll be helpful." His words are polite but I detect a note of reserve. "Speaking of your mother," he says, licking pastry from his thumb. "We had a chat about you wanting to be a chef."

A trickle of unease skitters down my spine. I told Cynthia Dad was being unreasonable. He is, but I probably shouldn't have bitched about it to her.

"She thinks I should let you use the education fund for Chef's Apron."

I'm surprised. She'd said she didn't want to interfere with Dad's parenting.

"She made some good points."

My mother is sticking up for me! How cool is that?

"I know this is important to you," Dad says. "So I have a proposition."

My optimism, long buried, peeks out. "What's that?"

"How would you like to study cooking in Paris?"

What? He won't let me go to California but he'll send me to France? "I don't get it."

"Paris," Dad repeats. "Where you can learn to make French pastries and baguettes and coquilles St. Jacques from the pros."

My mouth gapes. My mother has done what Nana couldn't. I owe her my life! In more ways than one. "Of *course* I'd like that. But I don't think I could get in for September. Plus I need to be eighteen. At least for Le Cordon Bleu. I guess I could defer for a year." Of *course* I'll defer for a year. For Paris? You bet your sweet macaroon! "I'll need to look into their qualifications. And what about money? My education fund won't cover it."

Dad laughs. "Slow down. I wouldn't touch your education fund." He finishes the last bite of his lemon square and brushes the icing sugar from his hands.

How would that work? Dad's income as a professor is modest. I haven't suffered but there's never been much left for extras. "Where would we get the money?"

He hesitates. That's when I know: my mother will help. She's back in my life to stay, she *does* want to be a mother and she's going to share tuition costs. Wait'll I tell Tegan!

But then Dad says, "I may have a chance to teach summer school. If not, I'll take the money from my retirement fund."

He'd break into his retirement fund? "But why?"

"I'm not talking about Le Cordon Bleu," he interrupts. "I'm talking about the Ritz Carlton in Paris. They run courses in the summer for people your age. There's still space. I checked. And the school can arrange a monthly billet."

I crash back to earth. "Go for a month in the summer?"

"And spend a few weeks afterward in England. Your mother suggested it. She'd be happy to tour you around."

I stare at him in disbelief. He's offering me a month in Paris followed by two weeks in England to make up for not doing what I want with my life.

"Your mother really is trying, Cate. She wants to get to know you better."

He's misunderstood my shock. "And after six weeks I'd come home and go to a college or university you think is appropriate."

The tips of his ears turn pink. "That's the plan. Yes."

His plan. My mother's too? I can't believe it.

"Think of it as a graduation present. Six weeks to have some fun and see Paris and England before coming home to work on a degree."

I should be grateful Dad is trying. Instead I'm so angry I can't speak. Why doesn't he get it? Why doesn't he get *me*?

He rests his elbows on his knees. "I want you to be happy, Cate."

"Then let me use the money in my education fund. Let me go to Chef's Apron."

"That's for a formal education."

My chest tightens. "A trade *is* a formal education."

"Now we're getting into semantics." He shakes his head. "I thought you'd appreciate the sacrifice I'm making for you."

Tears sting behind my eyes. "I feel manipulated."

"I'm not trying to manipulate you. I don't understand why you're so upset."

"I'm upset because it's my life! I want to make my own decisions! I don't want you to sacrifice for me."

"You're my daughter, Cate. I'd do anything for you. I thought you knew that."

Anything that fits into his view of what my life should look like. "Is that why you chose English over photography? For me?"

The colour on his ears spreads down his neck. "Cynthia told you." His voice is tight.

"Yes. And she told me you guys were totally in love once too and she thought you could make it but mistakes were made. On both sides," I emphasize.

I wait for him to admit the mistakes were more his than hers, because I am sure that was the case. But he steers things back to work. "It's hard making a living as a photographer, especially when you're raising a child alone. It would have been a mistake going down that road. Becoming an English professor was the right thing to do. I'm asking you to do the right thing too."

The right thing. I've lived my life trying to do the right thing. And this is where it gets me? "Dad! Why aren't you hearing me? I want to go to Chef's Apron. I want your blessing."

His mouth gapes. "What has gotten into you, Cate? You're so argumentative tonight."

"Honestly, Dad, I think this is more about you than me."

"What are you talking about?"

"You don't love being an English professor. You always talk about how you can't wait to retire so you can travel and take pictures. I think the fact that I want to follow my dream reminds you of what you gave up."

His lips thin. "Don't be ridiculous."

"I'm not being ridiculous. I think you're angry and disappointed and I think it's too painful for you to think about it so you're punishing me." Nana's right. I might have to move forward without Dad's blessing. For sure I need to think outside the box.

"Sending you to Paris isn't a punishment."

"No. It's a bribe." I stand up. "And I don't take bribes."

His silence follows me out of the room.

"So you have parent issues," Tegan says when we leave school and head to Starbucks at lunch on Wednesday. "Big deal. Join the rest of us mortals."

Behind the counter the barista fires up the espresso machine. I wait for the hiss to fade before I say, "At least your parents are reasonable."

"Hahahaha." Tegan snort-laughs. "Maybe ten percent of the time."

"Be serious! My dad's being rigid and irrational. He thinks life should go his way and only his way. I told him he wasn't listening to me. It did not go well."

Tegan licks a trace of cappuccino foam from her top lip. "Of course it didn't. He thinks he's saving you from a mistake."

Like I think I'm saving Max? The thought leaves a sour taste in my mouth. I pick at the corner of my chicken panini. "And what's with my mother agreeing that a month in Paris is a substitute for Chef's Apron? Since when do they even get along? This is the most they've spoken in fifteen years. And they're ganging up on me? What is that about?"

"A, they're parents. They work as a unit."

"Mine don't. Cynthia said mistakes were made. I'm betting Dad made them."

Tegan ignores me. "And B, you don't know they ganged up on you. Maybe your mother tried to stand up for you and your dad railroaded her too."

"Probably. He is *such* a tool."

"The fact that she even brought it up with your dad is good though, right?"

"I guess."

Tegan tucks a chunk of hair behind her ear and changes the subject. "Anyway, never mind that. What's the deal with you and Noah? You guys haven't been hanging out together much lately."

"We had a disagreement."

"What about?"

I fill her in, detailing Noah's hands-off attitude. "He thinks I'm meddling. That I'm being arrogant."

"He's a guy," she says. "You need to cut him a break. They don't get the nurturing thing."

"That's a totally sexist comment."

"Sue me. I don't care." She shrugs. "Anyway, that's a dumb reason to fight."

"We're not fighting." Now I change the subject. "Did I tell you Cynthia is helping me with my speech?"

"Twice." She downs the last of her cappuccino before

pushing the cup away and giving me that intensely owlish look of hers. “You must be totally into him.”

“What are you talking about?”

“Noah.”

Heat hits the back of my neck. I pick up my coffee. With Tegan, sometimes silence is the best option.

“Normally you’re way more talkative about the guys you date.” She continues to stare at me. “The fact that you’re so quiet says something. Plus you’re already fighting, so you must totally like him. You usually manage to hang in a few more weeks before you start finding reasons to bail.”

I put my cup down. “I’ve told you. We’re *just* friends.”

She gives me a knowing look. “Right.”

“You’re reading way too much into this, Tegan. And why are you getting involved?”

“I like him. I like you. I like the two of you together. I think you’ll look great together at prom next Saturday.”

“Who said anything about prom?”

“I did.” She smiles. “When I asked Noah to pay his share of the limo, he said sure. Obviously you guys are going together.”

~

Tegan’s comment about going to prom with Noah totally blindsides me. She knows I’m not going to prom with anybody. I’m still thinking about what she said when I leave school to meet Cynthia at Qualicum Sushi.

I walk into the restaurant at exactly three thirty. She’s already there, sitting at a corner table reading a menu. Her blond hair is pulled into a loose chignon; she’s dressed in cream trousers and a bright orange shirt.

"Hello, darling!" She jumps up and kisses my cheek. Her perfume, this time light and floral, tickles my nose. "I'm so glad you're here."

Her enthusiasm makes me flush. I'm not sure if I'm embarrassed or pleased. I smile and sit down beside her, my thoughts about Noah and prom completely gone. "Thanks for helping me." I pull the draft from my bag and put it on the table.

"I'm happy to do it," she says.

The server, a woman with close-cropped hair and almond-shaped eyes, materializes in front of us. "What can I get you ladies?"

My mother looks at me. "Green tea? You drink that, don't you?"

"Yes, I do."

"How about something to eat?"

"I'm fine, thanks. I don't have a lot of time. I start work in less than an hour."

"Don't worry about that. I'll drive you over." She looks back at the server. "We'll have the seaweed salad, an order of gyoza and the Parksville roll."

When the woman walks away my mother looks at me and smiles. "We can't have you going into work hungry now, can we?"

I grin. "I guess not." It must be a mom thing. Tegan's mom always feeds me too.

Cynthia picks up my speech. "Let's have a read, shall we?"

I sit quietly while she reads, grateful when our tea arrives so I have something to do with my hands.

After a few minutes she says, "I absolutely love what you've done here." She flips to the second page and lays a manicured finger on the middle of the page. "It's very powerful."

"Thanks."

"But I think your intro could use some fleshing out and the end needs a better wrap."

"Okay."

For the next twenty minutes we toss around ideas for the opening and the ending. The food arrives and I find myself nibbling at the gyoza and sushi as I take notes. By the time we've finished eating I have a better structure for the speech. "I can't wait to get started on another draft," I say as I slide the papers back into my bag.

"Feel free to email your next draft if you'd like me to have another look at it."

"You don't mind?"

"Not at all." We head outside. She shifts her purse from one shoulder to the other. My gaze lands on the large, square-cut emerald on her ring finger.

She sees me staring. "Beautiful, isn't it?"

Beautiful is an understatement. The emerald, a brilliant green, is the size of a grape. "Is it—?" I stop. The question is far too personal.

"From a man?" she asks as we reach Memorial.

I nod.

She laughs. "Not a chance, darling. I adore men but I don't want to be owned by one."

I can relate to that.

"How about you? Anyone special in your life?"

A picture of smoky green eyes pops to mind. "No. I'm fine on my own too."

"Good for you. You have to love yourself before you can love anyone else," she says.

I wonder if that's why she left Dad. Why she left me. I'd like to ask but we're now surrounded by giggling girls streaming into Qualicum Nails.

"They're getting a jump on prom," I tell my mother once the sidewalk clears. "Tegan wants to go to the Grotto at Tigh-Na-Mara. A bunch of us are booked in before prom next Friday."

As we head for her rental car my mother quizzes me about my dress, my hair, my plans for the night. When she drops me off at Fine Foods it occurs to me that it's the first time we've been together that she hasn't asked about Max.

We talked the way mothers and daughters are supposed to talk. And as I walk in to start my shift, the thought is as comforting as the smell of warm cookies.

Dad loans me the car on Thursday. I have a spare before lunch so I pick up burgers and fries and drive out to the shack to see Max. It's the first time I've been there since we dropped him off almost a week ago. The place is a mess: ash on the floor by the woodstove, food-encrusted dishes piled in the sink, wet towels balled up in the bathroom. After I eat I spend a few minutes gathering up the towels and sweeping before tackling the dishes.

"What about your pills, Max?" I dry the last bowl and turn to look at him. He's at the table, his head bent over his plate. "Aren't you supposed to take some at lunch?"

He doesn't answer. When I look more closely I realize his eyes are shut. I walk over and touch his shoulder. "Max?"

His head jerks up. His bloodshot blue eyes fly open.

"Huh?" His skin is sallow. White-grey stubble dots his chin. It looks like he hasn't shaved since he left the hospital.

An ache rolls through me. "Your pills," I repeat.

He gives me a vacant stare. Max has been off since I walked in the door.

"Don't you need to take some with lunch?" I ask again.

"Maybe," he finally says. "I can't remember."

My sadness gives way to frustration. How can he not remember? He's supposed to take them several times a day.

His hand is shaking as he pushes a French fry around his plate. He has no appetite. That's weird too. Max is always hungry. I wonder if he's been drinking. He doesn't smell like alcohol. I haven't seen any bottles and I don't know how he'd get booze out here anyway.

I retrieve the pills and skim down the list of instructions. Two are supposed to be taken with food and four are to be taken on an empty stomach before bed. I check the blister packs. They look virtually untouched.

I pop out the two pills he needs now and put them beside his plate. I set out the four he'll need for later too. "Are you feeling okay, Max?"

"I'm fine." He's still pushing the fry around his plate.

I don't want to force him to talk. I put the kettle on and straighten up his bed. When I turn around he's scraping the last of his lunch—most of it, I suspect—into the garbage.

"Did you have enough to eat?"

"Lots, thanks, Catie."

The piercing sound of the kettle's whistle makes us both jump. "I'll make you tea before I leave."

"That would be good." He hops his way back to the table and sits down. As I grab a tea bag and pour water I tell him how my scholarship speech is coming, about Dad's offer to send me to Paris for the summer. Max grunts a few times but mostly he stares out the window. His shoulders are slumped; his energy is low. I don't like the way he looks.

"There's fruit in the fridge for you," I tell him as I'm getting ready to leave. "And I brought you some fresh buns and old cheddar too, remember?"

"Right." His face brightens. "I'll make myself a nice cheese and jam sarnie for breakfast tomorrow." He pours himself some tea.

That sounds like the Max I know. "And don't forget to take your pills. They're beside the sink, remember?"

"O'course I remember. You just told me." He sounds indignant.

The ache in my chest eases. I laugh. Maybe he's just tired. "I'll see you again soon, Max."

"Thanks, Catie girl. Toodle pip."

I smile. I love that crazy goodbye of his. "Toodle pip, Max."

"Oh, could ya do me one more favour before you leave?"

"What's that?"

"Grab me another tea cup from the shelf." He gestures to the empty chair in front of him. "My buddy here needs a cuppa too."

At first I think he's kidding. "Right, Max," I joke. "Sure thing." But when I look into his eyes my stomach bottoms out. Max is looking at me like I'm the crazy one. "Max," I say softly. "There's no one there."

His blue eyes flash. "O'course there's someone there, Catie. My buddy, Fred. Goddamn it." He pushes his chair back and struggles to get up. "Never mind. I'll get it myself."

I gesture for him to sit down before hurrying to grab a second cup from the shelf. Kids see imaginary people all the time. It's not a big deal.

Except Max isn't a kid.

By the time I get in the car and reach the end of the driveway, I can't deny the truth: Max should have gone to a rehab facility. Instead he's at the fishing shack. Guilt weighs me down like a thousand-pound sack of flour. And I helped put him there.

14

Fine Foods is running a promotion when I get to work that afternoon, and it seems like everybody in Qualicum is taking advantage of it. Tegan's working cash. I see her in the office as I'm punching in and I quickly tell her about Max. "That sucks," she says. "Let's talk more later."

There's a long lineup at the bakery. "It's two for one on garlic bread," Karen tells me as I pull on my apron. "And two complimentary doughnuts when customers buy a dozen."

Even though I'm super busy with customers I notice the produce department is getting slammed too.

Okay, so it's Noah I notice. My heart does a little pirouette at the sight of him hoisting a carton of strawberries.

I need to talk to him about prom, but I'm still choked that he thinks I'm meddling in Max's life. Mixed up in my hurt is a mushrooming sense that he might be right. Maybe I have gotten too involved. Maybe I *have* screwed up.

After work Tegan and I are walking to Dad's car when I spot Noah leaning against his Civic. He's eating his way through a pint of strawberries.

"Hey." He nods at Tegan and then looks at me. "Do you have a minute?"

I can't read his expression. It's getting dark and his face is shadowed.

Tegan plucks the keys out of my hand. "I'll wait in the car. Don't be long, 'kay? Owen's waiting for me." She hits the unlock button; my car chirps its welcome. As she walks away she looks over her shoulder and mouths, *Prom.*

Noah offers me a strawberry. I take one and bang his elbow. I step back, acutely conscious of how I must look. My black shoes are covered in flour, my hair's a mess and for sure there's a crease in my forehead from the stupid hairnet.

"I'm sorry I upset you the other day." He's out of the shadow now; the expression on his face is intense.

My mouth is suddenly dry. "It's okay."

"No, it's not. And you're obviously not okay with it because you've been avoiding me."

Busted. There's no judgement in his eyes, only an acknowledgement of the facts. But I feel like I've let him down. "I'm sorry."

"Ditto. I didn't mean to be harsh. I know you have Max's best interests at heart, but..." He shrugs. "I guess I'm touchy about it because of my grandma."

A space opens up in my chest. "I get that. And I'm super sorry about your grandma, I really am." I grab another strawberry. It's cool and moist against my palm. "But you understand about Max? You can see that I need to help him?"

A tiny frown puckers his forehead. "Be a friend? Help him help himself? Sure. But I still think Max has the right to live his life the way he wants to."

Disappointment weighs me down. I don't think anybody should live on the street or scrounge food from dumpsters if they have options. And I'm not the only one who thinks that way. Mrs. Chen agrees. My mother does too. "I saw him at lunch today and I'm a little worried." I give Noah the bare-bones version of my visit, ending with how Max was sure there was someone sitting at the table across from him.

"Max always talks to himself," Noah says.

"This was different."

"Huh."

He's a guy. Tegan's words rattle through my brain. *They don't get the nurturing thing*. "I kinda feel responsible."

"Max isn't your responsibility."

Mrs. Chen said the same thing. "I know but I pretty much organized his move out to the fishing shack."

"That's true." Again, no judgement.

I almost tell him I'm calling Mrs. Chen tomorrow but I don't. Tegan's right. He doesn't need to know everything. "Well. Anyway. That's all."

"Okay," he says.

My car horn beeps. We both jump. It's Tegan.

Noah lifts the pint of strawberries out of the way. He inches closer. His shoulders block out the light. I feel both protected and vulnerable. He touches my hair. "So we're good?"

My heart stutters. For a second I think he's going to kiss me. And for a crazy second I want him to. "I'm not sure what good means since we're just, you know, hanging out casually and stuff but I, ah, I guess."

A tiny smile flutters at the corner of his mouth. "I'm glad."

He dips his head toward me. His breath hits my cheek, all fruity and soft. My knees start to shake. Kissing Noah will be different from kissing any other guy I've known. The thought terrifies me.

The car horn sounds again, long and shrill. The spell is broken. "Except for the prom thing," I blurt as I step back. "Except for that."

He blinks. "What are you talking about?"

I fiddle with my purse strap. "Tegan thinks we're going to prom together and we're not. I'm not going to prom with anybody. I told you that before. I'm going alone. It's a thing." The words rush out of me as if speaking will erase this feeling that Noah is special. Special scares me too. "I mean, prom isn't a thing but not going with anyone is a thing because of Owen and the barista and, well, you don't want to know the rest."

He's staring at me like I'm insane. Heat hits my cheeks. "Prom is off the table," I repeat. "As a couple. Us." Obviously Noah doesn't put much weight on the whole prom thing either or he would have firmed up his date months ago. We have that in common. But still. "Because Tegan said you're coming in the limo and she implied that...you know."

"That we'd be together?" He lifts a brow.

The heat in my cheeks races down my neck. "And that's dumb," I quickly say to cover my confusion.

"It's not so dumb. I told you before we should go alone together. That it would be the best date of your life." He grins.

Man. Talk about arrogant. I want to be annoyed but it's impossible. I am drawn to Noah like icing to cake. I struggle to keep my tone light. "So even though we're sharing a limo it doesn't mean anything."

"Okay."

"Even if we dance together and stuff."

"Oh, we'll dance together."

There's a wicked gleam in his green eyes. "And stuff."

My heart leaps. *Stuff.* This conversation is getting way too personal. "I gotta go."

As I walk away he calls out after me, "Even though we're not going *together* together, how about I buy you a corsage?"

Is he for real? "Save the forty bucks. You don't even know the colour of my dress."

"It's blue," he hollers.

How does he know? But before I can turn around to ask, he shouts, "I'm psychic, remember?"

His laughter follows me all the way to my car.

~

On Friday morning I call and leave a message for Mrs. Chen. I don't go into detail or tell her I'm worried. I simply say I visited Max on Thursday and that I'd like to talk with her. If something's wrong with Max, Mrs. Chen can help. She may not have the resources but she might know where I can turn.

She doesn't call back. Thoughts of her and Max slip my mind as the day goes on. The teachers seem intent on pushing through as much work as possible before prom. We have a review in English and a surprise pop quiz in French. I pick up a shift at Fine Foods that night and two more on the weekend. Cynthia drops me a text midday Sunday to ask how my speech is coming. I tell her I think it's going okay but add that I'm nervous about speaking in front of so many people.

She tells me everyone is nervous about public speaking and she knows I'll do fine.

"You're working a lot," Dad says when I get home on Sunday night.

"I need tuition money for Chef's Apron." I give him a hard stare, hoping he'll challenge me and we can hash it out.

Dad doesn't bite. "Make sure you leave enough time for studying," he says. "You've got three finals next week and those grades matter."

My grades are more than good enough for chef's school, I almost say. But I swallow my sarcasm and head for my room to study.

Mrs. Chen returns my call Monday just before Foods class.

"Your message said you wanted to discuss something," she says. "What can I help you with?"

I tell her about my visit to Max, how he seemed to think someone was sitting at the table with him. I say I'm not sure he's taking his pills, and I tell her that I don't know how much he's eating because I saw a lot of food in the garbage.

I hear her typing as I talk. After a minute she says, "I share your concerns. I took Max to the bank on my lunch hour last week so he could take over the trust fund. It was difficult. He seemed to be in a great deal of pain, which doesn't surprise me. He's been refusing to work with the physiotherapist. Every time she shows up he tells her to leave."

My heart sinks. "That's terrible."

"It is, and without physiotherapy his recovery is compromised. I explained that, along with a number of other things, but Max was extremely argumentative. He insists he has no money and no options."

"That's not true. There's money at the credit union and money waiting for him in England."

"I know," Mrs. Chen says. "And he has a third option as well. Several reporters have contacted me to say they'll pay Max for the rights to his story."

Really? Has my mother?

"Max has refused them," Mrs. Chen continues. "Which is his right and I respect that, but my boss told me this morning that Max is no longer classed as destitute. That means we won't pay for the additional medications he needs."

Max needs more medication?

"And they won't allow me to cover his therapy for much longer either, so Max has to take some responsibility for his own..." Mrs. Chen pauses. "I'm sorry, Cate. I'm way out of line. I've been speaking to you as if you're Max's family and that's unfair."

"That's okay." *If the government won't help Max, who will?*

"It was unprofessional of me. Max thinks of you as family and my guard was down. I apologize," she says again. "I've noted your concerns. I'll see Max after work on Thursday. We need to go back to the credit union. I'll talk to him again about seeing a lawyer. With any luck he'll be more reasonable."

Max, reasonable? I'm not so sure. I say goodbye and make my way to Foods to write my final exam, but it's hard to concentrate with thoughts of Max weighing on my mind.

On Tuesday I meet with Mrs. Kaneko to talk about another possible scholarship, I suffer through a brutal final in Environmental Studies and then I catch a ride to work with Tegan. When we're heading home later that night I tell her the latest about Max and how frustrated I am that he won't accept any of the money that's there for him.

"He's nuts!" Tegan says, shaking her head. And then she switches the topic to prom.

On Wednesday, before my shift at Fine Foods, I meet Cynthia at Bailey's for cappuccinos and dessert (date square for me, carrot cake for her). It takes her less than five minutes to read my speech and pronounce it perfect.

"You've worked hard on this and it shows." She's wearing jeans this afternoon and her hair is long and loose; she looks relaxed. "It's a wonderful speech. You should be proud of yourself." She scoops up a piece of cake and pops it into her mouth.

"You helped," I say, feeling shy. But her input made a difference and I need to acknowledge that. "And I appreciate it. Thank you."

"You're welcome, darling."

Will she ask me about Max? I wonder. I almost *want* her to. I want to know if she's found out more about the million pounds in England. I want to know if the UK News Group has offered to pay him to tell his story. And I want to tell her how worried I am about him. But she starts talking about how she'll have to work extra hard at the gym after such a big piece of cake. I'm thinking about how I can switch the topic to Max when her cell rings. She stares at the call display and wrinkles her nose. "I'm sorry, darling, but I need to take this."

"Sure."

By the time I get the word out she's talking into her cell. "Yes, I got your email and I'm doing the best I can."

Her finger taps out an impatient rhythm against the table. "I'm working on it, but I don't have quite the right angle yet and—."

An angry voice interrupts her. Male, I think.

I don't want to stare so I glance left. An older couple is debating politics in the United States. Yuck.

I look back at my mother. Two bright spots of colour sit high on her cheeks. "Don't talk to me like that, Lance." Her tone is sharp, her frustration obvious. "I've been living with deadlines since you were in diapers." The man speaks again but she talks over him. "Cut me a break. I know what I'm doing. You'll have something within the week."

She disconnects, puts the phone down and gives me a brittle smile. "Where were we?"

We were talking about her workout routine. "I can't remember," I lie. And then I gesture to the phone. "I assume that was about a story?"

"Yes." She drinks her cappuccino.

"About Max?"

She puts her cup down and gives me a tiny smile. "I thought you didn't want to talk about him."

My face tingles. Busted. "I don't, exactly." I stop, not sure what to say. I wait for her to interject, to help me out, but she gazes silently back at me, waiting. "I heard some reporters are offering to pay him to tell his story," I finally say. "I wondered if you were one of them."

"Where did you hear that?" she asks.

I almost say I have my sources too, but I don't want to be snarky so I tell the truth. "The hospital social worker told me."

She raises her eyebrow. "That's inappropriate."

"I know, but Max considers me next of kin."

"He does?"

"Yeah."

I stop. We're getting into dangerous territory here. "I just wondered if, you know, you were one of the reporters?"

She hesitates. "Yes. I am."

I figured. *Your mother wants to get to know you*. Dad's words bubble up from somewhere deep inside. I wish that was all she wanted. I wish I was the only reason she was here.

"You know I want to interview Max," she continues. "I'd be lying if I pretended otherwise. Max might be a big story but it's also in his best interest to talk to someone. He's sick, he's isolated and he needs support. He's going to need money. It doesn't matter whether that money comes from me or another reporter or a trust fund. He needs a permanent place to live and a way to buy food and medicine."

I frown. How does she know all of that?

"Don't ask me how I know," she says, reading my mind. "I just do. I know more than you think. Max has his secrets. And one way or another the world is going to learn about them."

I'm equal parts annoyed and intrigued. Tegan's mother is a mind reader too. "What kind of secrets?"

She grimaces. "Look, darling, Max is your friend and I don't want to betray that trust. I know you want to protect him. I want to protect him too. I care about him because you care about him."

I want that to be true. I want my mother to care about everyone and everything that matters to me. As mothers do. "I can't do anything about the interview," I tell her. "It's up to Max." I'm relieved in a way. Feeling responsible was starting to weigh me down.

"I know. I understand. But it's too bad because with the kind of money we're offering..." She stops, bites her lip. "Well. It would help him, that's for sure."

"What kind of money?" I ask.

"One million."

"A million *dollars*?"

My mother nods. "Yes. UK News Group is offering Max one million dollars for exclusive rights to his story."

Wow. Life sure has changed for Max. Or it would if he'd take what was offered. "It doesn't matter. Max doesn't want the money."

"He doesn't want the money that's been collected here or the money in England because he thinks he's not entitled to it," she says.

Once again she has surprised me with how much she knows.

"But if he sold his story he would earn the money himself," she says. "And he'd be paid within twenty-four hours of the interview."

15

Tegan Talks to CD Sheridan: *OMG, I called the Grotto at Tigh-Na-Mara to confirm our appointment and our ENTIRE bill has been paid by your mother. #IloveCynthiaPatrice*

Rowing Fox to CD Sheridan: *I got you a wrist corsage, not a pin. Hope you're cool with that.*

Administration@Chef's Apron to CD Sheridan: *Attached is a list of possible student accommodation in the Los Angeles area. Please note, the school does not recommend or endorse accommodations.*

Blue Skies Nana to CD Sheridan: *Are you willing to defer Chef's Apron for a year? If so, I have a proposition.*

On Thursday morning I'm running late so Parker offers to drive me to school.

"It's not like you to sleep in," he says as we drive past the golf course. "Did you stay up studying or was it pre-prom excitement?"

I can't believe prom is tomorrow. The last few weeks have flown by. "Neither," I say, chewing the last of my marmalade bagel. "I forgot to switch my alarm on."

In truth I stayed up late texting Tegan about my mother picking up the bill for the spa. I think it's weird. Tegan thinks it's wonderful.

Parker coasts to a stop at a crosswalk to wait for a pedestrian. "Are you worrying about Max?" he asks.

"A little." I tell him about my last conversation with Mrs. Chen. Then I tell him about UK News Group offering to pay Max to tell his story. "And I don't think they're the only one either. Mrs. Chen referred to reporters plural."

"She's not pressuring you, is she?" Parker asks.

"Mrs. Chen? No, if anything she's encouraged me to step back."

"I'm talking about Cynthia. Is she pressuring you to meet Max?"

Parker always calls her Cynthia.

"Not at all."

"As long as you're sure." Parker starts to drive again.

"I'm sure." We have way too many other things to talk about. Like my speech. Prom. And the past. "She told me about meeting Dad the other day."

"That's interesting." But his voice lacks enthusiasm.

"Did you know her back then?"

"No. I met your dad when you were five, remember?"

"Right." I had wondered if Parker was the mistake Cynthia mentioned. "Do you know anything about why they broke up?"

"That's your father's story to tell," Parker says. "Not mine."

"He's not exactly happy with me right now," I mutter. I change the subject. "Cynthia paid for our entire spa afternoon." Parker is the only person who doesn't seem to be under the Cynthia Patrice spell. Maybe that's why I want to tell him. "The whole bill for Alana, Rachel, Tegan and me."

"Wow, that's a big chunk of change."

"No kidding. It's, like, a grand for the four of us." In spite of feeling weird about it, I'm thrilled at not having to pay. That money's going straight into my Chef's Apron fund.

"Pretty nice," Parker says. But his comment seems lukewarm.

"Yeah, it is."

It also feels—I don't know—overly generous. My mother doesn't know my friends. She's only met them once. No other parent would spend that kind of money. But like Tegan said last night, no other mother has that kind of money. And no other mother is Cynthia Patrice.

I know Tegan's right. But I'm way more comfortable being on the giving side of things.

~

"The French manicure is perfect," I tell Tegan on Friday afternoon at the Grotto. Tegan is in the mani-pedi chair to my left and frowning at my still-tacky fingers. "I think it looks elegant."

Rachel and Alana are on my right. Nail techs sit at our feet studiously clipping and polishing our toes. Our hair and makeup have been done. Our dresses are on hangers in the back. The spa sets aside a room where we can change and the limo will pick us up here. It's a sweet deal. Like being Cinderella for an afternoon, thanks to my mother.

"You should've gone for some colour," Tegan says. "Your mom upgraded us to the premier package. You could have any colour you want."

"I know but I'd have to take it off before my next shift in the bakery and that would be a waste of money."

Unimpressed with my practicality, Tegan wrinkles her nose.

"French manicures are classy," Rachel says. "Besides, Cate is getting Blue My Mind for her toes."

The deep blue polish will look great with my prom dress. I watch the manicurist start on my second foot before I look into the mirror across from us.

My blond hair is in a fancy updo. A few curly tendrils swoop down around my cheeks. My eyes pop from eyeliner, shadow and three—count 'em, three!—coats of mascara. My lips are outlined and coloured and glossed. Who knew what a difference lip liner could make? A tiny ripple of excitement skitters down my spine. I look different. Beautiful almost. I wonder what Noah will think.

Don't be a dumb-ass.

In my lap my cell phone vibrates. That's the fourth time in five minutes. I reach for it but Tegan slaps my hand away. "Your nails aren't dry yet!" I stare at the soft curls framing her face. Scowling owl has been replaced by feminine owl. But still owl with attitude.

Two minutes later my phone pings, signalling a voice message. Somebody's determined to reach me. I glance at my phone again.

"We're at the spa," Tegan reminds me. "*For prom*. You shouldn't be on the phone."

"That hasn't stopped you."

"I have a hands-free." She watches the nail tech slick a coat of Rouge Rubies onto her toes. "Somebody has to be on top of the details. Without my phone I wouldn't have been able to let the limo guy know we're running late."

Or talk to Owen a bunch of times either. The nail tech slides my foot into the portable nail-drying machine. When she's done I'll borrow it for my nails so I can check my voice mail.

"*Of course* she's not answering her phone," Tegan says a minute later. "We're getting our sexy on. I've told you to stop calling me, Owen. Come on!" She's back on her bluetooth. "No. I mean it. Quit distracting us. This is the *most* important day of our lives."

I manage, just barely, not to snort. *Seriously, Tegan?*

She shoots me a look. "It'll be another twenty before her nails are dry enough. And then we have to get our dresses on. She can call from the limo."

What's going on? I mouth.

She holds her finger up. "What's so urgent?" A tiny frown puckers her brow. "That sucks." Another pause. "He's okay though, right?"

My heart skips a beat. He? I stare at Tegan. Has something happened to Dad? To Parker?

"Can't someone else deal with it?" She pouts at Owen's answer. "Okay. Fine. I'll tell her." Her gaze slides to me. "I don't know. That's up to her." Her voice hardens. "Now don't call me again unless somebody dies! I'll see you for the pictures."

"At least nobody died," I joke. But my heart is stuttering and I'm starting to sweat. "What's going on?"

"Some guy named Gabe's been trying to reach you," she says. "When you didn't pick up he called Noah. Max is having a meltdown. And Gabe is seriously pissed."

When the limo drops me at the fishing shack forty minutes later, Max has gone from rage to simmering anger. He's sitting at the table, staring out the window and drinking a glass of water. At least he's quiet. When I arrived he was ranting and making no sense. It took him almost five minutes to recognize me.

To be fair, with my face made up and in my prom dress, I hardly recognize myself.

"I can't be getting calls like this," Gabe says as I throw out the last broken bits from one of the dinner plates Max smashed.

A fisherman called Gabe saying somebody was trashing the place. When he arrived Max was throwing books and breaking plates and hollering. Tillie was there too. Gabe says she'd shown up with beer and bad news. That Tillie. She's like a doughnut. Crusty on the outside, sweet on the inside and the killer of good intentions. I glance at the eight empties on the counter. The beer is accounted for but I've yet to learn what bad news she brought.

"I don't need the hassles," Gabe adds.

Neither do I. Especially tonight. I turn to look at Max again, the satin of my blue dress swishing against my legs. His glass wobbles as he puts it down. His hand is shaking so much the water almost spills. I bite my lip. Why did Tillie bring him booze? And how did she know where he was?

"He can't stay here anymore," Gabe says. "I'm giving Max his money back. I want him out of here tonight."

"But he has nowhere to go!"

"He can go to the shelter. I don't care. It's not my problem."

My shoulder blades tighten. "The shelter won't work," I whisper. "They kick people out after breakfast. Max needs to rest." *And stay sober.*

"Not my problem," Gabe repeats.

Tears prickle behind my eyelids. As awful as I feel for Max, I feel worse for myself. "I have prom tonight," I say.

Gabe glances at my dress. “I see that.”

“I don’t want to miss it.” It’s true. All those weeks of not caring about prom and now I do. Noah’s picking me up after he’s done with pictures on the boardwalk. Too bad I’ll miss the prom parade.

Gabe is silent.

“I don’t know where Max can go. It’s the weekend and I can’t find him a place on short notice.” I hate that my voice is wobbling.

Gabe sighs and rubs his chin. “Fine, I’ll give him the weekend. But he’s outta here first thing Monday morning. And if he ruins anything else while he’s here, I will hold you personally responsible. Do you understand?”

I hate this. “I understand.”

~

“How did Tillie know where you were?” I ask Max after Gabe leaves. I’m at the table drinking tea.

“I left a message for her at the shelter.” He’s still staring out the window, seemingly enthralled by a heron. “With that cell phone your fella gave me.”

I want to tell him Noah’s not my fella but Max’s tone is already belligerent. “You wanted to see her?”

“Not really. I wanted some beer.”

Trust Max to be honest. My tea is strong and bitter; it burns going down.

“Tillie has cab vouchers.” He looks at me, his face weary and drawn. “I didn’t think she’d mind.”

“You shouldn’t drink beer when you’re taking medication.” I smooth a crease in my dress.

“Says who?”

Says everybody. "You never know about interactions," I say, avoiding his question. "You could get sick."

"So what? I'm already sick."

So what? My breath stalls. He's taken off his cast. His skin is a mash-up of colours: purple and grey and a sick-looking yellow. But the leg itself doesn't look bad. Not thin and wasted like some broken legs I've seen. "You're getting better, Max. I'm pretty sure."

"I'm just a shadow man, Catie girl." He brushes his hair back from his forehead. His hand is still shaking. "And shadow men don't get better. They only fade away."

"Don't say that."

"It's true." He turns to look at me. His blue eyes are flat, resigned. I'd like to argue but I'm afraid to upset him. "I'm an old man. The end of the highway's coming up fast for me."

My breath catches in my throat. I don't like where this conversation is going. "You're not that old." I want to make him feel a little better before I leave.

"I'm a hell of a lot older'n you. And you shouldn't be worrying about me anyway. You have your own life to live. Starting tonight." He looks at my silver heels beside my chair. "With prom."

The silence, long and awkward, stretches out. After a minute I say, "I care about you, Max. I hate to leave you when you're upset." He doesn't respond. I take our mugs to the counter and my dress flares out in a carefree swirl. My irritation flares with it. As much as I care about Max I want to be having fun with my friends.

"Grab me another pint, would you, love?"

"No." I gather up the last four beers. "You shouldn't be drinking. I'm pouring these out."

"Don't! I need something to drown the bad news."

I don't care about his bad news. The yeasty smell of malt and hops drifts through the air as I open a bottle and pour the contents down the drain.

"Stop!" Max is beside me before I realize it. "I paid good money for those." He grabs two of the bottles. "That Tillie's a crook. She charged me a premium." He hobbles back to the table.

"You shouldn't mix beer with pills," I remind him again.

It's his turn to ignore me. "They're coming down hard at Rathtrevor." His shoulders slump as he settles back into his chair. "They're making everybody leave. For real this time."

I shake my head and empty the last bottle. I'm not sure what to do about the two he just grabbed. He's had five already.

"Park Services and a bunch of uppity-ups in some other ministry have gotten together and reached an agreement. No more fightin' between them. That's bad news for us." He pops the cap on one of the bottles. "They cleared everybody out today. They did a sweep of the forest too. I can't go back there and Gabe's kicking me outta here. I'm snookered now."

Snookered. Max's word for screwed. "You're not snookered," I say. "You have options."

He snorts.

My phone signals a text. I tap and bring up a picture of Tegan, Owen, Noah and a few of the others standing beside the water, the sand stretched out behind them. Looking all prom smiley. The lump in my throat threatens to cut off my air supply. Man, Noah looks hot in his tuxedo. Not a crumb on his lapel or anything.

Photos running late, Tegan has texted. *Noah says he'll be another thirty minutes.*

Thirty extra minutes to talk some sense into Max. I put my phone down. "You have a million options." I emphasize the words "a million." "Money is still coming in for you at the credit union. You've got over fifty thousand there already. And you've got money waiting in trust in England."

He guzzles his beer. "I have no right to that money."

"You've got reporters willing to pay you to tell your story."

"My story's nobody's business."

"You need to figure something out, Max, because the government won't help you anymore and you're not well enough to collect bottles."

He guzzles the last of his beer, the bottle tipping erratically when he puts it down. "I don't give a good goddamn. I don't need any help." He smothers a belch. "And I'm not leaving here either. I'm paid up until June and I'm staying until June. Gabe can piss off."

My anger erupts like a grease fire, blazing over my pity, my compassion and my restraint. "People are trying to help you and you're being unreasonable!" Without second-guessing how I might sound I lay everything out: the millions of dollars he's owed, how many options he has, how he can be the master of his own life now, how patient everyone—Mrs. Chen, me, Gabe—is being with him. I finish by telling him how disappointed I am that he won't even consider telling his story to a reporter.

"People are interested in you! They want to know what happened. Your story deserves to be heard. All you have to do is talk to one person. *Just one.* And you'll be paid a lot of money."

"I don't want to talk to any two-bit reporter," he mumbles.

"My mother isn't a two-bit reporter."

He frowns. "Your mother?"

"Yes, my mother is Cynthia Patrice. She's with UK News Group. She's an excellent reporter. She's honest and trustworthy. She'd treat you well and pay you well too."

He is silent.

"She did a ton of digging on your behalf. She found that trust money in England. She contacted your old business manager. She's looking into the property your band bought in Spain. She's doing everything she can to help you."

"She didn't have to do any of that." But his face is flushed and he won't meet my gaze.

"She *wanted* to do that. You could at least listen to what she has to say."

"You trust her, do you?"

I hesitate. And then I give my head a shake. I am my mother's daughter. We share the same core values. We are more alike than different. "Yes." There is a world of faith in that one little word. "Of course I trust her. She's my mother." If you can't trust your mother who can you trust?

His lips thin. "Well, bully for you. I'm still not seeing her."

Oh *man!* "What if I call her? Would you talk to her on the phone?"

He raises an eyebrow. "Now?"

"Right now!"

"All right, if it means that much to you." My heart leaps. "I'll talk to her."

I'm dialing before he gets the last word out. The phone rings forever; my stomach falls more with each ring. *Pick up*, I silently will. *Don't go to voice mail.* Just as I'm starting to wonder why her voice mail hasn't kicked in, she answers.

"Hello, darling! I thought you were at prom."

"Something's come up." With Max providing snarky background commentary, I give her the bare-bones version of events. "Max is willing to talk to you now," I say.

"That's terrific! I'm at the Mansion. Where are you?"

"He wants to talk on the phone."

"Oh." Disappointment flattens her voice. "All right then. Put him on."

I hold the phone out to Max. He looks at me for a long minute before accepting it. "This is Max Le Bould."

At least he's not hiding who he is anymore. That's progress. I go outside to give them some privacy. When I come back inside Max is saying, "You're probably right. I guess it doesn't make much difference." His words are oddly emotionless.

There's a sombre expression on his face. "I'm not going into town," he says. "You can come here. I'm in Nanoose. Out past Craig Bay."

What? He'll see Cynthia now?

"It's on the water between Madrona and Beachcomber. Cate can give you directions." He looks at me. "Yes, her fella's picking her up shortly. I'll put her on." He holds the phone out. His eyes are worlds away. The hair on the back of my neck prickles. Something doesn't feel right. How did Cynthia change his mind? "Come on, Catie girl. She wants to talk to you." He shakes my cell. "I don't have all day."

That's the Max I know and love. I push my apprehension aside and take the phone.

"Hello, darling. Good news. I'm coming out to see Max and you're going to prom."

16

"Thanks for being so great about picking me up," I say as we drive down the tree-lined street to the civic centre. Noah arrived at the fishing shack first and Cynthia arrived soon after with steak and kidney pie, a wedge of Lancashire cheddar and crusty bread.

"It's no big deal."

I sneak another look at Noah. He's totally gorgeous in his black tux. The other guys will look like snotty-nosed kindergarteners beside him. Plus he's wearing some kind of woodsy cologne that smells amazing. "It is a big deal. You missed the prom parade, which is huge. And you haven't once reminded me that Max's problems aren't my problems."

"Hey, I get that you wanted to support him. That's what friends do."

"Yeah, but I didn't mean for you to miss prom parade."

Months of planning go into the parade. Grads decorate whatever vehicle they can get their hands on: classic cars, trucks, golf carts. One year there was even a rickshaw. Then they ride them up from the beach and through town to the civic centre and everybody in town cheers them on. It's a part of grad even I looked forward to.

He turns in to the parking lot. "No worries. I figure you can make it up to me." He winks.

Instant face flame.

He grins. "I'm talking about a dance, Sheridan. You opposed to that too?"

My flush spreads down my neck. "You did that on purpose."

He just laughs and parks. I retrieve my pashmina and cell. Thank goodness it fits in the tiny purse I'm carrying.

Noah helps me out of the car. I start toward the entrance but he takes my hand and stops me. I frown. "What?"

"I haven't had a chance to tell you how great you look." His eyes are an intense, dark green. "You're beautiful, Cate. Really."

I feel a blush start. What happened to the guy who was joking with me a minute ago? This guy is smooth. From the single white rose on his lapel (looped with blue ribbon; Tegan's suggestion, I am sure) to the tips of his shiny black dress shoes, he is sexy as hell. And hell never looked so good.

"Thanks." The word comes out in a whoosh. He's standing so close I can see where he cut himself shaving. That makes me feel all kinds of tender—a dangerous thing to feel for Noah Fox. "You look kinda hot yourself."

"No crumbs on my shirt?" he asks.

I giggle. He smirks. And regular old Noah is back. "For a change, no crumbs."

We start to walk. He's still holding my hand. It feels right so I don't pull away. We're still connected when we reach the banquet room. The large, airy space is decorated in burgundy and white with a touch of yellow, our school colours.

I take in the sea of tables and spot Tegan sitting near the stage. As soon as she sees us she shoots out of her chair and waves us over.

We weave our way around the tables and past the buffet line where the caterers are filling steam tables and setting out huge bowls of salads and pickles and buns.

"Finally!" Tegan says when we reach them. "I thought you'd *never* get here."

"Cynthia is with Max," I say as I sit in the chair Noah pulls out. "I don't know how long she'll be there but she said she'd keep him company if he seems upset." I'm hugely relieved Max isn't just another story to her.

"Good!" Tegan says.

"But if he has another meltdown I may go back."

"No way!" Tegan leans into me and I catch a whiff of hairspray. "And you're not bailing on after-grad either."

I'm ambivalent about after-grad, but the ticket cost me seventy-five bucks so I'm inclined to go and get my money's worth. A group of grads organized a bush party somewhere out near Cameron Lake. The exact location is secret so we won't get shut down, and they've rented three buses to take us there and back.

I glance at Noah. He's going to after-grad too, though he's catching the earliest bus back so he can grab some sleep before his regatta. "No promises." I slide my cell from my purse and hit redial on Cynthia's number. She answers on the second ring. "How is he?" I ask.

"He's fine, darling." Her amusement is obvious. "We've had a chat and something to eat, and the camera operator is arriving soon. There's nothing to worry about." I don't hear Max in the background. That's a good sign. "Have a good time and forget about us."

Things are turning around for Max I tell myself as I hang up. Even if he doesn't touch the money that's waiting for him in England, or the money donated at the credit union, he'll be paid for telling his story to UK News Group. And that will change his life for the better. The thought makes it easier for me to enjoy prom.

The buffet is good; that helps too. As we gorge on cheese straws, spinach and pasta salads, beef smothered with mushrooms, and grilled sesame chicken, a slide show of our school years plays on a big screen. By the time we get to the dessert table (chocolate sheet cake, profiteroles, lemon mousse and strawberry shortcake), the slide show is over and Mr. Statski is onstage telling us what a privilege it is to share prom night with us. He encourages us to enjoy our celebration and reminds us to stay safe.

For the next several hours I dance with Noah and Owen and Ben and Josh. I even dance with Carter. The few times the DJ cues a slow song, I turn my back on the dance floor and take off to the bathroom or soda bar.

"Last dance is mine," Noah says after the prom queen is crowned and we head out to the patio to watch the fireworks.

"Sure." I'm too preoccupied by the light show to consider the implications of my yes. But twenty minutes later when the DJ announces the last song of prom—"Carry On" by Fun—it hits me.

Slow. Dance.

Oh crap. I can't slow dance with Noah. No way. "I got chilled outside," I say, stalling for time. "I need to go find my pashmina. And my shoes." I kicked them off a few dances back. I give him an apologetic smile but he drapes his jacket over my shoulders before I can turn away. It settles against my bare skin like sunshine. "That should help." And before I can repeat the word "shoes," he takes my hand and leads me onto the dance floor.

My heart is thumping so fast and so loud that when he pulls me into his arms, I'm sure he'll feel it. "Relax." His breath is a hot whisper against my skin. My insides turn to water. "You'll warm up faster that way."

"How do you know that? Have there been studies? Is that some kind of a logic thing?" I'm babbling, I know I am. But it's the only way I can deal with the weird things happening to my insides. "Seriously, I don't think you should say things like that because—"

"Sheridan?"

"Yeah?"

"Shut up."

"Hey!" But before I can say another word, his hand slides down my back, almost to my butt, and he angles me closer. I stop breathing. We are thigh to thigh, hip to hip, chest to chest. And Noah feels so good and dances so well that my discomfort dissolves. So as Nate Ruess sings about being lost and alone and finding our way home, I let Noah Fox take me wherever he wants to go.

~

"Nice shot, Reid!" Owen yells as Josh drop-kicks a plastic cup and sends it flying over the massive bonfire. The crowd cheers. Rachel and a few others clap. We're in a large clearing up the hill from Cameron Lake. Between the blaze from the fire and the lights strung in the trees, it's as bright as daylight here. But cold. I zip up my hoodie and grab my cell from my pocket.

"Put that away." Tegan goes to slap my hand but almost falls off the log we're sitting on. She's had way too many hard lemonades. "S'a party, remember?"

"And you're cut off." I stare at my screen. It's almost four a.m. and I'm ready to leave. I turn off my phone and slide it into my pocket.

"Oooh, there's Noah!" Tegan points. My heart flutters when I see him coming up the path from the lake. He's supporting one of his rowing buddies. Brent is so drunk I'm sure Noah took him down to splash some cold water on his face. "I'm gonna get up so he can sit beside you." Tegan starts to stand.

"Don't." I grab her wrist. She plops back onto the log. I hand her a cheese-and-cracker package I brought. "Eat something. The buses will be back soon and I don't want you puking on the way home."

"Not hungry." She hiccups. "Srsly, you need to sit with Noah. Just because me 'n' Owen had a fight s'no reason you have to keep me company." She hiccups again. "You've hardly said two words to him all night."

A hoot of laughter erupts from across the clearing.

"It's fine, don't worry about it." I'm surprised Tegan noticed given that she started drinking the minute she got off the bus. Like pretty much everybody.

"S'totally dumb 'cause you were practically in his pants during that last dance," she says.

"I was not!" I look at him again. Heat races into my cheeks. That last dance was amazing, but now I feel totally awkward around him.

Tegan is giggling between hiccups. "Were so! I couldn't have slid a piece of paper between you."

"Because he was holding me tight. I told you."

"I know. It wasn't your choice. Blah, blah." Hiccup. "Blah. Methinks—" Hiccup. "The lady protests too much." She wrinkles her nose. "Protesteth? Protested?" She lets out another drunken giggle.

I grab the still-sealed cheese from her hand and open the package. "Here." I force her to take it. "Eat."

"Men are s'pricks," Tegan mutters, rocking back and forth on the log. "S'worth holding onto the good ones." Her voice starts to climb. "Not the misogynistic jerks who only pretend to like women!"

"You're overreacting, Tegan!" Owen shouts from across the bonfire.

Why did Owen and Tegan have to fight on prom? Tegan stuffs the last piece of cheese into her mouth. I haul her to her feet. "Let's go for a walk. You need some fresh air."

She jerks her head toward Owen. "I'm not walking past him." She says it loud enough for everybody to hear.

Owen glares at her. "Mature, Tegan. Real mature."

Avoiding Owen means I'll have to walk near Noah and his rowing buddies, and Riley and Carter too, but if I steer her down to the lake I can avoid them. "This way," I say when we get close to the path.

"No. S'important I talk to Noah." Tegan pulls out of my grasp and lurches over to him. "You and Cate were so totally hot on the dance floor," she says. "Hot like you needed a room or—" Hiccup. "S'thing."

My throat tightens. But Noah simply nods. Two of the rowers start to laugh.

"Hot as in I could see you naked hot." Her laugh morphs into another hiccup.

I can't look at Noah.

"Honestly," Tegan continues, "I think—"

I grab her arm and pinch. “Time out.” And I steer her down the path to the lake.

When we walk back up thirty minutes later, Tegan’s starting to sober up and the first set of buses have arrived. Noah and I convince Tegan and Owen to take the first bus back. By the time we board and the driver is heading for the highway, Owen is begging Tegan for forgiveness and she’s lapping up the attention.

I can’t watch. Beside me Noah is talking to Ben. I’m glad. I’m so self-conscious about Tegan’s comments I don’t know what to say to him.

Josh weaves his way down the aisle to the back of the bus. Carter and Riley plop down in the seat kitty-corner to us.

Riley gives me a drunken grin and waves her phone at me. “I see your buddy Max isn’t the good guy everybody thought he was.” Her eyeliner is smudged and she has a streak of dirt on her chin.

“Right.” I smile and nod. No point arguing with a drunk. Being careful not to graze Noah’s shoulders I wiggle out of my hoodie. It’s about a hundred and ten degrees in here. And it stinks like a distillery.

“No wonder Max disappeared.” She thrusts her phone in my general direction. “He killed his bandmates. He’s a murderer. And your mom broke the story.”

17

I text her immediately: *I saw your story. WTF? Call me.*

When she doesn't answer I text her again. *IS MAX OK? Does he know what you reported?*

Cynthia answers as our bus arrives in Qualicum Beach. *Max accepted my terms and agreed to talk.*

We need to talk.

Eventually she replies. *Network wants me in London ASAP. I'm heading to the Nanaimo airport for a 7:40 flight to Vancouver. How about I call you next week?*

"She's flying out this morning," I tell Noah, not bothering to hide the angry swell of tears pushing against my lids. "She's en route to the airport."

He looks at his watch. "I can get you there by seven," he says. "If you want to catch her before she leaves."

I text Dad and explain what's happening and I leave a message on Gabe's phone asking him to check on Max later this morning. If Max sees the story I don't want him having another meltdown. Once we're on the road I text Cynthia again to tell her I'm coming. "She says she has to clear security in thirty minutes," I tell Noah.

"We'll make it," he says, pulling out to pass a green minivan. The airport is only a few kilometres away.

"As long as we don't get hung up looking for parking."

"It's a small airport. We'll find a spot." He's in the fast lane now, steadily passing the cars on our right. I'm surprised to see traffic at six thirty on Saturday morning but at least it's not rush hour.

A sliver of orange crests the eastern horizon. The clouds take on a light, pearly hue. I watch the sun slowly rise, turning the sky into a brilliant kaleidoscope of orange and pink and purple. Sunlight floods the car, replacing the bleak darkness of the last few hours with warmth, light and hope. I shut my eyes and say a silent prayer. *Please let things be okay for Max. Please take away this sick feeling in my stomach. Please.*

But when I open my eyes my stomach is still knotted and I know things will never be okay for Max again.

Max hadn't deliberately killed his bandmates, but he was driving the bus when it crashed. Cynthia had detailed everything, point by point, in her story.

I can't help myself. I need to see it again. I pull out my cell, scan through for the interview link and hit play. Max appears. His face is sickly white, like an old mushroom. His thin, reedy voice fills the car. "Our main bloke had the back-door trots and couldn't do the driving as usual," Max says.

"Gastritis, you mean," Cynthia interjects from off camera.

Max frowns. "Call it whatever you want." He pushes the hair out of his eyes. His hand is shaking. "He was sick so the rest of us were taking turns driving. Our next gig was in Idaho. We were driving through Montana."

"And you were at the wheel," Cynthia prods.

Max swallows. His Adam's apple bobs up and down,

though his face is devoid of emotion. "I was at the wheel," he says flatly. "I went off the road and I crashed our bus. And then, well, I'm not sure what happened after that."

A sick feeling rolls through me. Oh, Max.

"Turn it off," Noah says. "You've played it a billion times. You probably have it memorized by now."

"I'm worried about him."

"I get that. But playing it over and over doesn't help.

As well as being worried I'm also furious, mostly with myself. I'd pushed Max to talk to Cynthia. She said she had his best interests at heart. And I believed her.

I glance at the clock on Noah's dashboard. 6:38. "The next left is the airport."

Noah has been so supportive, driving me even though it means he'll be late for his regatta.

He takes the turn for the airport, heading east on Spitfire Way. A few minutes later we pull into the parking lot.

Parking now, I text. *Be there in 5–10 mins. Where r u?*

Not hard to find, she texts back. *This place is tiny. Near the coffee shop. Must clear security by 7:00.*

I check the time on my cell. My breath catches. 6:42. "We need to hurry." We get out of the car and start to run. The entrance is crowded with travellers wheeling suitcases and pushing trolleys. Once we get inside I scan the nearby seats.

There she is. Blond head bent over her phone. A takeout coffee on the floor beside her. My mouth turns dry. I come to a sudden stop. "What am I going to say?" I mutter. "This is insane."

"No, it's not." Noah's morning stubble is showing. He looks vaguely pirate-like. "Stay calm and find out why she did it."

She wanted a story, that's why she did it. Reporters report. That's what they do.

"I'll go get a coffee," he says. "I'll be back in fifteen."

Cynthia waves. My heart jams into my throat as I close the distance between us. She's crisp, clean, polished. Sitting down beside her I'm acutely aware that my jeans are dirty, my hair smells like bonfire and I have bags the size of plums under my eyes.

"Why did you do it?" There's no time for preliminaries. "I believed you. I *trusted* you." My voice cracks. *If you can't trust your mother who can you trust?* "You said you wanted to help Max."

"I did help him," she says. "I gave him a chance to tell his story, I paid him well and I gave him the names of people he can talk to about the British trust fund."

"You sold him out. You called him a murderer."

"Max called himself a murderer. I didn't sell him out. He agreed to talk. He knew I wanted to do the story."

"You manipulated him."

"Not really." But her eyelids flicker. Dead giveaway. Of course she manipulated him. "Max was relieved to talk," she says. "He's carried a burden for years. It's an amazing story, you have to admit."

According to Cynthia's report—Noah's right, I've practically memorized it—Max wandered for days in the bush before finding his way to an abandoned hunting cabin. A local hermit materialized to take care of him, giving him food and making a splint for his injured leg. Max claimed to have memory issues for more than a year afterward, though he remembers heading west and hopping a ride to Canada on a fishing boat.

When his memory eventually returned, he found it easy

to turn his back on his old life because, as he put it, that life had died when his friends did.

"I set the record straight," she adds. "That's all."

My mouth gapes. "That's all? You told the *entire* world he killed his bandmates."

"He didn't deliberately kill them. But he was driving the bus that night."

"Why tell people that? What purpose does it serve? They're dead." No wonder Max wants nothing to do with that money in England. He's wracked with guilt. "He has to live with the pain of what he's done for the rest of his life."

"The friends and families of his bandmates deserve closure," she says. "And the hundreds of thousands of fans. What about them?"

I only care about Max. I thought she did too. I thought she wanted to do right by him. I thought we shared that.

"The needs of one should never outweigh the needs of the majority," she says, coming eerily close to addressing my unasked question. She fidgets with the strap of her carry-on. "That's the driving force behind what I do. It's how I've lived my life."

She's not talking about Max anymore. She's talking about us. About me. Hot fury bubbles up from deep inside, dark and blistering like sugar crystallizing on crème brûlée. She's walking out—again—so what have I got to lose? "Is that how you justified leaving me all those years ago? By telling yourself that the needs of the majority outweighed the needs of a two-year-old?" I snort. "Nice one, *Mom.*"

She flinches but doesn't blink. "That's part of it, yes."

Tears burn behind my lids. "And this time, if I hadn't come to the airport you wouldn't have even said goodbye."

She said I was important to her. Is this how she treats

the people who matter? Do I really share DNA with this woman? *Really?*

"I find goodbyes hard," she says.

"So you just walk out?"

"I don't expect you to understand, but I don't want you to feel responsible." She touches my arm. I jerk back like I've been burned. "It's not you. It's never been you. It's me."

How many times have I said that to guys I've broken up with? I have that in common with my mother. And it sickens me.

"I need you to understand this, darling. Please."

My knees start to tremble. The first time she called me darling I was over-the-moon excited. But Cynthia calls everyone darling. I see that now.

"I wasn't meant to be a mother. God knows I tried. You were a sweet baby, a calm baby, and I would look down at your tiny face looking up at me with such trust and love. And I would cry because I knew that I couldn't give you what you deserved. It just wasn't in me. And then..." Her voice wobbles. "And then I was offered an opportunity to cover the Middle East. I knew I had to get back to work. War was breaking out; the refugee crisis was escalating. My skills were needed. Informing people is what I'm born to do. Like you were born to be a chef."

"Lots of women work and mother children."

"Not many of them go into war zones. By then your dad and I had realized our marriage wasn't working. I had to leave. It wasn't fair to take you into a war zone with me and I wouldn't leave you with nannies for weeks on end. Your father is a far better father than I could be a mother. I knew he would provide you with the stability and love I couldn't."

My anger has simmered to a cold, hard knot. The

tears that threatened to spill have been burned away by my fury. I don't buy it. She could have stationed herself in Los Angeles. Or New York. She could have seen me a few times a year. "So you left and didn't visit or call for fifteen years? What mother does that?"

A shadow crosses her face. "I didn't handle it well. But as your father told me very emphatically, mothering isn't a part-time proposition. You're either a mother or you're not."

My gut feels like I swallowed acid. Dad was trying to protect me. I see that now. "And you were not."

Her smile is the saddest smile I've ever seen. "Not in the classic sense, no."

The truth settles deep inside me. "You lied to me. You didn't come back to see me. You came back to get the story on Max. You used me from the minute you arrived."

She pulls on her ear. My heart lurches at the familiar gesture. "That's a little harsh don't you think?"

The lack of her denial makes me bold. "No."

"I saw it as an opportunity. A way to come back and connect with you without it being just about me."

It was never just about you, I want to tell her. *It was about me too. About us*. But she wouldn't get it. She's too focused on herself. I feel better, realizing that. She hasn't deliberately tried to hurt me. She's only being herself.

A disembodied voice rings out. "This is the final security call for WestJet flight 3340 to Vancouver."

"You need to go." There's nothing left to say. I glance over my shoulder, looking for Noah. He's surfing on his phone and drinking a coffee, waiting patiently. More tears surface, clogging my throat. But they're happy tears.

"It wasn't my intention to make things worse between us," she says.

There is no us, I almost say. I have a mother who isn't a mother at all. All these years I thought it was no big deal growing up without a mom. But I was lying to myself. Like those cards I'd tucked into my drawer, I'd tucked a secret wish into a corner of my soul. A wish that one day we really would be mother and daughter. I'd spent years hoping—believing those letters held promise like the dry yeast I use to make bread.

And when Cynthia had shown up, an ache I didn't even know I had melted away. But now? Now I'm deflated and empty like dough that never got a chance to rise.

She's talking about her story again. "Max still has a few secrets," she says. "I didn't report everything."

I don't care. The damage has already been done.

"And making everything public will be better for Max," she adds. "They can't charge him. The statute of limitations has run out on vehicular manslaughter."

I don't care about legalities. This isn't better for him. She's using that to justify her actions. I stare at her face, memorizing her razor-sharp cheekbones, her pointy chin and how her pearls look against her translucent skin. I know this is the last mental snapshot I'll have of her for a long time.

She stands. "I'll email."

I stand too. "Whatever."

Is that a flash of pain I see in her blue eyes? Before I can step away she reaches out and gently touches my cheek. "Goodbye, Cate. Take good care." She turns and heads for security.

My mother has called me Cate for the first time. I stare at her retreating back. And she's leaving me for the second time. She shows her ticket and passport to the guard at the gate, places her briefcase on the baggage belt. Seconds later she disappears from view.

I brace myself for a rush of tears, for a sense of loss. But I feel strangely empty. And then it clicks—how can you miss someone you never even knew?

Noah says nothing as we start to walk. Not trusting myself to speak, I'm quiet too.

Eventually I say, "I'm not sure what I expected but that wasn't it."

"Things rarely turn out the way you expect."

When we'd left for the airport I was desperate for answers, determined to make Cynthia see that what she'd done was wrong. I knew she couldn't retract the story, but I thought maybe she'd apologize or offer to make it up to Max somehow. For sure I expected some kind of resolution. A heart-to-heart connection. I didn't know what that connection or resolution would look like, but I knew how it would feel and this ache in my heart isn't it.

"My sister likes to paint," Noah adds. "She says it doesn't matter how hard she works, the final result never measures up to the ideal in her mind."

Baking is like that too. Sure there's a recipe to follow—which makes it a lot easier than life—but you can always find a flaw if you look hard enough. A muffin that's lopsided or a strawberry pie with the berries not positioned right. But this is big. This is a betrayal on multiple levels. I betrayed Max. And my mother betrayed me.

There's a mob of people by the rental car booth and

Noah and I are briefly separated. "I thought bringing them together was the right thing to do," I say when we're walking side by side again. "I was sure his life would change for the better after they talked." Tears jam my throat.

My own mother used me. I know she did. How sick is that? "I don't know how to make sense of it. Of her."

We walk outside behind a family of three. The little girl is eating a bag of potato chips. Watching her stuff the salty snack into her mouth reminds me that we haven't eaten since last night. Noah stares at her too. I expect him to crack a joke about being hungry but instead he says, "Some things are impossible to make sense of." He takes my hand as we step outside and head for the car. "What we need to do now is talk to Max before anybody else does."

We. Noah said we. The sun hits my face as we pass the ticket kiosk for the parking lot. Noah may not agree with what I did but he's willing to talk to Max with me. I'm a little in awe. Except Noah has a rowing regatta this morning so I'll see Max alone.

"Don't waste your energy trying to make sense of things," he adds as we start to weave through the parked cars. "You'll only make yourself nuts."

I almost smile. It sounds like something a wise old man would say. "When did you get to be so smart?"

"Last year."

I snicker through my tears. He sounds so matter-of-fact. "Really?" I ask. It's a relief to change the subject. "Any day in particular?"

"The day this hot chick in my math class told me where to find the best pizza in town."

I almost stumble. Noah tightens his hold on my hand. He's talking about me. We start down the row to his Civic.

He thinks I'm hot?

Noah and I talked about pizza for a whole month last year. He kept insisting the best pizza he'd ever had was some frozen thing that came in a box.

"And she said I had to go to Salt Pizzeria to try their thin crust. She said it was amazing. She called it brilliant. I asked her to come with me, I dunno, two or three times at least—and she kept blowing me off."

Four times. Noah asked me four times. I could never figure out if he was serious. I decided he was joking because it was easier. Even then I knew Noah Fox was different. And different scared me.

"So I went by myself and ordered the Della Carne. She was right. It was brilliant. One bite of that crust made me brilliant too." His car is three spots ahead. "Of course I didn't tell her that."

He's being silly. The hurting part of me wants to tell him to knock it off but the diversion is good. Maybe it's better to keep things light. To face the heavy stuff when I'm alone.

We stop in front of his Civic. I look at him, finally, and manage a smile. In fact he'd continued to insist his frozen crap was better which led us to have the same circular discussion for the entire semester. Our flirtgument.

"Why not?"

He stares down at me. His calm, green eyes are dark and unreadable. "Because I wanted to keep talking to her and I didn't know what else to talk about."

My breath stalls. He wanted to keep talking to me.

"And I kept hoping she'd take me up on the offer to have that pizza taste-off but she never did."

A car speeds by and the backdraft sends a clump of hair into my eyes.

Before I can push it away, Noah steps closer and tucks it behind my ear.

"So this year I did something kinda crappy," he says softly.

The way he's looking at me is making my heart stutter. "You did?"

"Yeah, I lied to you."

"Lied?"

"I said you were nice." His face is pink. "And you're way more than nice."

Blood whooshes to my head. "I'm good with nice. Nice is cool."

He sighs and looks up at the sky. "Nice is for ice cream. For French fries. For root beer floats."

"Are you comparing me to a root beer float?"

He doesn't take the bait. "I'm not comparing you to anything, especially not a dumb drink." He hesitates. "I like you, Cate. I like you a lot."

My face flames.

"And I was afraid if I told you that, I'd scare you off."

He probably would have. The tears are back, pressing behind my lids, threatening to spill. I stare down at our feet. Toe to toe. Touching. I like Noah too. So much I can't see myself walking away from him. That means he'd be the one doing the walking. Because people leave. Fact of life numero uno.

"It's okay," he says as he tugs me into his arms. He tilts my chin so I'm forced to look up at him. "There's nothing to be scared of." His hair is a mess of curls and his face is still tinged with pink but his green eyes are steady and true. "And there's nothing you need to say either."

I open my mouth, but he stops me with a kiss.

That kiss.

It goes on and on, opening up a sea of possibilities. Noah is safe. In a scary kind of way. I wrap my arms around his neck and pull him closer.

A minute—an hour?—later a faint discordant noise registers. Our phones are buzzing. Simultaneously. We break apart, stare at each other for a minute and grin like crazy fools. Noah digs out his phone first. I pull my phone out too but I don't look at it. Instead I look at him. At his lips. And I think: *I want more of that.*

"It's Gabe," Noah says, forcing me to snap back to attention. "He's at the fishing shack. Max isn't there."

18

Noah pulls out of the airport parking lot while I phone Gabe and get the details. He tells me there's no sign of Max at the fishing shack or anywhere along the shoreline. His walker is still inside and so is his cell phone. The bed is neatly made; all the dishes are washed. "Maybe Tillie came back and took him for breakfast," he says.

"I don't think so," I tell him.

I call Dad. He doesn't see the urgency until I tell him about Cynthia's story. He says he'll wake Parker and they'll go out to Nanoose Bay to see if they can find him.

Noah calls in a standby rower to take his place in the regatta. When I protest that he shouldn't miss it, he gives me a look and says, "You're more important to me than any rowing regatta."

As Noah speeds back down the inland highway, I watch for cops and talk on the phone. I call the local radio and TV stations. As soon as I say Max Le Bould is missing they're all over the story. I call Tegan and Rachel and Owen and anyone else I can think of to aid in the search. Some of the guys still sound drunk. Two hang up on me. But Tegan and a couple of others agree to help. I call the Qualicum Beach and Parksville police too.

With Noah driving I have way too much time to think. So much has happened in the last twenty-four hours. Max. Cynthia. Prom. Our dance. I sneak a look at his profile. That kiss. Heat creeps into my face. It's too much to process.

We're nearing Lantzville when I get a text from Tegan. *We're here. So are the cops and the media. Your Dad and Parker are just pulling up.*

Thanks, I text back. *We'll be there soon.*

A few minutes later, on the other side of town, Noah checks his speed and slows. The cops wait under the overpass at the bottom of the hill to catch speeding drivers. Sure enough, when we get close I spot a patrol car. The officer is ticketing the driver of a silver Porsche. "You'd think people would know better," I say as we cruise past.

"People tell themselves all sorts of lies." He steps on the gas now that the speed trap is behind us.

"Yeah, I lied to myself when I left Max with Cynthia. I should have known better."

"Max invited Cynthia over."

"But if it wasn't for me he never would have talked to her. He'd be sitting in the shack this morning."

"You don't know that. Besides, you had his best interests at heart. He's responsible for any fallout."

Guilt gnaws at me. "On Thursday he said he was old. That the end of the highway was coming up fast for him." A sick feeling rolls through me. "I think you were right when you said Max tried to ride into that truck." Suddenly cold I rub my arms. "I'm sure he did."

Noah says nothing but the sad look on his face is enough.

"I'm afraid he's going to do something stupid again." Before he can answer I add, "And I know you think Max has the right to end his life, but I'd like him to at least talk to someone. Maybe he's depressed. Maybe someone can help him."

"Maybe. But I think people do what they're gonna do."

I hope someone stops Max from doing what I'm afraid he's going to do.

Tegan texts me a few minutes before we reach the Nanoose cut-off. *KONO TV has a helicopter north of French Creek. I think they found something in the water.*

Something? My breath jams in my throat. Or *someone? Can you find out?* I text back.

Before Tegan can respond my phone rings. "Hello?"

"My name is Lindsey Leeshman," a soft voice says. "I'm calling from Oceanside Health Centre."

"Yes?"

"You're the contact person for Max Le Bould."

Breath seems to leave me in a giant whoosh. "That's right." I stare at Noah who is waiting to merge onto Northwest Bay Road.

"Mr. Le Bould has sustained a serious injury. They're bringing him in. You may want to come."

They put Max in a private room beside emergency. It's a windowless space with dreary green walls and bad lighting, and it's barely big enough for me, Noah and the doctor. And Max. His eyes are shut. There's a blue-grey tint to his skin. And he has a ventilator tube going down his throat.

They found him face down in the water. Lucky to be alive, they said when I got here.

"He was without oxygen for some time," the doctor says. "And he's in acute respiratory distress."

"Is that like pneumonia?" I ask.

The doctor clears his throat. "In a way." He's a wiry guy with thick black hair and trendy bamboo glasses. "It means his lungs are having trouble moving air in and out of his blood."

"That's not good," Noah says.

"No, it's not. The body is a complex machine and oxygen is critical." The doctor launches into a detailed explanation about the dangers of chemical and fluid imbalances on the body. His words blend into the symphony of other hospital sounds: a female voice floating out over the intercom, the wheels of a medical cart click-clacking against the floor in the hall.

I can't stop staring at Max. If it wasn't for all the machines and that ugly grey tint to his skin it would be easy to believe he's sleeping. His chest rises and falls in a rhythm I know is machine-induced. What a difference from the last time he was in hospital. Three weeks ago he was loud and argumentative. Tears sting my eyes. I wish he'd sit up and yell now. I'd give anything to see that.

But that's not going to happen. And there's no point in wishing for the impossible. "What does it mean for Max?" I ask when the doctor stops talking.

"We don't know yet the impact on his long-term recovery," he says. "Right now he needs to be stabilized and transferred to Nanaimo General. The next twenty-four hours will be critical."

"Your guilt is misplaced," Parker says that night as I poke at my hazelnut gelato. "Don't beat yourself up."

I stare past him, down the patio steps to the barbecue where Dad is gathering up his dishes. "Why not? If I hadn't gotten the two of them together, that story wouldn't have hit the news." Parker starts to say something but I talk over him. "And if the story hadn't come out, Max might not be in the hospital."

"You can't know that," he says.

"Yeah, I can. I never should have trusted Cynthia." I put my bowl down. A fly buzzes over to check it out. "She's an opportunist." Like the fly. I shoo it away.

Dad heads for the kitchen. He hasn't said much since I got home from the hospital. Duke comes over and sits between Parker and me. He eyes the steak scraps.

"She's your mother," Parker says sharply. "Of course you should have trusted her." His freckles are popping on his cheeks like they do in the first few weeks of hot weather. "Cynthia played on your caring nature. She took advantage of you. Max too."

"I know." All the anger I've been trying to suppress boils to the surface. "I don't know a mother in the world who does that."

"I do." Parker lifts an eyebrow. "Yours."

"It sucks."

"Yes, it does."

"I thought Cynthia wanted to help Max. I really did." And now Max is in a hospital bed unable to breathe on his own. "And maybe a teeny part of her did, but all she really wanted was the story."

Parker stares across the patio. “There’s no point in dwelling on it. The story’s out. What’s important now is Max.”

“I know.” I plan to be back at the hospital first thing tomorrow. Dad has agreed to let me skip school if Max is still in the hospital on Monday. He’s even said I can take the car and drive into Nanaimo. “But I can’t make sense of this. She’s my *mother.* I don’t know how I’m supposed to be around her.” My throat starts to close. She said she’d email. What if she does?

What if she doesn’t?

Parker scratches Duke’s ear. “That’s the wrong question, Cate. The question is how can you be with yourself?”

“What?”

“I wonder if your mothering of others comes from never being mothered yourself.”

“I don’t mother others.”

“Yeah, you do.” He smiles. “It’s not a bad thing so don’t take it as a criticism. But rather than giving so much love away you might want to give to yourself.”

“Oh my God, Parker, you’re starting to sound like Dad.” I’m not used to Parker analyzing me. “And it’s not attractive.”

He grins. “Fair enough. Just be careful that all the good you do for others isn’t driven by some need to bring your mother back.”

“I don’t—”

He holds up his hand and interrupts me. “I don’t mean Cynthia as she is now. I mean the mother you’ve always wanted.” He gives me a level look. “Because that mother doesn’t exist. And she never did.”

NO RIGHT THING

I get to Nanaimo General early on Sunday morning. My heart lurches when I walk into Max's room. His eyes are closed, he's deathly still and he looks cold. I hate this. I hate the whooshing and beeping from the respirator. The two IV lines in his hands. Yesterday he had only one. I straighten his blanket, pull it higher on his chest. Covering Max reminds me of what Parker said about me mothering others.

There's nothing wrong with doing that. I pull up a chair and sit down. *As long as it's not overdone.* His idea that I want my mother back pissed me off. I don't want Cynthia back. I watch Max's chest rise and fall; my fury rises with every breath. Why would I? She reminds me of a snow cone. Sweet on the outside but cold on the inside. And completely without substance.

The nurse walks in after a few minutes. "How is he?" I ask.

"He had a quiet night." She checks his IV lines, replaces a nearly empty bag with a full one.

"Is he stable?"

She gives me a guarded look. The tag on her pink uniform reads *Christine North, Night Supervisor*. "And you are?"

"Cate Sheridan."

Her face clears. "Of course. You're on his chart." She checks the tube in his throat, lays a slender hand on his forehead. A lump forms in my throat. Now that's maternal.

"The doctor said once Max was stable you'd have a better idea of his prognosis."

She nods. "That's true. The doctor has ordered a scan. Mr. Le Bould will be going down sometime soon. I'm sure the doctor will tell you the results."

I spend the next hour pretending Max is sleeping and trying to read the Sarah Dessen novel I brought. When they come to take Max for his scan I head outside and power up my phone so I can surf and answer messages. I have one from Noah, one from Dad and one from Nana.

Noah: *How's Max? How're you?*

Dad: *Hope Max is off respirator & improving.*

Blue Skies Nana: *Your father told me everything. I am so sorry, Cate. Call me when you can. Sending love.*

After I answer them I go to the cafeteria and buy an unfortunate chicken salad wrap and a large coffee.

It's after one when I go back to Max's room. My stomach dives when I see the empty space where his bed is supposed to be. *He's getting scanned. He's not dead.* But even after they wheel him back in, fear and worry burn like too many jalapenos on an empty stomach. Today feels different. I can't figure out why but it's making me nuts.

I want to talk to the doctor but he still hasn't shown up by three o'clock when there's a shift change. Max is assigned a male nurse who says almost nothing when he comes to check on him. The second time he shows up I ask about the scan. "You'll have to speak to the doctor," he says.

Around four o'clock a tall, white-coated man appears in the doorway. "You must be Cate Sheridan?" He's a grandfatherly type with a deep baritone voice and loose, basset-hound jowls.

I stand. "Yes."

A younger doctor with sandy blond hair follows him into

the room. Mrs. Chen, the social worker, walks in behind them.

"Hello, Cate." She comes to my side. She's so tiny she barely reaches my shoulders. "How are you?"

My palms start to sweat. I wipe them on my jeans. "I'm okay."

The younger doctor looks at Max and murmurs something to the older one. Both seem to be avoiding my eyes. My breath quickens. This room is too small for the five of us. I can't get enough air.

"Mrs. Chen has asked me to speak with you," Dr. Baritone says. "As you know, Mr. Le Bould had a scan this afternoon."

"Yes." I look at his name tag. *Dr. Malcolm, Critical Care.*

"I'm afraid it's not good news," he says softly.

I bite down hard and try to prepare myself.

"Too much time in the water...massive damage to his brain...very few options." The doctor's words are a waterfall of nasty. I shiver and tune him out, focusing instead on the whooshing and beeping of the respirator and on Max.

The younger man, Dr. Oliver, starts talking about lungs and oxygen and cerebral edema and something called ischemic hypoxia. "Do you understand?" he asks.

"Yes. Max has a brain injury."

The doctors exchange looks. Mrs. Chen clears her throat. "He doesn't have a brain injury," Dr. Malcolm says. "Mr. Le Bould has very little brain function left."

Those are ugly words. "'Very little' means he has some, right?"

"Minimal," the older doctor says.

Minimal is something.

"That means he can improve. And Max can afford the

best care money can buy." I rush to get the words out before they can disagree.

"It's not that simple," Dr. Malcolm says. "Mr. Le Bould's underlying condition left him in a weakened state."

"What underlying condition?"

The two doctors look at Mrs. Chen. "Max considers Cate next of kin," she murmurs.

"Max has Parkinson's disease and it's already had a significant impact on his brain."

Parkinson's. Like segments of an orange fitting together, all the pieces fall into place. Max's tremors. His spaciness. Maybe even those hallucinations. That must be the secret Cynthia held back. "But people can live with Parkinson's. They do it all the time." Rachel's grandpa has had it for years.

"True. However, we have new imaging technology called a DaTscan that allows us to measure the severity of the disease and its progression." He pauses. "The scan indicated Max was likely six to twelve months from being completely incapacitated."

Incapacitated? Max? "You can't know for sure. People make amazing recoveries."

"I'm sorry," Dr. Oliver says. His eyes are the palest, saddest excuse for blue I have ever seen. "Even without Parkinson's there's no hope of recovery here. Mr. Le Bould is brain-dead. He won't get better."

Brain-dead. My knees buckle. Mrs. Chen touches my arm, her small, square hand anchoring me to reality.

Dr. Malcolm clears his throat. "And since Mr. Le Bould listed you as next of kin, we'd like your permission to take him off the life-support machine."

19

"Doctors don't know everything," I tell Dad after dinner. "What if I make the wrong decision? This isn't a mistake I can fix. This is life and death."

Dad mutes the television. "You heard the doctors, Cate. He has no brain function left."

"Minimal," I correct. "That means some." In my mind I see Max lying in that bed, pale and still, the machine breathing for him.

"We've gone over this," Dad says softly. "Max has irreversible brain damage."

The older doctor and Mrs. Chen called Dad after they spoke to me. As a minor I'm legally unable to decide if Max's machine should be turned off. But since Max listed me as next of kin the hospital feels an ethical obligation to consult me. And since Dad is my legal guardian they're obligated to deal with him too. It's a weird Catch-22 that can only be changed if the hospital files to have Max declared a ward of the court. That would take too much time. And invite the kind of media attention nobody wants.

"Doctors make mistakes. People wake up from comas. I've read dozens of examples since I got home. Miracles can happen." And I want one. Desperately.

Dad switches off the TV. "There are no miracles to be had here, Cate."

I roll onto my side so I can see him. He's leaning back in his chair with his feet up on the stool. His face is grave. "Max can keep breathing hooked up to that machine," he adds. "But what kind of life is that?"

My tears start again, a silent trickle down my cheeks. "Who am I to decide?" I demand.

Dad doesn't answer.

"Max could go to a private facility," I tell him. "Get the best doctors money can buy. The best care. Money makes a difference when it comes to medical care. You know that."

"Money can't buy brain function. Money can't give you breath."

"But—"

"And besides," Dad interrupts. "You don't have access to Max's money. No one does. That money is in limbo right now."

And so is Max.

"You can let them appoint a public trustee," Dad reminds me. "And let someone else make the decision." He pauses. "But that would only prolong the inevitable. As painful as it is we both know turning off that machine is the right thing to do."

"I thought getting Max and Cynthia together was the right thing to do." Dad hasn't said much about Cynthia's story. Though he did point out that at least she'd not shared Max's Parkinson's diagnosis with the world. As if that excuses everything else she did. A dull ache is starting behind my eyes. "And look how that turned out."

Dad runs a hand through his hair. "Even if bringing Max

and your mother together was wrong, you did it for the right reason. Your motives were good."

"So that makes it right?"

He sighs. "Sometimes there is no right thing. Sometimes you're caught between two bad choices."

Like now. "If I turn the machine off I'm letting Max die," I whisper. "How do I look myself in the mirror after that?"

Dad is silent for a long time. Finally he says, "How do you look yourself in the mirror if you don't? Is it fair for you to let Max hang in some kind of half-life?"

I can't answer that.

Mrs. Chen said the hospital is prepared to wait a day or two for my decision. I don't have to decide tonight. But if I wait too long they'll start the process to get the public trustee involved. The media would know. And Max would hate that. "I need to talk to a friend."

"Of course. I don't want you to have any doubts or any regrets. This is much harder for you than it is for Max." His smile is sad. "From what you've told me it sounds like he made his decision a long time ago."

"I'll come find you after I make my call."

"Do," he says. "I'd like to hear what Tegan has to say."

"I'm not calling Tegan," I tell him. "I'm calling Noah."

"Who knew one good deed would turn out so bad," I say. A harried-looking waitress delivers four massive plates of fries to the group at the table across from us. Even though it's almost eight o'clock, Lefty's is still packed.

"Define bad." Noah bites into his double cheeseburger. He sounds matter-of-fact, blasé even. But I know he isn't because when I called and told him about Max, he said it wasn't the kind of thing we should talk about over the phone. He offered to come to the house but I figured if I was out in public, I'd be less likely to cry.

"Oh *come on!*" My voice wobbles and I feel those stupid tears again so I lean forward and stare hard at the ice cream slowly melting on top of my apple pie. Once I regain control I say, "If we hadn't rescued him, nobody would've known he was *the* Max Le Bould, Cynthia would've stayed in England, that story wouldn't have aired and we wouldn't be having this conversation. So in my books we did a bad deed."

"Max would say that's history and history is for old farts." Noah attempts a grin but it's a pathetic effort. "Why relive the past? It won't help."

"How is everything so cut and dried for you?"

"How is it not?" But he won't look at me and I can tell he feels bad.

"Life isn't just about facts," I add. "It's about feelings too."

After a minute Noah puts his cheeseburger down. "You said we did a bad deed not a good one. That means we should have done nothing at all, right?"

"You were the one who said it's wrong to help people who don't want our help."

His face fills with colour. "I didn't realize until afterward what Max was trying to do. I reacted in the moment, same as you. And if it happened again I'd probably do the same thing. It's one thing to let people make their own decisions and live their own lives, but when they're about to get hit by a truck, the right thing to do is to save them."

"But what about your grandma?"

She tried to kill herself. The unspoken words hang between us.

He looks as if he's gathering his thoughts. "If I've learned anything over the last while it's that life isn't black and white. My grandma was ready to die. I hate that my parents pushed her in a direction she didn't want to go, but who knows what would've happened without the surgery? She might have suffered just as much." He clears his throat. I can tell he doesn't believe it. He's trying to make me feel better. "We didn't know about Max's Parkinson's when we rescued him. And Max didn't know about his options. Maybe with money he could have gotten good care and lived a reasonable life. We don't know. So to your original point: no, I don't believe we did anything wrong. We did a good deed. *We.* This isn't all on you. I'm just as responsible."

By taking on some of the responsibility and by admitting that life isn't always straightforward, Noah has given me a gift.

I shove a chunk of pie into my mouth. The act of chewing and swallowing stops me from losing it. "You also said I can't know what's right for someone else," I say after a minute. "So how am I supposed to know—" My breath catches. My eyes fill and everything around me blurs. "How am I supposed to know what Max would want?" I whisper.

"Have you asked him?"

I snort out a half-laugh. "Yeah, I'll get right on that."

"I'm serious. Hearing is the last sense to go. Who knows if brain-dead people can hear or not? I talked to my grandma right up until the end."

Brain-dead. I hate that term. "Well, they sure can't talk." Sitting with Max today was hard. Yet the thought of talking to him suddenly feels right. "If I talk to him will you come with me? I know it might be hard because of your grandma and stuff but—"

"Let's go." He throws a twenty-dollar bill on the table and stands.

~

The nurses—three women and a man—are whispering when Noah and I arrive at the critical care desk.

"We're here to see Max Le Bould." The talking stops abruptly and all four heads turn to us. I recognize Christine North, so I talk to her. "I know visiting hours are over but we'd like to spend a little time with him." Before we can't. The unspoken words jam my throat like a cork. "We're hoping you can make an exception."

"Visiting hours don't apply to next of kin," she says softly. "You may visit any time." Her gaze flickers to Noah.

"He's with me." I reach for his hand. "We're together."

The male nurse smirks. A nurse in a pale pink uniform kicks him with the toe of her Croc.

"You can stay as long as you like," Christine North says, "providing you keep your voices down." Her footsteps squeak as she walks out from behind the desk. "Go on in. I'll get you a second chair." She disappears down the hall.

For a second I'm rooted to the spot.

Noah tugs my hand. "Come on," he whispers. My tummy quivers as he propels me across the hall to Max's room.

We stand at the end of the bed. The soft whoosh of the respirator bounces off the walls. The air feels heavy. I have the weird sense that something has changed. I glance around the room. Maybe it's the lighting. The curtains are drawn and the overhead lights are off. Only a couple of pot lights are on. One shines just above Max's head. He looks like he's wearing a halo. A nervous snicker bubbles up. Max would hate that.

Shoes still squeaking, Christine North arrives with a second chair. Noah takes it; I take the same one I sat in this morning.

I stare at Max's high forehead. His ski-jump nose. That long, stringy hair. Someone has tied it back since I left. Is that the difference? But things felt different this morning too. I still can't make sense of it. I study his skin. It's a pale, sickly grey now. Like a bleached oyster.

"Hey, Max." I pick up his hand. His fingers feel like frozen onion skin. "We brought you something." Noah pulls out the tiny basket of kumquats and the small wedge of triple cream brie. He places them on Max's side table.

At first when Noah suggested bringing them I thought it was weird. But he didn't give me a choice. "We gotta take something and Max wouldn't want flowers," he'd said as he pulled into the parking lot at Fine Foods. We'd selected the most expensive out-of-season fruit and the creamiest chunk of brie. I look at them now, sitting beside a plain black comb and an industrial-sized tub of cream. They vibrate with colour and life and goodness. I can almost hear Max saying, "You did good, Catie girl."

I pull my gaze from the table and look back at him. So still. So pale. No change from earlier in the day. And yet.

"They want to turn off the machine, Max. And they want me to tell them it's okay." The tears swell behind my eyes. I hate that I can't stop crying. I hate that Max wants to die. Because that's what this all comes down to. Max wanted to die when he aimed his bike for that truck weeks ago. "Because you listed me as next of kin, remember?" I squeeze his hand.

He doesn't squeeze back.

I hate that too.

I look over at Noah. His expression is stoic. But his eyes glisten and he's jiggling one knee up and down. This is hard for him too. He nods his encouragement.

"I don't know if you'd want that," I say, looking back at Max. "The machine turned off, I mean." But I'm lying. That's exactly what Max would want. *Get me outta here, Catie.*

But there's outta here. And there's never-coming-back outta here.

How can I make that decision for him?

Sometimes there is no right thing. I watch Max's chest rise and fall and stare down at the swollen knuckles on the lifeless hand I'm holding. Then I look at his face again. I stare hard. I'm waiting for a sign: a grunt, a snort, something that tells me there's hope.

But there's nothing.

I look at Noah. "Max wouldn't want this," I whisper. I know that. "The machine is living for him."

I glance back down. And I see what I've been too scared to see. Max is gone. My insides turn to water. That's the change. That's the reason for the weird heaviness in the air, the feeling that something is different. Max was gone this morning. On some level I knew it. I just didn't want to accept it. His soul has left the building. His body is the only thing left.

And it's up to me to let that go.

My tears start then. Silently they stream down my

cheeks onto the blanket, the bed, Max's wrist. Choking back a sob I lay my head on Max's arm. Noah stands behind me. When he puts his hands on my shoulders my last bit of resistance goes. I cry hard. I cry for Max and all those years he lost. For the first accident and the death of his band members. I cry for the mistake I made bringing Cynthia to see him.

And I cry for me.

Max is leaving. That's what people do. They leave. I've known it forever. I've hated it forever. That's why I've always tried to be the one who leaves instead of the one left behind.

But it's time for me to change. I watched my mother walk away a second time and it didn't kill me. It's okay to be left behind. It's time I accepted that.

It takes me a while to compose myself. When I'm finally able to speak I raise my head, wipe my eyes and turn to Noah. "I need to leave a note for Mrs. Chen."

I'm up before five the next morning. I text Nana to bring her up to date and tell her my plan, and then I email Chef's Apron. By the time Dad wanders into the kitchen shortly after six I have breakfast and my speech prepared.

He's wearing khakis and a button-down; about the only thing out of place is a small chunk of hair that's still wet from his shower. It sticks up from the back of his scalp like a tiny exclamation mark. If he knew it was there it would make him crazy. It makes me love him even more.

He glances at the stove, sees the eggs ready for frying, the cinnamon buns cooling on the rack, the coffee, and the cloth napkins laid out beside our cups. He turns to me. "Ah, Bean." The childhood nickname is nearly my undoing. He opens his arms. I fall into them, welcoming his hug, letting him stroke my hair. "Did cooking help?" he asks softly.

He knows that cooking is my salvation, the place I go when I'm happy, when I'm sad, when I need to find my centre. "Not really," I admit, gently pulling away.

"You were brave last night."

And I need to be brave again this morning. I'd texted him about Max before I drove home but now, as I pour coffee and cook the eggs, I fill in more of the details.

When I finally sit down across from him I say, "Dad, there's something you need to know."

He's halfway through a cinnamon bun. "What's that?"

"I'm going to Chef's Apron whether you like it or not." I sound calm but my heart is beating a rat-a-tat-tat in my chest. I've been rehearsing this in my head for the last hour.

"Not that again!" A tiny crumb of bun sprays across the table as he lists out, for the millionth time, all the reasons cooking as a career is just so wrong.

Rather than argue I let him talk. Finally he sputters to a stop.

"I know you disagree and I know you're disappointed," I tell him, "but it's my life and I get to live it my way." When he opens his mouth to argue I add, "Just like Max got to live his life his way." The irony doesn't escape me. I tried to get Max to conform to my idea of what was right and Dad is doing the same to me.

"That was different, Cate."

"Not really. What kind of life will I have if I can't live it the way I want?"

He doesn't answer.

"Besides, if I was mature enough to make the decision about Max's life support, then I'm mature enough to decide on the course of my own life too."

Pain flashes through his eyes. I see sadness and worry reflected there, but I see a world of devotion too. Tears feather the back of my throat. Dad might be a crazy control freak but his love for me is unconditional. That's what makes this so hard.

"I think you're making a mistake," he says.

"If that's the case it'll be my mistake."

"I can't let you use that money in your education fund."

My anger sparks. I hate that Dad's not being supportive, that he thinks he knows what's right, that he's refusing to give me money that's rightfully mine. But I would hate myself even more if I didn't stand up for what I wanted. "I know." I won't fight with him, not anymore. I need to focus all my energy on making things happen. "That's why I've deferred Chef's Apron."

He frowns. "I don't understand."

"Nana's buying me a ticket to Japan for graduation. I'll stay with her and tutor English until I save up enough for tuition and living expenses."

"*Japan!*" He sounds horrified. "But—"

"I've asked Chef's Apron to hold my spot for a year."

Dad's face is the colour of grape jelly. "But Japan's across the world!"

I reach for the coffee pot. "Whatever it takes to get to cooking school, Dad." I hold it above his cup. "More coffee?" I ask sweetly.

He pushes away from the table. "What time is it in Tokyo?" he mutters. "I need to talk to your grandmother."

20

A couple of weeks after Max's death and my conversation with Dad, Gabe takes Noah and me out on his boat. It's a sunny Saturday in mid-June, the perfect day to spread Max's ashes off Rathtrevor Beach. Tillie comes with us. She refused our invitation at first, but when we got to the marina this morning she was standing beside Gabe's boat, wrapped against the morning chill in her blue-and-orange poncho and carrying her ever-present plastic bag.

"A funeral with no one there is the saddest thing in the world," she'd said gruffly, her pie-shaped face flushed with emotion. "I figured somebody should come."

The water looked like liquid silver as we climbed into the boat and chugged away from the dock. Noah scanned the shore with his binoculars in case the media turned up, but all we attracted were a couple of noisy seagulls who cried mournfully as we headed for the point.

The press had hounded me for days after Max died, pouncing on me outside my house and at school too. Would there be a funeral? Did Max have a will? Say any last words? Express remorse about the accident?

My refrain was simple and repetitive: no comment, no comment, no comment. But by the end of the week I'd smartened up and added this: "There'll be a public memorial for Max later, maybe on the summer solstice since that was Max's favourite time of the year." After that they left me alone.

I wasn't used to lying. I was surprised at how easy it was.

Gabe cuts his speed. "This good?" he shouts. Rathtrevor Provincial Park is up ahead.

"Go a little to the left." Tillie motions to the port side; her poncho billows out with the movement. "Max always liked the west."

Gabe picks up his speed. The wind is cold. I hug Max to my chest and try to convince myself that the west is a very good place to be.

Noah monitors the shoreline with his binoculars. I follow his gaze but I'm barely able to make out the small brown shapes and blobs of colour that are the makeshift tents and lean-tos where Tillie and the others still live in spite of constant raids from the authorities. Farther on is the forest where Max spent the last few months of his life.

"It looks like the usual crowd," Noah says, lowering the binoculars. "Twenty people. Maybe thirty."

We're planning a small celebration with them after we scatter Max's ashes. Gabe will take us back to the marina and we'll drive over with the food I bought. "We should have enough then." There's a ton of cheese (the good stuff along with plain old cheddar), cold cuts and deli salads. Olives and pickles. Buns and all the condiments. Cookies and cinnamon twists. A great big lemon cake decorated with as much fruit as I could get on it. Juice and soda for those who want it. And beer too. Because Max would want that.

Gabe slows. "How about here?"

Tillie nods.

Gabe looks at me. My heart tumbles. This is it. "Okay."

Noah comes over and sits beside me. He's concerned. I see it in his eyes. I see something else there too. Something deep and a little bit scary. It makes my heart tumble too, but in a good way.

Gabe cuts the engine. The silence, after the scream of the motor, is startling. And the urn cradled in my arms feels a whole lot heavier.

For a minute I pretend this is just another boat ride. I shut my eyes and inhale the sharp brine of the morning air. I let myself enjoy the warmth of the sun on my cheeks, the swell of the water. The movement reminds me of breath. Up and down. In and out. That makes me think of Max. And why we're here.

I open my eyes. They're all looking at me. Tillie says, "It's time." She picks up her bag and stands. The boat rocks. "Max wouldn't want you pissing around about this."

Gabe chuckles. Noah smiles. I smile too. She's right.

"We need to stand upwind." Gabe leads us to the bow of the boat. "Otherwise—"

"Otherwise Max's ashes will stick to us like glue," Tillie interjects. She unties the knot in her bag. I glimpse something yellow. "And I'm sure as hell not taking that bugger home with me."

They all laugh. I don't. I clutch the urn and wonder how I can be holding the sum total of Max. The familiar prickle starts up behind my eyes. How is it that an entire life can be reduced to five pounds of dust?

I cradle the urn while Noah removes the lid. I take a deep breath and look inside. The remains aren't ash at all.

They're coarse sand. My stomach rolls. And jagged bits too. Bone probably.

Fighting the urge to cry I rest the urn against the edge of the boat. Noah stands on my left, Tillie on my right. The yellow in her bag is flower petals. Handfuls and handfuls of them. Yellow and pink and white and blue. Orange and purple. Bright red.

I tip the urn. *Safe journey, Max,* I say silently. My eyes blur. *Toodle pip.*

And I pour him out.

Max scatters in a puff of grey. Tillie tosses a handful of petals. Time slows. Max and the flowers swirl together, suspended in front of us in a kind of mystical dance before they gently float down to settle on the water.

We help Tillie scatter the last of the petals. And then we all stand in sacred silence as Max and the flowers drift slowly, slowly, into the distance before finally disappearing from sight.

~

"Are you sure you don't want something to eat?" Noah asks after we get to the beach.

I put my hand in my pocket and feel the letter I've been saving. It's time for me to read it. When Gabe and the authorities removed Max's belongings from the shack, they found two envelopes: one for me and one for Mrs. Chen. "No, I'll wait until after." I pull the letter from my pocket and toss my hoodie onto a log. It's not even eleven o'clock but it's already warm.

He grins. "There may not be much left."

I glance at the people clustered around the slab of

plywood serving as a table for the food. Within about two minutes of us arriving and Tillie announcing that we'd brought lunch to honour Max's memory, the plywood materialized from Gabe's truck, along with four plastic barrels to hold it in place. They were followed by folding chairs, blankets, a radio. Everybody within a ten-minute walk had wandered over.

"Don't bring out the dessert until I get back," I tell him. "If there's nothing else left, at least there'll be cake."

It's an easy walk from the beach to the forest, but I'm sweating by the time I reach the trees. When I step away from the shore and into the shade, the briny scent of seaweed gives way to the resinous smell of pine and moss and fertile earth.

Max's clearing is easy to find. The thick old tree with the low-hanging branches is unmistakable. Max's firepit is still there. I stare around the space remembering how quickly his tent had come down, how little he had to call his own. I settle at the base of the tree. One of the branches curls around my shoulder like a protective friend. In the distance a bird chirps an encouraging song.

Slowly I unfold Max's letter. I notice the date first. Wednesday, May 29. Blood rushes to my head. Before prom. Before Cynthia's story.

My Dearest Catie Girl,

If you haven't heard from Mrs. Chen yet, you'll be hearing from her soon. That money you collected for me at the bank? It's yours. It is my gift to you.

Gifts come with strings. We've talked about

> *this before, you and me. People always have an agenda when they give. I know you don't believe it, and you don't have to, but I believe it. Sometimes people give to make themselves feel superior. Sometimes they give expecting a reward, even a symbolic one, in heaven perhaps. Sometimes they give because they pity a person and that scares them and it takes them to a dark place. Giving is a kind of reassurance that they'll never sink as low as the person they're giving to. Sometimes people give because it's expected, or they expect something back, which is a kind of string too. And sometimes people give to make themselves feel whole when a part of them is broken.*

Tears blur my vision. There's a weight on my chest heavier than a sack of potatoes. I stare up at the tree canopy and wait for my eyes to clear. It's almost a minute before I can read again.

> *This gift I am giving you is no different. There are strings, Catie girl. Two of them.*

> *String #1. Some of the money is to be used to pay the tuition for Chef's Apron. And you are to go there and become the chef you want to be because that is what your heart is calling you to do. It doesn't matter what anyone else thinks. It doesn't matter if you decide, after it's all over, that you don't want to be a chef after all. That you'd rather*

grow potatoes in Peru. That the only thing you want to cook for the rest of your life is cheese pizza. No experience is wasted.

String #2. The rest of the money is to be used to heal your broken places. We all have broken places, my Catie. We all need healing. The best way to heal is to do the things you love. I don't mean drugs and booze and crazy sex, though I've done my share of all three. I mean you should do the things that make you excited to get out of bed every morning, even if they scare you. Some people call it a bucket list. That's a goddamn stupid phrase. Don't be thinking of what you need to do before you kick the bucket. Think about what you need to do to fill the bucket. To live. And do it every single day of your life. If someone complains tell that wanker to sod off. No one knows how to live your life but you.

Speaking of wankers, avoid them at all costs. They're usually male and easy to spot. I hope you find a good bloke one day. I hope you won't be alone because even though you talk that kind of talk, I don't see you walking that kind of walk.

Don't be sad for me, Catie girl. My life was over a long time ago. It ended when I was driving the bus on that mountain pass in Montana. I tried to pretend and for a while it worked. But the pain only grew, and with my body giving out, I don't want to be a burden. Yes, there's dignity in dying well, and several nurses promised to care for me until the end, but that was after they knew me as Max Le Bould. After they knew I had money. You were the only one who cared about me when I was just Max. When I was me.

That, my Cate, was your gift to me. And it was truly priceless.

Toodle pip,

Max

Noah is waiting for me when I walk back to the beach. Silently he hands me a tissue and waits while I dab my eyes and blow my nose.

I'm a mess. I don't need a mirror to tell me that. My eyes feel swollen and my nose is red, but there's a lightness in my chest I haven't felt for weeks. I stare down the beach to the people clustered by the table. The cake box is out and the lid is up. I hope there's some left.

"You good?" Noah asks after a minute.

Good? What an ironic choice of words. I don't trust myself to speak so I simply nod. He takes my hand and we start to walk.

Tillie glances up when we get close. She's cutting the cake. She slaps a wedge onto a paper plate and hands it to me. "It's good," she says.

Good. There's that word again. I grin. "You sound surprised."

"I am." She scowls. "Anything with that much fruit on it looks too healthy to be good." She cuts another, bigger, piece for Noah. "But what the hell do I know?" She hands him the plate. "I guess good and bad is all a matter of taste."

I break off a piece of cake. When it comes to dessert maybe, but when it comes to life? I don't think so. The sweet tart flavours of lemon sponge, kiwi and strawberry explode in my mouth. There's nothing good about the fact that Max is gone. I hate that he didn't see any possibility in living. I hate that Cynthia will never be the mother I'd like her to be. I don't even know if I can accept it or accept her.

And I hate that Max dying makes it easier for me to follow my dream. But if I'm being honest, Max didn't just give me money. He gave me a bigger gift. From the very start he saw me for who I was. And he always believed I could succeed. Whether I do or not, I need to give it my best shot. For Max. And for me.

June 28, Gymnasium, Madrona Secondary School

"Before I end this speech I'd like to say thank you." Sweat beads under the rim of my cap as I turn to the last page of my speech and look up at the crowd. "And there are many people to thank." Under my graduation gown my dress is sticking to me. It's sweltering in the gym. That's what happens when you put four hundred bodies in a room in a heat wave.

"Thank you first of all to the teachers and the administrators who selected me as this year's recipient of the Ruth Mackie Holland scholarship. Your belief in me means a great deal. Thanks too for making sure we got to graduation day and for preparing us for the transition to the next phase of our life. Thanks to our parents who have supported us in too many ways to count and kicked our butts when we needed it."

Laughter breaks out. I glance over to where Dad and Parker and Nana are sitting. My heart swells. My family. I've never appreciated them as much as I do today.

"Thanks to my friends who suffered through every minute of the last four years with me." More laughter. "My high school memories are stronger and richer because of you. And even though many of us are heading in separate directions now, I'll carry those memories with me forever."

I pause. This really is it. The end of twelve long years and the beginning of the rest of our lives. It's bittersweet. I don't want school to end. And at the same time, I do.

"Finally, I'd like to end this speech with a quote. This isn't a quote you'll find in any book or social media post or movie. These are words of wisdom from Max Le Bould." Pain stabs my gut. I wonder when I'll stop feeling his loss.

Someone coughs. The silence seems to deepen.

"Always follow your heart," I say. "Do the thing you're scared to do. Spend less time worrying about how you'll earn a living and more time thinking about how you want to live. Be kind to others but don't lose yourself in the process. Break a few rules. Cause a little trouble. When in doubt, choose love. And always remember to buy—" Heavy emphasis on the word "buy" "—the really good cheese."

~

When the ceremony is over I head for the side door along with the rest of the grads. We're meeting our families on the field but for a minute it's just us: a rowdy sea of red gowns laughing, crying and high-fiving. I search for Tegan and Noah but I can't see them. And I can't text either. Cell phones weren't allowed at the ceremony. I watch for my friends while I hug everybody else around me: Rachel and Josh and Alana and Ben. I even hug Carter, who says I gave an awesome speech and that he'll never forget me.

A minute later there's a tap on my back. "You were amazing!" Tegan screeches when I whirl around. "That was the *best* speech ever!"

I laugh. "I don't know about that." But I feel good.

"It was probably easier now that Chef's Apron is settled too, right?"

"For sure." In truth, Dad's still not happy about my plans and I'm hurt that he's hurt. But his inability to accept that I've grown up is his issue, not mine. I can't let Dad's feelings colour my future.

"I see Owen." Tegan points. I follow the direction of her finger and spot Owen off in the distance waving frantically at us. "Let's go," she says.

It takes us forever to get through the crowd. I watch for Dad, Parker and Nana, but mostly I'm looking for Noah.

Eventually I spot him. He's a few yards away, talking to a rowing buddy. Those shoulders are unmistakable, even under a graduation gown.

Tegan tugs on my arm. "Come on."

"I'll meet up with you guys in a few minutes," I tell her.

When I turn back, Noah is standing in front of me, his chestnut curls frothing out from under his cap.

"I was looking for you," he says.

Delight ripples through me. "Me too."

"You did great up there. Really. I'm not just saying that because, you know, of us."

Us. We haven't talked about us yet. I don't know how the "us" thing will work when I'm at school in California and Noah's at UBC. For now it's enough that there is an "us." And that I haven't found a single thing about him that bugs me.

"My parents want to meet you," he says. "You up for it?"

His parents. A tiny tic starts up at the corner of my mouth.

"You have to meet them sooner or later," he adds.

"Technically I could probably put it off. If you want to get all logical about it."

But Noah doesn't even crack a smile. Instead he studies me with an intensity that makes me flush. "What happened to doing the things you're scared to do?"

My flush deepens. I pull off my cap and fan my face with it. "I'm not scared." But I'm lying and we both know it.

He steps close and leans down. "I'm not asking you to marry me," he whispers. His breath is hot against my cheek. "Or to sleep with me." He pauses. "Although I have thought about one of those two things."

I have too. And that scares me even more.

He drops an arm across my shoulder. "But starting with my parents is an easy first step. And they're going to love you. Trust me, I know." Now he's smiling.

"Okay." Butterflies erupt in my stomach. "Where are they?"

"I told them to meet us by the coffee and snacks," Noah says. "I figured we'd be starving by the time all the speeches were over."

I smirk. "Why am I not surprised?"

He winks. "Maybe you're psychic too?"

I'm not psychic but I know one thing for sure. We all have broken places. Max was right about that. The best way to heal them is to do the things you love. Max was right about that too. But another way is to embrace risk. And I'm ready to start. "Let's go."

ACKNOWLEDGEMENTS

Thank you to Lisa McManus Lange and Tlell Macrae for valuable feedback on the manuscript, and to the BC Arts Council and the Canada Council for the Arts for writing assistance that enabled me to focus on this project.

AUTHOR'S NOTE

While I've made every effort to remain true to the setting of the Parksville-Qualicum Beach area, I have taken some liberties in telling this story. As of this writing, the Oceanside Health Centre is not an overnight hospital facility, nor does it provide any surgical services. As well, there is no local TV station in the area, nor is there a police bicycle patrol.

ABOUT THE AUTHOR

Laura Langston is the award-winning author of twenty-two books for young people including *Lesia's Dream* (HarperTrophy) and *The Art of Getting Stared At* (Razorbill). By the time she hit grade four, Laura knew she wanted to be a writer. So did the teachers. Her persistent daydreaming and invisible friends were the tipoff. Her first word was "cookie," her second word was "book" and her priorities haven't changed. A former journalist for the CBC, Laura currently lives in Qualicum Beach, British Columbia. For more information visit lauralangston.com.

ABOUT CRWTH PRESS

Crwth (pronounced crooth) Press is a small independent publisher based in British Columbia. A crwth is a Welsh stringed instrument that was commonly played in Wales until the mid-1800s, when it was replaced by the violin. We chose this word for the company name because we like the way music brings people together, and we want our press to do the same.

Crwth Press is committed to sustainability and accessibility. This book is printed in Canada on 100 percent post-consumer waste paper using only vegetable-based inks. For more on our sustainability model, visit www.crwth.ca.

To make our books accessible, we use fonts that individuals with dyslexia find easier to read. The font for this book is Helvetica Neue.